THE
TRADE

KAREN WOODS

Harper
North

HarperNorth
Windmill Green,
Mount Street,
Manchester, M2 3NX

A division of
HarperCollins*Publishers*
1 London Bridge Street
London SE1 9GF

www.harpercollins.co.uk

HarperCollins*Publishers*
Macken House,
39/40 Mayor Street Upper,
Dublin 1
D01 C9W8

First published by HarperNorth in 2025

1 3 5 7 9 10 8 6 4 2

Copyright © Karen Woods 2025

Karen Woods asserts the moral right to
be identified as the author of this work

A catalogue record for this book
is available from the British Library

ISBN: 978-0-00-868089-3

Printed and bound in Great Britain by
CPI Group (UK) Ltd, Croydon

MIX
Paper | Supporting
responsible forestry
FSC™ C007454

This book contains FSC™ certified paper and other controlled
sources to ensure responsible forest management.

For more information visit: www.harpercollins.co.uk/green

For my Uncle, Tony Price,
gone but never forgotten.

Chapter One

Gina Gilbert had prepared herself for this moment. She straightened her shoulders, determined to stand tall as the judge delivered his sentence.

Ten years. She felt the words as much as heard them. They were like a kick to her chest. But she was a fighter, determined not to flinch. She allowed herself one quick glance down and a moment to draw breath then raised her eyes again and looked straight at him. Her husband. About to be sent down for ten years in the big house.

Bastards they were, in her eyes. The whole courtroom had never listened to one bit of her husband's statement. They just had him down as a mindless gangster, ruling the area he lived in, earning a crust from criminality and fear. She was devastated, but there was no way she was showing anyone here today that her world had fallen apart, that she was vulnerable. No, her expression remained the same, straight back, chin up, just like she'd practised at home staring in the mirror this morning. There was no way these pricks were seeing her break, no way in this world.

Luckily, the court's attention moved on quickly. Sure no one was clocking her, Gina sat chewing at her finger-nails, trying to control the anger raging inside the pit of her stomach. She'd always bitten her nails when she was stressed, and to say she was bubbling with rage was an understatement. 'Ten Years,' she repeated over and over in her mind. 'Ten fucking long years.' How could she tell her kids that their dad wouldn't be home for a long time, would miss their birthdays, miss Christmases? They weren't little anymore but still their dad would miss the moments that mattered, even as young people they still needed their father.

The courtroom was in uproar by now from all the friends and families of the men being sentenced. The case had been long and drawn out and the media were all over it. There were ten men in the dock, each of whom had played their part in the crimes they were being sentenced for. Conspiracy to supply class A drugs, firearms, threats to life, the list felt endless as the charges were read out. Then, as the sentences were handed down, each was met with jeering and heckling, a few tears mixed in too. But not from Gina.

Despite the adrenaline still flooding through her, a smile formed briefly on her face as she took in the scene. It looked like an episode of *Shameless* in here. There were girls in miniskirts caked in make-up, men dripping in gold and snarls, old women looking like they were chewing a wasp, sunbed queens, guys with the kind of old leathery skin that takes a lifetime of sun-worshipping. All with their eyes on the men in the dock.

'It's a fucking joke, you old git,' a middle-aged man roared from behind her, his stale tobacco breath warm against her cheek. There were plenty of dibble in the courtroom today spread about and, as soon as the words fired out of this geezer's mouth, the police were dragging him out by his arms, team-handed, him kicking and screaming. Zero tolerance.

'Let me go, no-good bastards the lot of you. Our kid is innocent. You set him up, and you know it, you bent twats,' he screamed at the top of his lungs.

The journalists would have a field day, Gina thought, each of them sat gripping their pens in their hands ready to scoop a front-page story. They'd already splashed stories when the arrests were made, writing about how the police had done well piecing all the evidence together and that, after nearly a year of surveillance, they'd caught a gang whose arrest they said would clean up half of Manchester. Gina dropped her head into her hands as Judge Wymott continued sentencing the rest of the men. She shot her eyes to the side as Big Tommy Seymour got ready to hear his fate. Jess, his girlfriend, crossed herself and closed her eyes as the judge started to speak, her mouth moving but no words coming out. Maybe she was praying to the big man in the sky, maybe not. But Gina could have given her the heads up and told her that her prayers had been wasted. For weeks she'd been down on bended knee praying to God, pleading with him, telling him she just needed her Scott at home with his family, told him she would help him mend his ways, keep him on the straight and narrow. But God never listened to her prayers, hadn't done for the last forty-odd years – that was why she'd relied on Scott to provide rather than any heaven-sent gifts throughout her life. So she shouldn't be surprised he hadn't answered her prayers this time, hadn't given her husband his freedom. Perhaps God knew Scott Gilbert would never change his ways and she was trying to pull the wool over his eyes. After all, if God really did see everything, he'd have a pretty long list of all the times her husband had broken the Ten Commandments. She wasn't a church-goer and the only time she ever prayed was when she needed something. But she wasn't too proud to ask, just in case. Gina would have done anything to protect her man. He was her world.

Scott was fifty-two years of age and had been hailed for years now as the main man in Manchester. 'The Butcher' he was known as in the world he moved in. It was in his blood to earn money any way he could, in his genes that he had to be at the top of his game and rule his empire with force and not let anyone get one over on him. His father had run the place before him and with his dying breath he had made his son pledge to keep his family name strong, never let anyone take what he had worked hard for all his life. The tattoo on Scott's chest read, 'You just can't beat the person who won't give up,' and he never would, never let anything slip away that he loved or wanted. The whole family was well known in the area, head-the-balls the lot of them. Scott might not have agreed though – he liked to class himself as firm but fair when he was dealing with the people who had crossed him. That was what he told the Mrs, anyway. Gina never ever asked him any questions when she scrubbed at his clothing to remove the blood stains. After all, it was all in a day's work in her eyes and, if someone had wronged her man, then they had to face the consequences, didn't they? She'd rather a man who worked hard and provided, than one sat on the sofa skiving, so she felt she couldn't complain over the line of work he had chosen. And to be fair, the blood stains and bruises had lessened over the years. Whether that was because her husband had mellowed or because he had more people to do his dirty work, she didn't know. He'd never hurt a man who didn't deserve it, is what he'd always told her, and it was what she chose to believe.

Gina let out a laboured breath and twiddled the gold chain on her navy-blue Chanel clutch. Her eyes met Scott's in the dock, and they clouded over. He'd been her world for as long as she could remember and he'd always made sure she had everything she wanted in life: cars, handbags, designer clothing, perfumes – yep, she'd had it all. She was going to miss him, but she'd be lying if she pretended she wouldn't miss the money too.

The judge had nearly finished running through Tommy's crimes now and was nearing the sentencing. Gina watched Jess licking at her lips frantically. Jess was stunning, long legs, long raven-black hair, big chestnut eyes. More than a trophy girlfriend, she was a proper beauty. Tommy was punching above his weight when he bagged Jess and he was paranoid that she would leave him. Jess had always told him straight that she was a free spirit and nobody owned her, not even Tommy Seymour. Gina supposed that was why he was always buying her gifts, taking her on holiday. Jess sat forward now and clutched the cold metal rail in front of her, looking one way then the other. Bloody hell, this was all taking so long. Why didn't this old fella just get to the point, Gina thought. They all knew what these men had done. What did this judge want, a round of applause for reminding everyone about how dangerous these blokes were? The journalists here today were hanging on every detail though, eager to squeeze this story for all they could. Vultures they were.

Gina could see the headline now. 'Ten men jailed. Manchester's most notorious criminals behind bars.' A reminder to all the other grafters in the area that they would be next, and the police would be booming their doors down anytime soon. Reporters would be camped outside her front door, taking photographs, hounding her neighbours for more gossip. The judge coughed slightly to clear his throat and sipped another mouthful of water. Gina's eyes flicked back to him.

'Tommy Seymour, I am sentencing you to ten years in prison.'

There it was, he'd said it at last. Jess had closed her eyes but still tears were flowing from them, uncontrollable.

Gina reached over and patted her knee. She whispered, 'Chin up, love, don't let these wankers see any emotion. Be strong for our men. Get a tissue, dry your eyes and sort yourself out. Cry on the inside for now.'

Jess's meal ticket was gone, no more fancy nights out, gifts or luxurious holidays. She was going to have to toughen up. Gina's words were sharp and maybe she should have been a bit more sympathetic, but that wasn't her style. No, she would cry tonight when nobody could see her, when she was alone in her bed. Public tears were for the weak. Jess snivelled and bit down hard on her bottom lip. It was all getting too much for her, Gina could tell, anxiety surely flooding her body. Gina was right, though: no number of tears would bring her Tommy home now. She just had to grin and bear it.

The judge moved on again. Gina looked to her other side and already she knew that Lola Turner was struggling to hold it together any longer. She had two kids at home and every day the women had sat in this courtroom listening to the trial, they were all she spoke about, her kids and how they would cope. Gina was lucky in that way, she supposed. Her kids, Bethany and Jenkins, were grown up now, even if they hadn't properly flown the nest yet. She could only imagine how it would have felt to have two young children to bring up on her own when their father was locked behind bars for a real stretch.

Lola screamed like a banshee when Judge Wymott passed sentence on her Mike. She stood up and pointed a long finger over at the prosecution. She was going sick, letting them have it. 'It's a bleeding stitch-up. You pricks set my man up and you fucking know it. Read the evidence, listen to his barrister. He's telling the truth.' She twisted her head over at the jury and growled at them, showing her pearly white teeth, 'I hope you lot can sleep tonight knowing what you have done to my children's lives. Two kids I have. How am I going to tell them that their dad won't be coming home, won't be coming home for years. Bastards the lot of you.'

Scott jerked his head forward and snarled over at Gina, fuming he was. 'Sort her out,' he mouthed.

Gina flicked her honey-blonde hair over her shoulder and stood up too. She gripped Lola by the arm and squeezed it, the skin turning white. She was eye to eye with her now as she spoke through clenched teeth. 'Sit the hell down, Lola, and stop making a scene. We're all in the same boat here so button it. Now, park your arse. Everyone's watching us.'

Gina's words were strong, and her nostrils flared as she helped Lola to sit back down. Lola was a hot-head for sure and she was well known for speaking her mind whenever she needed to. Lola and Mike were a toxic couple, Gina and all their friends knew. They were either head over in love with each other or scratching each other's eyes out. Lola didn't trust her man as far as she could throw him, and she was forever accusing him of cheating on her. Everyone knew the signs of a partner playing away and many a night her man had come home stinking of perfume, lipstick on his collar. Mike was a good-looking man, though, gift of the gab, big, toned body and he always had had an eye for the ladies. What did she expect? Gina had heard a few stories about his antics and she'd told him straight to sort himself out before Lola found out because she knew more than anyone, she would kick off big time and cause World War Three.

Gina studied the courtroom. The usher was going out of his mind today and already four people had been removed from the public gallery for the noise they were making. Gina nodded over at Scott, a look that told him she was alright. She stared at her husband and studied every inch of him, trying to drink him in before he was sent down. He was a big man and, to look at him, you would have thought he was a force not to be messed with, exactly like the prosecution had described him. That hard-as-nails look was held deep in his eyes. But, to her, he was a real romantic. She'd known him since she was sixteen years old, childhood sweethearts, and they'd never really been apart in all the years since. Of course, Scott had been in the slammer before, but only a few months here and a few months there, motoring offences, small potatoes. Scott had always made sure she was taken care of and she never wanted for anything. He was like that, Scott was, always made sure his Mrs had a smile on her face. Happy wife, happy life he told everyone. But they both knew this time was different.

Scott winked back at her then dropped his head low as the rest of his firm was sentenced. This was his worst nightmare; he had only a few men now on the out keeping his empire ticking over, and he knew how it all worked more than anyone. His opponents would see his weakness and strike hard. He'd done the same thing himself, always looking for more areas to take over when their boss man had been taken down. Only give what you can take sprung to mind.

This time though it wasn't only his rivals who'd be on the take. The Proceeds of Crime team were all over him already, taking anything of value he owned, anything he could not prove where it had come from. Even his family home was not safe and, if the police took that, then what? His loved ones would be homeless. Of course, he had money stashed away, but was that enough to look after his family for the time he would be in jail? He wasn't sure. The POCA team, as everyone called them, were often a more dreaded knock at the door than normal coppers. Scott had been sloppy, he realised now, too confident in the world he'd built. He'd thought he was untouchable, and that no one would ever take his empire away. He'd been watching his back for his enemies – not the POCA guys. The police had already frozen their joint bank account and taken anything that was of any value from their home: Gina's coats, her handbags, her jewellery. All she had left were the things friends had borrowed that she'd had to call back in. The Gilberts were vulnerable, no longer safe on the streets they used to run. The news would be out already that Scott Gilbert was going to the chokey. The clock was ticking. It was only a matter of time now before the other grafters in the area would be at Gina's door. Would they have her back or put a knife in it?

Chapter Two

Gina had to watch her husband being taken away from the dock by the Group Four guards. After one last chance to lock eyes with his wife, Scott didn't look back again. His head was in the game now and he knew he would always have to watch his back. Being a big name in the area came at a price and, behind prison doors, he would be a sitting target for all those men he'd hurt or had over in the past. No, Scott would be sleeping with one eye open from now on.

Tommy wriggled about as security led him down the stairs. 'Fucking pull me like that again, you wanker, and I'll end you. I'll walk at my speed, not fucking yours. You understand?'

The officer escorting him down the stairs didn't reply but backed off slightly. He'd heard the court case, knew these men weren't bluffing. They had less to lose now they were going down. Added to that, the wages he got were poor and certainly not worth a belt from one of these gangsters. No, an easy life was all he wanted, no bother. He looked at the shuffling line of gang leaders. Each one was clearly taking their sentences differently.

Mike Turner was the first man down the stairs, and he froze on the spot waiting for Scott and Tommy. He looked petrified, had been suffering with his mental health for months now according to his defence statement. But he stood tall, pretended he was still the man. One look at the guards told them to leave them alone for a few minutes, let them have a last chat before they were thrown into a holding cell.

Scott blew out his breath and his nostrils flared wide. 'It is what it is, lads. Could have been a lot worse. I was expecting a fifteen-stretch shoved up my arse. So, when I think of that, I'm buzzing. Good behaviour and all that, we'll be home before you know it.'

Tommy spoke through gritted teeth. 'Jess won't wait for me. She has more or less told me that, the slapper. I swear to you now, one word I hear that she's banging somebody else, and I'll end her, honest, on my life. Why did I even get involved with her? You both told me what she was like, and I never listened to any of you. Gold-digging bitch. Fucking hell, I can't even think about her without knowing she's going to do me dirty.'

Mike chirped in, trying to cheer them all up. He was like that, no matter what had happened he always made a joke out of it. 'You love the woman, that's why you didn't listen to us. It was only last month you was going to put a ring on her finger. Chill out, Tom-lad. Worrying about our women is the last thing we should be stressing about right now. Are you forgetting that Zac Manion and a few of his boys are in the Ways?'

Tommy growled and his fist curled at the side of his legs, forgetting instantly about his own worries over Jess. Strangeways Prison was not far from Manchester city centre, and he knew already that's where they would all start their sentences before they were shipped out. A shit-hole it was, a place all of them knew well – they knew the cells and they knew the local boys occupying many of them.

Scott nodded slowly, just the mention of Zac Manion's name already sending shivers down his spine. The two gangs had had beef going on for a long time now and to say there was bad blood between them was an understate-ment. Even Gina had beef with Zac's wife Sadie, both protecting their families like two preying lionesses. 'That cunt is mine, do you hear me, mine. He'll know we are on our way so, from now on, never take your eyes off the ball. We stay together and see how the land lies when we reach the slammer. Once we are in the main jail, then we will see what's what. We know a lot of heads too, remember that, so let's round them up and get that prick sent home in a body bag.'

Mike cracked his knuckles, ran his hand down the side of his face and felt the deep scar there. Zac had done that to him, caught him off guard and nearly gouged his eye out. Twenty-five stitches he'd had, hours of plastic surgery and even now when you looked at his face the scar was one of the first things you noticed.

The guard nodded over at Scott: it was time to move on. The prisoner respected him for having given them a minute's peace. He slowly paced forward and winked at the man. 'Make sure we all get on the same bus to the Ways, boss. You know the score, don't you?'

The officer looked pale, clear he wanted this man locked away in his cell so he could feel safe again. He nodded and kept schtum. It was showtime now and Scott was there for everybody in the holding cells to see. He might as well have been a celebrity for the reception he got from his fellow cons, most of whom who were shouting at the main man through the hatches in their doors.

'Anything you need Scott, just shout me. The name's Jamo, I'm from Moston.'

More voices joining in. 'Alex from Harpurhey here too,'

'Pluto from Monsall if you need me, mate.'

Scott was like a gladiator returning from the arena. Already his army was forming, and he'd not even stepped foot inside the jail yet.

He shouted back at them. 'If you land in Strangeways, lads, come and see me and I'll look after you boys.'

Tommy shook his head. Most of these wasters weren't Scott's friends, or even useful allies. They were small-time grafters all after a piece of the action, a piece of the pie, his fucking pie.

The guards stopped at an open door. Scott looked inside and inhaled deeply. He walked inside and stood with his back against the wall as the guard closed the door after him. The sound of the door banging shut rippled through his body, drilling his ears. He'd been through this before, but the first moments never got easier. He looked up at the ceiling and then at each of the four walls. There was a small bed to the right of him and a blue blanket. He'd been up early this morning and he was ready for sleep, exhausted physically and mentally drained. He moved towards the bed and plonked down on the edge of it with his eyes still fixed on the door. The hatch was still held up and he knew eyes were still on him trying to get a look at one of Manchester's most notorious criminals. 'Close the fucking hatch,' he roared.

Jingling of keys outside his door, low voices, the ray of light from outside the door slowly fading. He was alone now, alone with his thoughts, and could finally stop stamping down his emotions. He dropped his head into his hands and ragged his fingers through his thick dark hair. His voice was low. 'Bastards, fucking bastards.' He fell back onto the bed and dragged the thin blue blanket over his head.

Tommy sat staring at the grey wall in front of him and screamed at the top of his voice. Then he jumped up from the bed and started punching the door, kicking it, nutting it, prison life already suffocating him. 'Open the door, open the door, you pricks.' There was no reply and Tommy melted down the back of the dark grey steel door like hot wax melting from a candle as the sentence hit home. After a few minutes, he drew his knees up to his chest and covered his mouth as he sobbed his heart out. 'Ten years, I can't do ten years,' he wept. Tommy had always been the emotional one out of the gang and he cried openly when he was upset. Mike always said he could never get his head around it and couldn't understand how this tank of a man could cry at the drop of a hat. But Tommy knew that, though they showed in very different ways, Mike had his weaknesses too. Everybody did.

Chapter Three

Gina walked out of the courtroom and was met by more journalists, all after a photograph of her, a story. She held her palm out in front of her and barged her way past them, not arsed if she knocked any of them over. They already had her down as a gangster wife. Might as well live up to it. She looked back and snarled at Lola and Jess. 'Hurry up, will you? Bleeding hell, get me out of this place.'

Lola was being dragged by the arm by Jess who rolled her eyes at Gina. She needed a hand to keep the other woman moving. Gina turned on the spot and rushed back to where they stood. She whispered in Lola's ear, 'We need out of here, so pick those feet up and start bleeding walking. Do you want these pricks to get a snap of us looking beaten for the front of the newspaper, or what?'

Lola gave a small shake of her head, put her Prada sunglasses on and hurried forwards.

'Move out of our way,' Gina hissed as another reporter tried to get a photograph of the three women together.

Gina started the car up and took a few moments to regain her composure. She slammed her hand on the steering wheel and shot a look over at Jess in the passenger side. 'A shit day for all of us. No point pretending otherwise when it's just us. Let's go back to mine and try to get our heads around this.'

Jess nodded as Gina looked in her rear-view mirror at Lola, her eyes red-raw through crying. She used a softer voice now, one she'd always used when her children were upset and needed comforting. 'Lola, it's just the shock of it. Give it a few days and it won't be as bad. We are all in this together and we will support each other.'

Lola burst out crying. 'It's alright for you two. Mike has left me with nothing. All the money he had went on that daft bleeding car he bought and his new watch, and they're both gone. He's a dickhead. I always told him to save some money for rainy days and look at us now, bleeding skint.'

Gina was right back at her. 'Lola, you were on holiday every other month before he got nicked, and, if I was to look in your wardrobe, every bit of clothing you own is designer. You have to take the rough with the smooth in this game, love. You lived the high life. Now let's find a way to avoid the low.'

Jess fanned her fingers out and admired her almond-shaped nails. There was no way she was giving up habits like her weekly trip to the salon. 'Like Gina said, the rough with the smooth. Tommy wasn't any kind of saver either, so give it a few months and I'll be in the same boat as you, Lola. Well, unless I hook up with some new rich bloke,' she chuckled.

Gina slapped her arm playfully. 'Oi, bloody yo-yo knickers, we'll be having none of that. Tommy's head will be mashed enough without him having to worry about you too.'

'Oh, lighten up, Gina, I'm only having a laugh, where has your sense of humour gone? What did my mum always say – if you don't laugh, you'll cry…'

But Gina was miles away, already making plans as she flicked the engine over and drove them out of the multi-story car park.

Gina pulled up outside her house relieved the kids had both said they'd be there waiting when she got home – knowing she'd need the support. She'd have to tell the kids now, get it over and done with, like ripping off a plaster. She expected tears from Bethany, but she knew Jenkins would hit the roof. Her son was twenty-four and she'd always done her best to keep him well away from the world his father lived in. Not an easy job at all. He'd wanted a piece of the action from an early age, as soon as he'd clocked what his dad really did for a living, though she'd begged her husband to promise her that her boy would never be involved in the same world he was.

But Jenkins had crime in his blood. He wanted a name just like his father had, and Gina suspected he was already earning money breaking the law.

Gina spoke to Lola and Jess before she got out of the car. 'Right, I'm not looking forward to this. Jess, you might need to comfort Bethany after I've told her, and I'll concentrate on Jenkins. Come on, let's get this over with.'

The three women got out and already Gina could see her daughter at the front window looking distressed. She took a deep breath and walked down the long driveway. Theirs was a nice house set in a lovely area of Manchester. Gina knew from the moment she viewed it that this would be her forever home: four bedrooms, spacious living room, and a magnificent garden. Woodhouses was a place she'd been as a child with her father and, even then, she knew this was a place she would love to live. It had been her dream – and there was no way she was letting go of this place, whatever happened next.

The front door opened and a rich, warm scent of cinnamon enveloped her. Gina loved the smell and said every day she wanted to be reminded of Christmas because, in her eyes, living in this house every day was her birthdays and Christmases all wrapped into one. Bethany stood in the hallway with her arms wrapped around her body, already on the verge of breaking down crying.

'Mam, please tell me Dad is with you,' she snivelled in a low voice.

Gina walked to where she was stood and placed two hands on her shoulders. 'Babes, we spoke about this, and your dad spoke with you too. The evidence was damning and we all knew one way or another that he wouldn't be coming home today.'

Bethany started sobbing and Gina held her tight in her arms as her legs melted from under her. 'How long, Mam, tell me how long?'

Jess and Lola both stood watching and already Lola was getting upset just hearing Beth weep. This would be her children soon enough and she didn't know how she was going to tell them their dad wasn't coming home.

Gina swallowed, the sentence still stabbing her deep in her heart. 'He got sentenced to ten years, love, they all more or less did.'

Her words stabbed into her daughter's heart, and she howled out like an injured animal. 'I want my dad home, I want my dad,' she sobbed. She looked like a little girl again, not a grown woman.

Gina shot a look over her shoulder to Jess. This was her cue to come and comfort Bethany. Jess was on the ball, and she led her into the front room as Lola followed close behind. Gina looked up the stairs and slowly peeled her coat off. She could hear music and knew her son would be waiting in his bedroom for the news. D-Block was his favourite group and, whenever he was stressed, she would always hear the tunes filtering through his bedroom door. He had begged her to let him come to court, pleaded with her to see his old man one last time, but she'd refused point blank. It was hard enough for herself to watch Scott getting slammed, never mind putting her children through it. She headed up the stairs and slowly walked along the landing. She could see his bedroom door was open slightly.

'Jenks,' she said as she pushed it fully open. There he was, an image of his old man when he was younger, toned, tanned and big blue saucer eyes staring back at her. He looped his hands above his head and, by the look on his face, he knew what was coming.

'How long?' he asked.

Gina walked over to the bed and sat on the edge of it next to him. She stroked her fingertips along his arm. 'Ten, son.'

Jenkins swallowed hard and stared up at the ceiling, holding back any emotion that he felt. 'I need to step up now, Mam. Please don't be pecking my head about what I get up to, because you know better than me that my dad will be wanting all hands on deck until he's home. I'm not a kid anymore, Mam, remember that.'

Gina's expression changed. 'I'm not saying anything at the minute, son. I need to get my head around it all myself. Things will be different around here for a while but we all need to pull together and do the best we can. We'll find out soon enough if the police are taking our house away from us, so my mind is all over that for now. I just hope your dad has all his ships in order when it comes down to the house, because they'll take it, you know, put it all down to proceeds of crime, if there's a single loophole we've missed.'

Jenkins sat up on the bed and sucked hard on his gums. He hugged his mother and pulled away from her, looking deep into her eyes. 'It's all going to be fine, Mam. Trust me.'

'I hope so, son, I hope so.'

Back downstairs, Gina opened a bottle of red wine and poured three glasses out. Lola and Jess were still sat there and none of them were speaking, still in shock, all thinking about the days that lay ahead. Gina passed them a drink each and sat down on the large cream leather sofa. Gina looked over at Lola. 'If you want, Lola, I'll come home with you to tell the kids. Jess, you will come too, won't you?'

Jess hunched her shoulders, checking her silver Rolex. 'Erm, I really have to go home soon and sort some stuff out. I suppose I could come for an hour or so?'

Gina ran a single finger around her glass. 'It's going to be hard for us all and we need to be there for each other, that's what the boys would want. We were all together through the good times and we need to be there for each other through the bad times. The good times will come again, eh?'

Lola finally started smiling, remembering times when they were all happy. She smoothed her red hair over her shoulder. 'We've had plenty of good times, ladies, eating at the best restaurants, drinking the best wine and all dressed to the nines anytime we went out. I bet the women hated us around here, we were like the Cheshire Housewives. I mean, just look at us all. It takes hard work to look this good. We've all had our teeth done. Jess has had her tits done, and we've all had work done on our faces. Some more than others,' she said as she directed her look over to Jess.

'I've only had my lips done once, and that was for the shape. You've got about three mils in yours, Lola, so don't point the finger at me, you cheeky bitch. I think you should have them dissolved and start again, anyway. They're like bleeding sausages.'

Lola's back was up. She hated that Jess was having a pop at her again. It was always the same anytime they were all together. They would be having fun then one comment, the mood would flip and they'd be at loggerheads. 'And, if we're putting it out there, then your airbag tits are too big, but you don't hear me going on about them, do you?'

'Whoah,' Gina snapped before this got out of hand and the two of them were scratching each other's eyes out. 'Stop bloody having a go at each other all the time. Let's just have a quiet drink and try and work out what comes next.'

Lola dug her hand deep into her pocket and pulled her fags out. 'I'm going in the garden for a ciggie. I need to clear my head for a bit.'

Gina reached for her cigarettes too. 'Wait up, I'm coming too.'

Jess knew she'd upset Lola and held no remorse for it. She picked up her mobile phone and started scrolling through her social media. Lola was a mard-arse and needed to get a grip.

———

Gina lit her fag and blew out a large cloud of grey smoke. She looked around her garden and smiled. All the solar-powered lights were coming on now and they shed a gentle light on the garden in its full glory. Everything was neat and tidy, no overgrown grass or a flower that needed deadheading. Gina loved gardening. It was right after buying her first plant that she got properly into it. It calmed her down and gave her some head space when she needed it most. There was a large tree just outside her garden and nesting in it were a couple of wood pigeons. At this time, she knew they would be huddled together sleeping. She'd watch her feathered friends for hours some days, watching them peck at each other, fly away and come back together. She'd read somewhere that wood pigeons mated for life and they reminded her of herself and Scott.

Lola was quiet, sucking hard at her cigarette, long hard puffs, fuming. 'She's a right bitch, Gina, and I don't know how I keep my hands from her sometimes. She knows how to press my buttons and I can't help but want to punch her lights out.'

'I don't think she thinks before she puts her mouth into gear, love. She's still young and she means no real harm. Jess is just Jess, take her with a pinch of salt.'

'Still doesn't stop me wanting to one-bomb her though, does it?' Lola stressed.

'I think we are all on a short fuse tonight, love. The last few weeks have been horrible sitting in that courtroom every single day. It's drained me, I'm not going to lie. I've not had a decent night's sleep for months with all this going on. My head feels like it's going to burst.'

Lola looked up at the winter moon, serene in the night sky compared to all the crap that was going on down here.

'You always seem to cope with anything that life chucks at you, Gina. I fall apart at the slightest thing. Mike has zapped all my energy lately and, if it's not him, it's the kids. I never find time for me anymore.'

'You're much stronger than you give yourself credit for, love. I've promised Mike and Tommy that I will look out for you both and I'll keep to my word. We all need to stick together. I'm frightened to death, if I'm being honest, Lola. What will I do if they take our home? I've not slept proper for as long as I can remember, and it's constantly on my mind, I can't rest. I could strangle Scott sometimes for leaving us open like this. You see, he tells me not to worry and he sorts everything out, but he's not sorted this, has he? So God knows what else he has left open. The police have taken most of my stuff – my labels, my bags. It was a good job I had a few pieces lent out or stashed away, the same with my jewellery, otherwise I would be fucked too.'

Lola nodded. 'I had my Rolex on, and I stashed a bag of my rings in my knickers just before they searched upstairs. A good job really because, if it all goes tits up, I'll have to sell what I can to keep our heads above water.'

Gina could see Lola was getting upset again and patted her shoulder. 'You'll be fine, Lola. Something will come up; it always does when we need it.'

Lola smiled. 'I've calmed down now. Should we go back inside and see what Mrs Tits-and-Teeth is saying?'

They both giggled and headed back inside. Jess was already stood up looking in the mirror, coat on. 'I'm sorry but I'll have to get going. I'll give you a ring tomorrow and see what's what. No doubt we will be on a reception visit taking the boys all their stuff into the prison. I'll tell you both now, if Tommy starts with all his demands again, then he's getting told he can piss off. He only did six months the last time he was inside, and he made my life a misery. Honestly, constant phone calls, wanting to know where I was every second of every bloody day, he done my head in. I'm not doing years of that. He might as well know from day one that he needs to mellow out and trust me, or I'm walking.'

Lola smirked and nodded. 'Tell me about it. It's like we're prisoners now too. The fellas will want to know where and what we're doing. Well, I don't know about you two, but I can't be thinking they've got their lads on the outside watching our every move. Tell you what, I could do with a girlie weekend away. Before POCA clean us all out of everything. Let's get away for a couple of days – we deserve something to mark getting through the trial. My mam will have the kids, so clear your diary and we can piss off for a few days in York or something.'

Jess perked up, clearly liking the sound of this. 'Yep, put my name down for it. I'll tell Tommy when he rings me. I can tell you now, he'll see his arse as always. He'll probably say I'm meeting some man.'

Gina chirped in, 'Girls, if you are both with me, it should be alright. They see me as the sensible one.' She chuckled.

'You're probably the worst one out of us, Gina,' Jess giggled.

'Oi, I don't mind a bit of a laugh and a joke with the guys, but that's as far as I go. My knickers stay on, as you both know.'

Jess kissed Gina on her cheek and made her way towards Lola. Their beef seemed over for now and they had forgiven each other.

'See you soon, Jess. Take care, love, go get some rest.'

Gina hugged Jess too and they both watched as she left the room. Jess's car was parked on the street opposite and they could see her through the large bay window getting inside it. 'Bloody trouble, isn't she,' Lola chuckled. 'Gorgeous, and she knows it.'

'Yes, she sure is. I just hope she doesn't give Tommy a hard time now he's locked away. You know more than me what she's like. To tell you the truth, I won't hold my breath before we start hearing rumours about her again. A ten-stretch is a long wait without a ring on your finger.'

'Exactly what I was thinking too. I wouldn't like to be in her shoes if Tom hears she's doing him dirty. He'll put her six feet under without a shadow of a doubt. It's too effing easy to meet with a little accident round here if you piss off the wrong person.'

Gina looked at the empty space next to her in bed that night and her fingers touched the white pillow. Here it was, the emotion she'd caged for weeks bursting out from her. She'd waved Lola off who'd decided she'd face her own kids alone, then Gina had gone straight upstairs, the silence deafening when she closed the door and let the night darken around her.

The bedroom door opened slowly, and she quickly dried her eyes.

'Babes, go and get back in bed. It's late.' She didn't want her daughter seeing her in pieces.

But Bethany came over, pulled the duvet back and got in next to her mother. She cuddled in close to her and they both had a cry. Gina kissed the top of her daughter's head. 'Everything's going to be fine, baby girl, everything's going to be fine.' Gina stared at the street outside her window. The blackness beyond the pools of light from the streetlamps looked more ominous than usual. She was going to have to always think who might be lurking in every shadow from now on. The days ahead were going to be hard, but something was stirring in her. Something that told her she had the grit, the determination it would take to make sure her husband and her family still stayed Manchester's number one. Her eyes flickered as she slipped into sleep. Tomorrow was a new day.

Chapter Four

Scott Gilbert opened his eyes slowly and rubbed his knuckles deep into his sockets. A pain deep in his heart, a dull ache, wouldn't shift. He turned his head and looked over at his cell mate. Tommy was still sleeping. It had been a long night for sure, their first after being transferred, and Scott felt knackered. There'd been noises all night keeping him awake, grown men crying, doors being booted in. A nightmare, but it was his reality now and he knew he couldn't let anyone see the pain he felt. Scott hung one pale leg out of the bed and lay there scratching his nuts. He looped his arms above his head and yawned. The noise from outside on the landing was constant. Inmates shouting to one another, whistling, singing. Scott threw a pillow over at Tommy and gave a half-hearted smile. 'You go and put some towels on the sun-beds, lad, and make sure we have a sea view. Welcome to Hotel Strangeways.'

Tommy groaned and moved the pillow from his head. 'Was it a dream, or what? Please tell me I was dreaming, and I'm not banged up?'

Scott scoffed. 'I'm afraid not, Tom-lad. I'm as gutted as you are. I swear all night long I was tossing and turning. I got about an hour's sleep. Ten fucking years. I still can't get my head around it.'

Tommy folded his wafer-thin pillow under his head, then sat up and looked around the cell. 'It's a shit-tip in here. They better fucking sort this shit out and get us hooked up in a better cell. I'll make a few enquiries later and get things moving.' He inhaled and immediately regretted it as a sour smell filled his lungs. 'I can smell the misery in this place already. Once I'm on the landing, I'm going to start seeing what's what. Firstly, we need to see where Zac Manion is. If he's in this jail, then the shit will hit the fan. The runt's going down, no question about it. The moment I see him, he's getting it.'

Scott rolled on his side and licked at his lips. 'Just chill ya beans, Tommo. Let's find our feet before you go in all guns blazing. I'm the first in there for that twat, but I need a bit of time to sort my self out. Things have been crazy lately and I just need to breathe and clear my napper.'

Tommy sneered over at Scott and spoke through clenched teeth. 'Yeah, whatever, but you know how things work in here, mate. It's a dog-eat-dog world and we need to get to him before he gets to us. I wonder how Mike slept. I think he's padded up next door. I heard him shouting last night so fuck knows what's going on.'

Scott started laughing and jumped up out of bed. 'I'm sure he will fill us in.' He stepped near the door and stood back as he heard the jangling of keys from the other side. 'Ay-up, opening time, Tom.' Scott stood back from the door, facing the screw. He nodded slowly and examined every inch of the officer. 'What's the script, boss, how long are we out for?'

The man, who was in his mid-forties and looked like he'd rather be anywhere else but here, swallowed hard. He wasn't even meant to be working on this landing: he was covering today for his colleague. He wanted no hassle and, after reading the files on these two guys, he wanted away from here sooner rather than later. 'About an hour, lads. Go and get some breakfast down at the canteen and the staff there will fill you in on how things work in here.'

'Nice one,' Scott said. The officer was gone, and the door was open wide. Scott started to get ready and urged Tommy to do the same. Mike was here now, and he didn't look happy. He paced the cell, ragging his fingers through his hair. 'A fucking smackhead I've been padded up with all night. The cheeky twat was rummaging through my stuff trying to have my baccy away. I was asleep and heard him.'

Tommy growled and sat on the edge of the bed cracking his knuckles. 'Nah, do these muppets think we are some kind of pricks, or what? We need to start as we mean to go on in this gaff. Tell the screw if he brings anyone near your door again who's on gear then you'll do him in.'

'Mate, I don't need a screw to sort it. I whacked the fuck out of him last night, kicked ten bags of shit out of him.

Don't tell me you didn't hear him whinging. I made him sit at the door all night long and told him, if he moved an inch, I'd cut his dick off and shove it up his arse.'

Scott shook his head and made his way to the door. 'Nice way of making friends you've got there, Mikey. Now let's see what's what and then we can start planning our time here. You both know as much as me that these screws are bent bastards and all out to earn a few quid. Let's suss out who's who and get them on the books.'

Scott and his boys left the cell and walked along the landing, shoulders back, a cocky look in their eyes and as much swagger as they could muster on a terrible night's sleep. It worked. Their presence was felt straight away, men whispering as they walked past, doors being closed by men who didn't want any beef.

Scott sat at the graffitied table and started to eat his food. His eyes were all over the place and he clocked everyone who was sat in the room. When you were on the inside, you never took your eyes from the ball, always alert.

Tommy played with his food, stirring it around. He pushed his away. 'I can't eat this shit, it's fucking tasteless.'

Mike reached over and stabbed his fork into Tommy's sausage. 'I'll have that, then. No point in it going to waste.'

Tommy sat back in his chair and folded his arms in a strop. 'We should be getting a visit today from the girls, shouldn't we?'

Scott nodded and spoke with a mouthful of food. 'Yep, I rang Gina last night and told her what she could bring in. She said she would tell Jess and Lola.'

Tommy looked deflated. 'I bet Jess makes up some excuse why she's not brought me any stuff in. She's a thick cow and doesn't realise I will need socks, boxers and all that.'

'Just wait and see before you start moaning. Give the girl a chance.' Mike was still looking at Tommy as it became clear that the word was out that Scott and his boys were here. Already the brown-nosers were starting to appear in the canteen, all wanting to get on the good side of these guys.

'You need anything, give me a shout,' a man said as he walked past.

Scott nodded over at him and that was all it took.

Mike nudged Scott and he sat up straight, alert. 'Yo, eyes to the left. I'm sure that's one of Zac's wingmen.'

Tommy stretched his neck and eyeballed the man on the opposite side of the room. 'I've seen his face about too. We need to move quickly, Scott, and sort our shit out before these clowns ambush us. And you know they will, it's just a matter of time.'

Scott shot a look over at the prisoner and studied him, gave him a look that told him he was ready for whatever he had to throw at him. 'We need a couple of mobile phones. Have a word around the landing and see what the script is. Mike, you suss out which of these screws are snide and get the ball in motion.'

And that's how easy it was to get things you shouldn't have in jail. The men finished their breakfast and headed out of the canteen. Until they were tooled up, they were sitting ducks, and they knew it. This was their home now and they had to make the most of it if they were ever going to survive the years set out in front of them. Only the toughest survived in places like this and it was up to Scott now to make his mark and take down his opponents. It was dog eat dog.

Chapter Five

G ina Gilbert sat looking in the mirror, twiddling her hair, fed up. She pulled at her eye-bags and grimaced as she touched the wrinkles around her eyes. All night long she'd been crying, and her eyes looked swollen.

Bethany came into the bedroom and stood behind her. She draped her arms around her mother's neck and kissed her cheek. 'Mam, I still can't believe my dad is not going to be here with us. I miss him already; the house doesn't feel the same without him. Is there anything we can do to get him out of that hell hole? Can't he appeal against the sentence? I've seen it on the TV. Anyone can appeal against the time they have to serve.'

Gina turned round and looked deep in her daughter's eyes. 'I know you miss him, love, but your dad will be fine. It's up to us now to be strong and support each other until he comes back home. If there was a way of getting him home, I would have found it. Stop worrying.'

Bethany's eyes clouded over. 'I'm not strong like you are, Mam. You can deal with everything, and you don't get stressed like I do. Dad paid all my bills, my car insurance, my phone bill, my clothes. I'm going to be lost without him. I don't even have a job, so what the hell am I supposed to do?'

Gina raised her voice. Tough love needed. 'Stop it now. We'll sort it out. No matter what, we will make sure we are all alright. And maybe it's no bad thing if you start thinking about looking out for yourself a bit more too. I don't need you giving me grief when I'm only just about functioning myself this morning.'

Bethany snivelled and Gina used her finger to wipe away the tears. She turned back to the mirror and sighed. 'I've got a visit today with your dad. I'm not looking forward to it one little bit – it'll break my heart to see him in there, and it's even worse when I have to leave him, but he needs me.'

'Why didn't you say? I'll get ready and come with you.'

'No, love, I need a bit of time alone with him today. We have a lot of things to talk about and I need his full attention. You can come on the next one.'

Bethany knew when no meant no and backed off. She sat on the bed and watched her mother applying mascara to her long lashes, fanning them out with her eyes wide and her mouth half open.

Gina had aged well, and she was still a beauty. Everyone was always telling her how good she looked for her age and they were right. She was still a looker any man would have been glad to have on their arm and she knew she had to make an effort for Scott – show him she was up to the job ahead of her.

In the corner of the bedroom was a pile of white papers. Bethany leaned over, picked up a bundle of them and started to flick the pages over. 'What's all this, Mam?'

Gina looked at her in the mirror. 'Put them back, love, and don't mess them up. It's all the depositions from your dad's court case. I'm going to read through them and see exactly how the police managed to nick them all. Hopefully there might be something his barrister has overlooked in them.'

'Bloody hell, good luck with that, you'll be there for years.'

Gina shrugged, trying to make light of the matter. 'Well, I've got lots of years to read them now, haven't I?'

Bethany put the papers back where she found them and stood up. 'Tell Dad I love him, Mam, and make sure he rings me. I won't rest until I've spoken with him.'

'I will, love, don't worry.'

Bethany looked like her mother – the same strong features, almost masculine, until she glammed up. Her passion was the theatre and transforming into different characters. She'd loved acting since she was a kid – school plays had been her favourite thing to do. She had bagged some great parts too, although her largest roles had been male. The teachers always said they had more girls than boys so she was used to taking on any part she could get. When she put on her male voice, it was spooky. Gina and Scott had invited the world and his wife to come and watch their daughter on stage for her latest performance and had told them all that in time Bethany would be a film star. For now though, she had to make do with the local theatre company, where she auditioned for everything. She'd need it more than ever to take her mind off her dad.

Bethany left the bedroom and Gina carried on getting ready. To the side of her, folded neatly on the white drawers, were Scott's belongings that she'd be allowed to take in: socks, boxers, tracksuit bottoms, t-shirts, everything her husband needed. She quickly checked the clock on the wall and stood up to get ready. She'd better get used to this routine – once a week she would be making the journey to see her husband in the nick. This was her sentence too; all the family would do time now in one way or another. That was the problem with prison – the family was punished as much as the prisoner.

Gina loaded the car up and made sure she had everything she needed, giving herself a pep talk as she did: it was an effort to get her game-face on. She took a last look at the bag: passport, clothes, money, cigs, yep, she was ready to go. She was meeting Lola outside the jail soon and no doubt she would have to help her check all Mike's property in too. Lola was never the sharpest tool in the box and found it hard to cope with rules and regulations – plus she had a brain like a sieve. Jess on the other hand, was as sharp as a tack but hadn't replied to any of the texts she'd sent her. This was all she needed, her not turning up. Tommy would go ape. He was sure to kick off if she ghosted him on the first visit.

The car came to a halt as Gina pulled the handbrake up and sat staring at the prison across the road. She rubbed her arms as goosebumps started to appear on her skin. The prison spooked her, made her stomach churn. Behind those walls were men who'd done bad things: murderers, robbers, fraudsters. It was hard facing up to the fact that Scott was in their number now. She couldn't turn a blind eye to the darker things he'd done, not now he was doing time for them. But she knew Strangeways was packed with more than just the guys like Scott – she told herself he'd only ever taken out people who knew the risks of the life they led. No, the cons who really made her shudder were the ones she thought were the dregs of society – the rapists, the wife-beaters, the kiddie-fiddlers. She hated the thought of Scott having to share breath with those blokes. Then of course there were the plain weirdos, ones no one could understand, ones who should have probably been on a psych ward. And there were the quiet ones who were just trying to keep their heads down for short sentences, the old lifers who knew all the secrets, and the guys who spent their whole stretch telling everyone they were innocent. Yes, you could find pretty much every stripe of criminal in this jail. Gina looked up at the looming tower then paused, her eyes closing slowly, imagining what her husband must be going through behind the walls. He wasn't a danger to society, in her eyes, he was just earning a crust to look after his family. He was a danger only to anyone who tried to step on his turf. Well, that's what she told herself. She opened her eyes, the vision of her husband crying in his cell disappearing. She pulled her fags out of her coat pocket and opened the window slightly. She was ten minutes early and, if she knew Lola, she would turn up late anyway. Gina checked her phone and started looking at photographs of her family when they were all together. She zoomed in on one shot of her husband and smiled at the photograph. 'I'm going to miss you so much, Scott.' Gina choked up and quickly turned her phone off. She had to pull herself together, stop being soft. From the corner of her eye, she clocked Lola heading towards her. Bleeding hell, she was dressed to the nines, high heels on, low top showing nearly all her knockers, short skirt that would flash the lot if she crossed her legs when she sat down.

The car door opened, and Lola jumped inside. She dropped the large black sports-bag on the floor in front of her and slid the seat back. 'I can't be arsed with all this. On my life, I've not stopped all morning, I had to drop the kids off at my mam's, iron all Mike's clothes and not spin out thinking about what's going to happen next. Stressed out I am.'

Gina smiled and flicked her fag ash out of the window. 'No sign of Jess. I've texted her about ten times. She's not answering my calls, either.'

Lola looked sceptical. 'Probably on her back with some guy, that one. I'm not being funny but we've both heard the rumours about her, and, if Tommy has chosen to ignore them, then that's his problem, not ours.'

'I know she was fed up before he got nicked, thinking he was never going to pop the question, but she's stood by him while this case has been going on, so I thought they'd sorted things out between them.' Gina could do without Tommy kicking off – Scott needed to be finding his feet on the inside, not talking his mates down from a flip-out.

'Jess is a money-grabber. While Tommy was on the out, she was still getting treated like a princess. Now that he's gone and the money has stopped, she knows she will need another hand to feed her. Think about it, Gina, I know her of old.'

'I'll have a word when I see her, see what's going on in that head of hers.'

Lola sighed and looked over at Gina. 'Let's face it, Tommy was punching above his weight with Jess anyway. She's drop-dead gorgeous and she could have any man she wants.'

Gina looked confused. 'So, why did she end up with Tommy? Ask yourself that, because he's not the best-looking guy out there, is he, and there are other minted guys around if that was all she wanted?'

'She told me he makes her laugh but, come on, I'm not buying that, are you? She gets everything she wants from Tommy and she's a freeloader.' Gina frowned. 'She probably thought she'd just wait until he was sent down so she could bin him off without a fight.'

'He'll have her out of that house if she starts messing with his head. Worse than that, if he thinks it's because of another fella. Come on, you've seen him before slinging her clothes on the street when she's pissed him off. The guy's ruthless.' Gina started laughing and shook her head. 'Bleeding hell, do you remember that all her knickers were all over the street and every single neighbour was out watching it all. The talk of the estate they were for months.'

'Crazy man that one is. I wouldn't like to be in her shoes if she's ditching him.'

'We keep out of it; we know nothing if Tommy asks. Leave them to it,' Gina said.

Lola glanced at the clock. 'Come on then, let's go and do this. I'm not looking forward to all this palaver for sure. But this is what for richer for poorer means, I guess.'

The screw had a face like a smacked arse when Gina approached the reception desk carrying the clothes in her arms. 'I'm here to see Scott Gilbert and I've got property to hand in too.' Lola was stood behind her and already she was fed up with waiting in this shit-hole. Gina started placing the clothes neatly on the counter. She'd spent ages ironing them and she wanted to keep the creases out.

The officer spoke to her with attitude. 'Other window for property, love.'

Gina huffed at him, and he could see he'd rattled her cage. 'You could have told me that when you saw me putting them on here. It would have saved us both the ball ache.' She snatched the clothes back and placed them under her arm, fuming she was. 'Tosser,' she mumbled under her breath as she made her way to the next queue. Some of these officers needed to learn some bleeding manners. Just because they were visiting someone in jail it didn't mean they were criminals too. Wankers. Her patience wasn't going to last a day, let alone a decade.

Gina and Lola sat waiting for their names to be called and looked around the visiting centre. You got all kinds in places like this. Young women dressed to the nines not caring that their children were running about the joint and bothering the other visitors. Lola covered her mouth with her hand and whispered under her breath. 'Oh my God you can see her bleeding arse, someone should tell her to get a skirt that fits her. Imagine letting your daughter out looking like that?'

'I was just going to say the same thing,' Gina replied. Not wanting to mention that Lola's skirt was probably only an inch longer. 'If that was our Bethany she would have been dragged back inside the house and made to change her clothes, bloody walking about like that. Slapper.'

Lola shook her head as she watched the young girl finally get up to grab her kid who was bothering a man at the end of the row. Gina went quiet, thinking, just digesting everything that had gone on to bring her to this point. Lola nudged her as the names were read out for the visitors to go over to the main jail. Gina stood up and looked back at the officer still manning the reception desk. 'Prick,' she whispered under her breath.

After what felt like endless security checks, the girls walked into the visiting centre, and Gina finally spotted her man sat at the far side of the room. It had taken nearly half an hour to get through all the inspections and searches. She was sick to death of it all already, being treated like a second-class citizen. But it was worth it all when she saw Scott. He stood up and smiled at her.

'Come here, my girl, and give me a big fat sloppy kiss. I've missed you so fucking much already.' Scott hugged his wife and sat down facing her. She could tell just by looking at him that the sentence had knocked him for six. It was up to her now to fix him, get his head straight and tell him everything was going to be alright. She was good like that, she could always calm her husband down and make him think differently about any situation that was bothering him. Countless times she'd talked him out of kicking off at someone or giving one of his lads a second chance. She reached over the table and touched his strong fingers. 'How's it been?'

He dropped his head low and replied without meeting her eyes. 'First night and all that. I've not been out in the main jail long enough yet to get myself straight but give me a few days to adjust and I'll be in the gym and sorting my head out. You know what I'm like, it takes me a bit to sort my napper out. I'm buzzing now I've seen you though. I could take on the whole wing now I've had a look at you.'

And there it was, her big strong husband was back again. 'Bethany said to ring her. She was upset this morning, missing you – although half of it is just her worrying about paying all her bills. Sometimes I think we've been too soft on her.'

Gina could see Scott's face crumple. Thinking about his daughter, his baby girl, was always his soft spot. 'Tell her I'll carry on paying everything like I always do. We should have a couple of phones on the wing later so, once they land, I can start phoning you both each night after bang-up rather than standing in the queue with every man Jack listening.'

'Jenkins has been quiet about it all. I've told him you don't need him to do anything, but you know what he's like, he doesn't listen. I don't want him doing anything stupid. Ring him too when you get the chance – he'll listen to you. Who's your cellmate – one of the boys?'

Scott shot a look over at Mike and Lola and then at Tommy sat at a table on his own. 'Yeah, it's me and Mike. Which might be for the best if Jess has not turned up. Tommy will go apeshit if she's done one.'

Gina raised her eyebrows. 'I tried messaging her last night, but she never replied, she's just blanked me. She might turn up late. You know what she's like: she likes to make an entrance.'

Scott shook his head. 'Not what Tom needs, is it?'

'We can't make her come, love. She knew it was a visit today. It's up to her if she comes or not.'

Scott moved in closer, inhaling the floral perfume from his wife, the smell reminding him of home, his place in the bed next to her, his safe place. His voice was low. 'I'm gutted, babes. On my life I woke up this morning and it all landed on me like a ton of bricks.'

'Scott, you will be fine. You're the strongest man I have ever met, and you can deal with anything that life throws at you. I'm here with you all the way of this sentence and I'll never let you down. You can always depend on me. We're a team, remember?'

He swallowed hard and kissed the ends of her slender fingers. 'I just hope the money we have left is enough to last. I've still got a few men on the out looking after things so hopefully we have nothing to worry about. There should be cash coming in – we might just have to be a bit clever about how you get your hands on it.' He didn't sound too confident, and Gina could sense it in his voice.

'As long as we keep the house, I can deal with everything else. I need a roof over my head – somewhere to think and plan and wait for you to get out.'

But Scott was hiding something, she could tell: no eye contact, fidgeting about. 'Scott is there something you're not telling me? If the house is going, then I need to know. I need to be prepared.'

He looked her directly in the eyes and sighed. 'Babes, the barrister was speaking to me about it, and I have no way of proving where the money came from that we put down for the house. It was a dodgy mortgage, wasn't it. He told me he would try his best but it's not looking good.'

Gina felt a physical pain, like a knife had stabbed deep into her heart. Panic was setting in and the colour had drained from her face. The noise in the visitor centre suddenly felt deafening, talking, kids screaming, mothers shouting at them.

Scott looked over at the door to the canteen. 'Go and get me some decent scran, babes. The food in this place is rotten. Tommy's not eaten a thing yet. The weight's going to fall from him.'

Gina looked inside her black coat and pulled out a twenty-pound note. She stood up. 'Should I ask Tommy if he wants anything while I'm going? Look at him, just sat there on his lonesome.'

'Yeah, get him a butty and some chocolate, anything to put a smile on his face.'

Gina headed towards Tommy's table. He had a concerned look as she stood over him. 'Don't tell me she's sent you to tell me it's over. Gina, do yourself a favour and don't get involved. If that rat is carting me then let her do her own fucking dirty work.'

Gina placed one hand firmly on her hip and replied with a stern tone. Who did this idiot think he was talking to? 'Tom, I'm here to see if you want anything to eat. I've not even spoken with Jess so wind your neck in. I belled her last night and texted her, but she never answered. She might be ill for all we know.'

He let out a sarcastic laugh. 'Like fuck she's ill. I bet she's getting shagged by someone else. I knew that tart would have her knickers down the moment I got slammed.

'Bleeding hell, do you want something to eat or not?'

Tommy realised he was taking this out on the wrong person and started to calm down. A screw was nearby and already he was making his way over. Probably ready to throw the rule book at them both. 'Get me a couple of butties and a bag of crisps, would you, Gina love? I'm Hank Marvin, the food in here is shite.'

That was better. Gina smiled softly and patted his shoulder. 'I'm sure Jess will be in touch. It's hit us all like a ton of bricks so she might need time to digest it all. If I know her, she will be on the phone to me later.'

Tommy nodded and watched Gina walk off. The screw was at his side now and gave him a serious look. 'No one's allowed at your table unless they have booked a visit. There are rules here for a reason, so follow them next time. I'll give your visit another ten minutes to book in and if they're not here then you'll have to go back to the wing.'

Tommy spoke through clenched teeth, ears pinned back, chest expanded fully. 'Move out of my face and stop badgering me. If my visit isn't here when my food comes back, then I'm walking anyway. So, wind your neck in and get back in your box.'

The officer jerked his head over at his work colleagues. The look that told them an inmate was ready to kick-off. It all happened so fast: four men in uniform stood around the table. Dave Planer was leading this. He was well known as a bit of a bastard, the toughest screw in the place. Ex-military, always out to make a name for himself. He gripped Tommy by his arm and twisted it up his back. The others restrained him too, his head pressed down on the table. He was trying to talk but it was hard to hear what he was saying. The officers were team-handed and they dragged the inmate from the visit. All the other inmates were in uproar now, shouting insults at the screws.

'Dirty bastards, takes a bunch of you to deal with one man,' one prisoner shouted.

Scott sat up in his chair. Eyes were on him already and he knew if he made one slight move, he'd be dragged from the visit too. Mike shouted over to him from a few tables away. 'Leave it, Scott, it's not the time or place, that twat will keep.'

Gina was back at the table, and she was distraught. 'Jesus H Christ. I was gone two minutes and all hell breaks loose. I've got Tommy some food, will they let you take it back for him? What kicked off?'

'Not sure, love, but these pricks are out to prove a point today. They want to show the new inmates they're on us – try and scare visitors from bringing anything in. But it's better they've taken Tommy back than him chinning someone on day one. I'll sort it out when I'm back on the wing.'

Gina passed the snacks over to Scott and sat down looking flustered. She knew, if this had happened on the outside, all the screws involved would have been twisted up and ten bags of shit kicked out of them. But this was prison rules, not Scott's, and he had to learn that inside these walls his rules meant fuck all. He had to pick his battles. Gina was quiet, her head doing overtime. 'Scott,' she said in a quiet voice. 'What you were saying before. I can't lose the house. It's my everything: me, you, the kids, it's where my heart is.'

'I know, babes, just keep your fingers crossed they don't take it. I'll speak to the accountant, do everything I can to make sure it doesn't happen, but,' he paused, 'I can't promise.'

Gina swallowed hard and took a few deep breaths. She could do this, hold her tears back, pull herself together. She'd done it a hundred times before when she had to. Scott reached over and kissed her softly. 'We've had a good run, haven't we, Gina? Holidays, clothes, cars? This is just something that happens eventually in the world we chose to live in. You get the highs and you can't avoid the lows forever. But we'll get back on top again – no one keeps a Gilbert down.'

Gina nodded. But was this really the life she'd chosen or was it one that had crept up on her? Scott had been a small-time player when they met. She'd never imagined she'd be a mob wife – but then again, she'd never told him to quit. By the time she realised how deep into the life he was, she was too dependent on the things it bought her.

The visit was coming to an end and, as she looked over at Lola, she could see her sucking face with Mike. There was no way she was kissing Scott like that in front of everyone. Those kinds of kisses were private, for when she was in bed with her man. No one would have ever guessed, but Gina had always had a shy streak went it came to sex and she was proud to say she'd only ever slept with one man in her life and that was her husband. Sure, she'd had a string of boyfriends before she met Scott and, yes, she'd had a bit of slap and tickle with them, but nothing as serious as when she met Scott. Scott had claimed that he'd never slept with any other woman and she'd decided she'd rather believe him than know otherwise. Over the years, she'd had reason to doubt him some-times – there was a particular time when he'd acted differently and changed towards her, gone cold in the bedroom. She never confronted him about it, decided to wait it out and, soon after, he went back to normal. She could have called him out, but she figured sometimes it hurt less not to know. Maybe she was overthinking it, maybe not. All her friends said they wished they had a relationship like Gina and Scott's. He was always the perfect gentleman with his wife. He opened doors for her, pulled her seat out at the table before she sat down. But those days were over. Now she was alone, and would have to fend for herself. This was the first time in her life she would have to step up to the mark. She'd never worked a day in her life, had no formal skills, no qualifications, nothing in this life that would earn her a good wage. Perhaps she could be a cleaner, she thought suddenly. She loved cleaning and mopping and polishing. Anybody who came into her home always commented on howcleanitwasandhowfreshitsmelt.Shewouldbealaughing-stock if the high and mighty Gina Gilbert was found cleaning other folks' home and she knew it, but she had always told her kids be careful who you meet on the way up because you will meet them on the way back down. True words. Now she'd have to live by them.

Scott kissed his wife's hand, and she was back in the moment. 'I love you, Gina, for now and always. Please don't worry.'

She coughed to clear her throat and managed a half-hearted smile. 'I'll try, Scott, but you know the only thing me and the kids have while you're gone is that house.' She pulled away and started to put her coat on. Bleeding hell, Lola was still kissing Mike and he was copping a feel of her tits. Gina blushed and turned her head back to her husband. 'I'll get going, then. Try and phone Bethany later. Give Jenks a bell, too.'

'I'll sort it. Like I said, I just need to see what's what, then hopefully I'll be running my wing. If I get it right, I'll be sending you some money home each week.'

Gina leaned in and kissed his warm cheek. 'Love ya,' she said as she started to walk away. She didn't want him to start telling her his plans for the wing – not with the screws listening. She'd have to trust him to play his cards right. He'd always had a good instinct for when to make a move. She only hoped she'd picked up that instinct – it sounded like she was going to need it.

Gina waited in the car for Lola; she was taking ages to come out. She turned her mobile on and there was a missed call from Jess. 'It's a bit late to be ringing me now, love,' she muttered under her breath. She sparked a cigarette up and opened the window. She needed this fag for sure. Cheeks sank in as she dragged on it. She looked over at the prison and spotted Lola. She honked the horn.

Lola plonked down in the passenger side, looked in the mirror and started to straighten her hair. 'Bleeding hell, he was all over me. I swear, if they'd have let him, he'd have had me over the table. I wouldn't have said no, either.'

Gina chuckled. 'It was like watching a live porn show. I couldn't even look. My face was burning up when I clocked you two.'

'It is what it is. I've got to make the most of my time with him because, let's face it, I won't be getting any for a lot of years, will I. My fanny will be like a mouse's earlobe by the time he comes home.'

Gina creased up. She hadn't realised how much she'd needed a laugh. She might have been a good girl herself, but Lola had no shame and Gina loved her for it. 'You're a nutter, you are, Lola, you don't half have a way with words.'

Lola was laughing too. Even at the worst moments, a proper giggle with friends was golden.

'I've had a missed call from Jess. Let's call around on the way home, if you're up for it?' Gina said once she'd got her breath back.

Lola grimaced. 'I'll give it a miss. I have to get home for the kids.'

'No worries. How was Mike, other than randy?'

'You know what, he seemed in good spirits, laughing and joking. But he did say his anxiety was through the roof, not sleeping, over-thinking and all that.'

'I wish I could say the same for Scott, that he was in high spirits. He tries to hide it, but I can see in his eyes that he's struggling.'

'Give him time, love, he's only been in there two minutes. He has to find his feet, adjust to prison life.'

Gina flicked her fag out of the window. 'Do you want me to drop you off, or what? I don't know why you didn't let me pick you up this morning instead of getting a taxi?'

'I can't stand rushing about. I knew you would be outside waiting for me, and it would have done my head in.'

'I don't mind, I would have waited until you were ready. Like I said, we've got to rely on each other now.'

Lola put her seatbelt on, and Gina gunned the engine.

'It's going to be hard, Gina, isn't it? I mean, no man, no sex, no one to support us?'

Gina pulled out onto the road. 'Yep, Christmas, birthdays, anniversaries, they are going to miss them for a lot of years.'

Lola looked forlorn. 'What if I fall out of love with Mike, what then, what if I meet someone new?'

'Bleeding hell, Lola, you had his tongue down your throat two minutes ago and already you're thinking about shacking up with someone new. Sort it out, woman. Buy a vibrator or something if you can't do without the sex.' Gina hissed.

'Oh, lighten up, Gina, I was just saying, that's all. I'm still a young woman and, if I need more sex than you do, it's not a sin, is it? Stop being like bleeding Sandra Dee.' she sang the last part. Gina realised she might have overreacted and backtracked. 'I know, love. Sorry, my head's all over the place today. Scott said we might lose the house. I'll be devastated. Imagine if I've got to go back to living in Harpurhey with my mam. I thought that chapter of my life had closed a long time ago. My mam has always wanted me living back near her, but I don't think I could ever go back to that life, if I'm being honest. Don't get me wrong, there is nothing wrong with it. I grew up there for how many years and I love visiting mates, but living where I do now, come on, Lola, it would be a giant step back in my life.'

'Harpurhey is tidy, Gina, and you would fit back in no problem. So what, people will talk about you behind your back but fuck them, fuck them all.'

'Can you imagine Paula Noble's face and the old crew when they see it's all gone tits up for me? They would love it.

I swear to you, one comment from her scruffy mouth and I'll rag her all over. She's nothing but a skip-rat that one is, in my eyes, and she's had more knob-ends than weekends. Proper sperm bank she is, nothing more.'

'I'm glad I stayed in my council house now, Gina. Mike was always saying he would buy us a house, but you know as well as me that, if we had one argument, he would be slinging me out on the streets. He's like that, Mike, loves to have one over on me.'

'I'll just have to grin and bear it, won't I? I'll think of something to get us out of the mess if the worst comes to the worst. I always do.' Gina shot a look at the diamond ring on her finger. Over twenty-five thousand pounds her husband had paid for it. He told her she was worth every penny of it too when he placed it on her finger after twenty years of marriage.

Gina swerved in and out of the traffic and they were minutes away from Lola's house. 'If you can get a sitter tonight, come around to my house and I'll cook us something nice. A few bottles of wine too.'

Lola looked downcast. 'I wish I could. My mam is already moaning about having the kids today. She'll have kittens if I ask her again. You can come to mine if you want, but I'll warn you now, the kids will do your head in. I'll have to start getting them in some kind of routine now Mike isn't here. Every night it's ten or eleven o'clock before they get in bed.'

Gina shook her head, remembering her own children growing up. She always had a strict routine, bath and bed every night at seven thirty, no messing about. She liked to think she was a good mother. She read every night to her children, always took them to different clubs after school. Jenkins was into martial arts and every Wednesday night of his childhood she would sit with him and watch him train. He was good too, agile and quick. Bethany had loved acting and, on a Monday night, Gina did exactly the same for her, sat and watched her like the proud parent she was. Scott never really had time to go with her. He was home late most evenings, and it was her who sorted the kids out. No, from the moment Scott walked in, his tea was on the table, his bath was run, and he wanted for nothing. Gina treated him like a king and even Tommy and Mike commented on how well Gina looked after him. But who would look after him now?

Lola got out of the car and looked back through the open door. 'If my mam changes her mind, I'll come around for a few hours, but don't hold your breath. Let me know what Jess says too.'

The car door closed, and Gina was on her own once more. She turned the music up and found her favourite Celine Dion album on her playlist. The singer made the hairs on the back of her neck stand on end. Her voice was something else and Scott had always said when she was on tour in Manchester next he would get them tickets to go and see her. Then she'd got ill. Proof that life could throw challenges at you however rich or famous you were. As 'The colour of my love' came on, Gina sang along, really going for it. For the short time she was singing, her problems seemed to disappear and she was back to being herself again.

Chapter Six

Jess looked at clock next to her bedside and gasped. She picked her mobile phone up and started to text.

I enjoyed last night. We need to do it again soon.

She sent the message. She could hear knocking at the front door and sat up straight. Quickly, she checked the doorbell camera app on her phone. She examined the screen and pressed the green button to speak. 'Gina, give me two minutes to get dressed.' She jumped up out of bed and glanced in the mirror to straighten her hair. Jess had the kind of tanned legs that seemed to go on forever and, even in her loungewear, she looked stunning. She tied her hair back, shoved on her fluffy slippers and headed downstairs.

'Come on, get inside, it's bloody freezing and you're letting all the heat out,' Jess said. Gina walked in and headed straight into the front room, followed by Jess.

She perched on the big grey sofa and placed her hand-bag at her side. 'Go on then, why didn't you make the visit?'

Jess sat down on the chair facing her and tucked her legs under her bum. 'I couldn't face it. For weeks I've been sat in that courtroom and every day it's been about Tommy. I needed some me time to process it all.'

'So, you should have said that instead of blanking me. Tommy might have understood if you were tired or stressed out, but to ignore me and give me nothing to tell him is a piss-take.'

Jess dropped her head low. Gina was like her older she'd and in all the time she'd known her she'd always put her in her place when she was wrong. 'I'll go on the next one. No doubt he'll be on the phone later hurling abuse at me. Honest, on my life, if that man starts with the name-calling, then he's gone. I don't have to listen to his bullshit when it's me doing him the favour. Ten years he's expecting me to wait for him. That's a long time, Gina. I'm a young woman and should be having the time of my life at this age. Surely, he must know that. It won't be long before the demands start again, telling me what time I should be home, asking who I've been talking to, stopping my money.'

Gina nodded; she knew this woman was right but she was here to try and smooth things over not add fuel to the fire. 'Turn up for visits for now. I get what you're saying but I can't go back to Tommy and repeat what you've just said, can I?'

'But it's the truth, Gina. I can't be expected to put my life on hold because he's in the chokey. I'm going to do me from now on.'

Gina folded her arms in front of her and changed the subject knowing she was fighting a losing battle. She couldn't make Jess love Tommy or wait for him; this was for them two to sort out, not her. 'I think we're going to lose the house. Scott is trying everything he can to sort it out but I'm not daft. He won't be able to prove where the money has come from to pay for it. He's not worked an honest day in his life, has he?'

Jess's eyes were wide open. She knew how much the house meant to Gina. 'Bloody hell, Gina, what are you going to do?'

'I don't know, I have to look at the options. I can't get that much money together to get a mortgage in my own name. And, even if I can, they will want to know where the money has come from. It's a no-win situation. I could strangle Scott for this. He should have boxed it off, made sure we were safe in our home. I mean, half the businesses round here are laundering – why couldn't he have put more of his takings that way, set something up the rozzers or the taxman wouldn't take?'

Jess could hear the anger in her friend's voice and tried to soften the blow. 'You're Gina Gilbert – you'll think of something. You can buy a new house, do things properly this time so nobody can ever touch it again.'

'I can't, Jess. Where would I get money like that from? POCA will be watching like hawks if they think I'm living the good life. I think I'll pack up what's left before they come and take the house, and go back to my mam's. Imagine the shame of everybody watching us being evicted?'

'Yeah, that would be hard, Gi, I get it. That's the thing about men like Scott and Tommy: when they fall, we fall with them. I could have had my own salon and been a success on my own, but it was Tommy, you know, who stopped me opening one. He wanted me to be kept by him and me, like a fool, agreed to it.'

'We've all been kept women, love. We let our men call the shots and now we've got nothing left for ourselves. I could kick myself when I look back. I was naive to think this would go on forever. I never stashed any money away, never put anything away for a rainy day, did I? My mam always told me to have my own money that nobody knew about. I should have listened to her. I'm an idiot, a bleeding daft idiot who thought we were untouchable.'

Jess sat in silence for a few seconds. Then it was as if a switch had flicked. She sat forward in her seat as she spoke. 'Let's do it now, then. Let's set up our own business, make our own money. Buy our own dresses, be our own success and all that. We could open a sunbed shop like I was always going to – get someone doing nails, facials and all that. It won't cost a lot to get up and running and if that is a success then we can go bigger. Open a string of beauty lounges.'

Gina shook her head. 'That might be alright for you, Jess, but I don't bring anything to the table. I have another idea, but I need to work it all out yet and I'll get back to you. An idea that could be a game-changer for us all because, let's face it, we're up shit creek without a paddle.'

Jess looked intrigued. 'Tell me more, I'm interested already?'

Gina sucked on her gums and looked down at her hands, twisting her gold wedding band around her finger. 'Not yet, let me work it all out and I'll get back to you. One thing for sure though is we tell nobody: not Tommy, not Mike and definitely not Scott. It'd knock him sick if he thought I was grafting, that he wasn't providing for me. And your Tommy would send his boys round if he thought you had a side-hustle. No, we have to look after things our way now. I'll wait for Scott forever – but I'll never depend on a man again, mark my words.'

Jess started smiling. 'I like it already and if it can earn us all some decent money then I'm in. Maybe I won't have to find myself a sugar daddy after all.'

Chapter Seven

Jenkins was sat watching television as Gina came into the front room, his eyes still on the box as he spoke. 'How was my old man? Did he say anything about me? What's happening about the house? Has Dad got a way of stopping them POCA scum getting their hands on our stuff?'

'Give a woman time to get in through the door, lad.' Gina took her coat off, placed her handbag on the corner of the sofa and collapsed down next to it. 'Son, just back off, will you? My head is going to pop if I have any more stress. Your dad will ring tonight so I'll know more then. My head is battered with it all so, like I said, chill out and let me relax for a bit before you start going on at me with a thousand and one questions.'

Jenkins was on one. He stood up, pacing about the front room. He wasn't a little kid anymore and his mother needed to start remembering that fact. He was sick of it, sick of his younger sister calling him a mummy's boy, fed up with everyone thinking he had no backbone. This was his time to shine and there was no way on this earth anyone was going to stop him. He knew about the world out there, knew more than he was letting on. How on earth did his mum think she could keep him away from it all when day in and day out he listened to the conversations his old man was having? He'd seen it all – how the drugs flowed in and out, which people paid up when they were 'politely' asked for protection money. He'd seen the blood on his dad's hands when he came home late at night, and the hard silhouette of firearms stuffed in waistbands. No, this was his world now and his mother could like it or lump it. 'Nah, Mam, this is serious. I know you are stressed and it's up to me now to put bread on the table and make sure we keep on top. My dad is locked up and what can he do from behinds bars?' He paused and eyeballed her. 'Not a lot.'

Jenkins was getting right on her nerves now and she glared at him, ready to blow. The two of them had always had a fiery relationship – he'd been a tearaway as a teen and had driven Gina to the edge. And this woman could blow. She'd launched things at his head in the past, put him up against the wall, nose to nose with him when he got gobby with her and thought he was Charlie Big-spuds. She hadn't taken any shit from him when he was younger and she wasn't going to start now. This was her home, for now at least, and her rules. He needed reminding of who she was. 'I've told you time and time again that I don't want you involved in anything like that. It's your dad's mess, not bloody yours. Give your dad a bit of time and he will sort things out like he always does. You don't need to do anything.'

'I do when the house is being taken from us, Mam. There's a letter come this morning telling us it's getting taken by the dibble. And you expect me to take that lying down, do you? Because I'll tell you something for nothing – I'm not sitting here waiting for it to happen.'

'Oh, have you heard yourself, Jenkins? Give it a bleeding rest, will you. You're still a baby and know nothing about the real world out there. I made sure of that when you were growing up and now you think you can step up and run things like your dad did. You'd be eaten alive out there, son, and you know it, so do yourself a favour, take a back seat and let the real men sort things out. If your dad thinks you can help, I'm sure he'll be on the phone telling you so. On my life, if brains were dynamite, you couldn't blow your bleeding nose.'

Jenkins sat down on the edge of the sofa and cracked his knuckles, his cheeks bright red. He was fighting a losing battle with his mother and tried his best to keep quiet. Gina flicked the channel over, searching for something on the TV to calm her down, a gardening programme, a DIY show, anything. She sat back on the sofa; she could feel her son's eyes on her.

'Mam, I know you're upset and it's hard for you, but it's hard for us too.' His tone was softer now. 'I know you have done your best to keep me away from my dad's world, but it's in my blood like it was in Grandad's blood too. The Gilberts never give up. We fight to the death. My dad has drilled that into me from being a kid and it's stuck with me. Like it or not, I'm going to fight to keep what my dad has grafted his balls off for.'

Gina kept her eyes on the television and spoke in a sarcastic tone. 'Are you still talking?'

Jenkins stood up and stormed out of the room, banging the door behind him. He'd show her, he'd show them all.

Gina scanned her eyes over the dining table. She saw the letter her son was talking about. She stood up and walked over. She read every word of the letter, and finally flung it back where it had come from. She marched back to the sofa and sat staring into space as if the answer would simply come to her about how she could fix this mess. Nothing.

Bethany walked into the front room and clocked the look on her mother's face straight away. 'Mam, what's up, is it Dad?'

Gina saw the worry etched on her daughter's face. 'No love, it's bleeding Rockefeller up the stairs thinking he can sort everything out. He's chatting shit so do me a favour. When you talk to him, tell him to calm down and leave things well alone before I lose my rag with him. I'll swing for him, on my life. If he carries on, he'll see a side of me he won't like.'

Bethany sat down and played with the cuff of her jumper. She had a good circle of friends and up to now she'd never given her mother any trouble.

'Before you ask, your dad said he will ring you later and he said stop worrying about your bills. He will continue paying them.'

Bethany looked relieved. Without her dad bailing her out all the time she wouldn't have a carrot. Her life was the theatre, but she very rarely earned a wage from her performances, just dribs and drabs.

'I'm here if you need me for anything. You keep it all in, Mam, you need to stop thinking you can deal with everything on your own. Tell you what, why don't you go out with the girls tonight? I bet you could all do with a break from worrying. It's been ages since you've let your hair down. I know Dad is banged up, but it doesn't mean that you are too. Go to the club that's just opened on Deansgate. Everyone's talking about it. I'll do your make-up and hair, if you want?'

Gina had to admit her daughter was right. These last few months had been hard, day in day out all about her husband and the court case. It would be nice to get her glad rags on. 'You know what, Beth, you might be right. I think I need a good blow-out, dance the night away. I'll ring the girls, but Lola has already said she won't be able to get a sitter.'

Bethany jumped in. 'Then I'll babysit. Hayley and me were only going to chill here tonight anyway and practise our lines for the show. Go on, ring the girls and see if they are up for it.'

An hour later, Gina looked stunning. Her make-up was on point and Bethany had styled her hair so it was full of bounce and looked sexy as. She was wearing her white jeans and an off-the-shoulder red top. Gina had blushed when Lola arrived and called her a MILF. Jess walked into the front room now and whistled at her. 'Check this sexy mama out. You're looking hot tonight, girl.'

Lola was sat on the sofa still finishing her make-up when Gina's mobile phone started ringing. She answered straight away. 'Hiya, babes. It's so good to hear your voice. Didn't take you long to sort out a phone.'

Lola peered over at her friend, trying to suss out what Scott was saying.

'Actually, I'm on my way out in a few minutes so I'll probably speak to you later when I come back home.' Gina looked anxious as she listened to her husband's voice at the other end of the phone. 'I'm going out with Jess and Lola. We needed a cheer-up so we're all going to that new club in town. Why is that a problem?' It was clear all was not rosy in the garden, and the girls glanced at each other and rolled their eyes as Gina raised her voice. 'Listen, Scott, let's get one thing straight before you start ballooning at me. Of course I'm not rubbing it in your face. I've not been out for as long as I can remember and I've been stressed, we've all been stressed, so don't get on the phone to me shouting the odds. You should be telling me to go out and grab some life instead of sitting in the house staring at four bleeding walls all night. I'm not dead, you know.' Gina was listening now and, whatever her husband was saying, she didn't like it. 'Right, ring me later when you're in a better mood. I can't be arsed with drama when

I'm going out. I'm off for a few hours down Deansgate, not going to the bloody Maldives, you know.'

The call ended and Gina stood on the spot for a few seconds.

Finally, Jess spoke. 'Is everything alright, doll?'

Gina walked to the mirror to apply her lippy. 'What the hell is wrong with them lot? You should have heard him telling me what I can do and can't do. Honest, on my life, he said he wanted me home for twelve.'

Lola burst out laughing. 'Like we have ever been home for twelve o'clock. Who does he think you are, bloody Cinderella?'

'Exactly,' Gina hissed. 'There I was earlier telling you not to give Tommy an excuse to blow and then it's Scott who starts pecking my head. Anyway, fuck him and his mood. We're going out tonight whether they like it or not. If he wants to make a scene about it then so be it, I'll deal with it when I have to.'

Lola's phone started ringing and then Jess's. They all looked at each other. Jess answered her phone like it was a hand grenade. Tommy's voice was loud, and she had to hold the phone from her ear. 'Are you done?' she said finally when Tommy's shouting had died down. 'I'm not the one locked in prison so don't treat me like I am. If this is going to work between us, then you need to sort your head out. This is a you problem. You need to end the call and go hit the gym or something, because I'm not listening if you are shouting at me like this.' She stabbed at the screen to end the call.

Lola's phone was still ringing and she winked at her friends and put the call on silent. No, there was no way she was listening to any abuse from Mike just before she went out. He'd ruin her night, put her on a downer. The three of them sat there realising they'd broken the habit of a lifetime and said no to their men. Gina stood and grabbed her coat. 'So ladies, we can either sit here for hours worrying about how we're going to sweet-talk the fellas round, or we can say sod them, get our coats on and go paint the bastard town red. I know what I'm doing, what about you two?'

Lola gathered all her make-up and flung it into her bag. She ruffled her hair up and stood up next to Gina as she swigged the last bit of wine in her glass. 'I'm ready to party. Fuck them, let's go and dance.'

The music was pumping, and the clubbers out in full force tonight. The wine they'd had getting ready had hit them now and they were all tipsy. Gina walked up to the club and was met by two bouncers. She never queued or paid in clubs once she threw her husband's name into the mix. She would walk in, no questions asked. Doormen were often the fixers of the scene – they always knew who was barred, which gang would kick off if their main guys weren't let in. They knew who was dealing and who was buying. Scott had always had the best ones in his pocket, but she didn't recognise these guys.

A lean, muscled man stood in front of her. She'd definitely not seen him before. Maybe she was getting out of touch.

'Twenty quid, darling.' He held his hand out and looked at her.

'I'm Scott Gilbert's wife, love, and these two are with me.' She was like royalty, and she loved that feeling that she was important, that her face and name meant something in this city.

There was a pause. The young guy was obviously a bit wet behind the ears and was full of attitude. 'And that means what to me? You could be King Charles's wife, but it's still twenty quid each.'

Gina was flustered, looking one way then another. She had never had this problem before. She peered into the moodily lit corridor inside, clocked a familiar face and beckoned him over. 'Greg, this one doesn't know who we are. Can you have a word and sort him out? And make sure we don't have the same problem again. Embarrassing, it is.'

Greg whispered something into the younger bouncer's ear, and you could see the look on his face change. His tone was different immediately. 'Sorry, darling. Yep, you and your friends go straight in. Sorry, it won't happen again. I'm new here, don't know the crack yet.'

A few of the other clubbers lining up were shouting abuse now. They'd been queuing up for ages in the cool night air and these three women had walked to the front of the line and gone straight in. But Gina didn't look back.

Jess went to the bar and nodded at the barman. 'Have you got a table for us, love? Send over a bottle of champers when you're ready.'

The barman was a known face on the scene and knew the score. 'Yes, no worries, there is a table. I'll get one of the girls to bring the drinks over.' He pointed to the left of them, then grabbed another staff member and worded him up.

Gina tried not to look relieved. Her heart had been racing back at the door – to think all the respect she'd earned could have vanished like smoke overnight. Thank god some of the older guard still knew which side their bread was buttered.

Jess sat down and looked about the room. She nudged Lola and kept her voice low so Gina couldn't hear her. 'Do you fancy a bump?' Lola licked at her lips and nodded. This was the norm on a night out for Jess. Coke was part and parcel of any night out she had. Rich man's whizz they called it, something to give them more energy and confidence, both of which they needed tonight, she figured. Jess scanned the crowd. Most of the clubbers would be on something tonight – Ket and Magic and sniff were never far from any night out. Why should she and Lola miss out just because Gi was too straight-laced to take anything?

Jess stood up and walked away. Gina watched her from the corner of her eye. She wasn't born yesterday. 'Where's she off to, powdering her nose?' she asked Lola with a sarcastic tone. She hated that they tried to hide that they were drug users from her. She wasn't daft.

Lola stuttered, not looking directly at Gina. 'Probably, it's only a bit of sniff, Gina, relax.'

Gina watched the drug deal taking place in the corner of the club with an inquisitive look. 'So, who runs all the drug dealing in this place these days? Is it one of our boys, or someone else?'

Lola hunched her shoulders. 'Honestly, I bet there are people scrapping over it – the younger ones who want to make a bit of a name for themselves know Scott's not here to fight back. Mind you, most of the time I just get twisted and, as long as it's good stuff, I'm not really arsed where it come from.'

Jess was heading back over, and Gina's eyes were still on the dealer at the back of the room. Lola stood up ready to go to the toilets to have a sniff. Gina however had other things on her mind. She stood up with her drink and hid away in the shadows watching everything that was going on. Hold on, this was a familiar face she'd spotted, and worse, he'd spotted her. Sonny Lawson was headed straight towards her. Bleeding hell, this was all she needed. Sonny was an old friend, she knew him from school. They'd even had a bit of fun behind the bike-sheds all those years back. He'd probably want to dig for gossip and see how the mighty have fallen.

'Gorgeous Gina! How's long's it been? And who's let you out on your own?' he chuckled as he barrelled up to her.

Gina flicked her hair over her shoulder and tried to keep calm. 'I'm always out, love. I've not seen you around for ages, though. Where have you been hiding?'

'I've been abroad for a few years, Gina. Once I knew there was no go with you, I had to go and try and mend my broken heart in another country, didn't I?' He winked.

Gina giggled. 'Shut up, you daft bugger. You've not changed, I can see.'

'Nope, bigger, older and no wiser. Anyway, how are you? I've heard your Scott got a ten-stretch?'

'You heard right, Sonny. I knew it wouldn't be long before the gossip got out.'

'It's not really gossip. It was all over the newspapers and on the radio.'

Gina stood with her back against the wall and studied him. He was still good-looking, dark brown hair, big blue eyes. His clobber looked like the good stuff – she'd heard he earned his money the right way, as a property developer. Sonny was a success in his own right and, some nights when Gina was feeling fed up, she wondered what her life would have been like if she had chosen the path with Sonny Lawson. Him and Scott hadn't been so different when they were all kids. She'd heard it was the drug game that had taken him aboard. But someone had told her Sonny turned his life around years ago, couldn't stand the life of crime anymore, valued his freedom and got out of that world before it was too late. She'd always felt the life she'd chosen was a one-way street and yet here was living proof you could take a u-turn.

She wasn't sure if it was the wine, old time's sake or the fact he'd shown that there was a way to make some honest wedge, but something inside Gina flared. A heat. He gripped her hand and led her to the dance floor. 'Come on then, I'll have that dance now, the one I should have had all those years ago before big Scott Gilbert stepped in and ruined my game plan. If he wasn't such a big lad, I might have put him on his arse and taken you back.'

Gina burst out laughing. 'Sonny, we were kids, not what I would call a romance., We shared a few kisses, that was it.'

Sonny pulled her towards him by the waist and swung her about. 'A few kisses that I never forgot, Gina. You're the one who got away.' Sonny started dancing, pretty good moves too, snake hips.

She was dancing with him and for a few minutes she forgot about her own problems. As always there were eyes on Gina Gilbert from every corner of the room. Scott's boys were watching, and she knew this dance would be reported back to her husband. She didn't care and for now she enjoyed the dance. Jess and Lola were dancing too, and the DJ started to play some old tracks, songs from her era. Sonny was not sitting down, and one song slipped into another. Gina was making the most of tonight: and this was just what the doctor ordered, a bit of laughter, some harmless flirting. Finally, the DJ started playing stuff she didn't recognise and they all headed back to the table. Jess was on another level, busting out moves like a cage dancer. The men were like flies around shit, all trying their best to get her on their arm. Lola was drunk as a skunk. She had never been a big drinker. She flopped at the table.

Gina yanked her up – she knew this would be reported back to the boys in Strangeways too. 'Lola, sort your shit out, love. Go and wash your face in the lav and see if that livens you up. You're too old to be getting yourself in this state. Jess,' she shouted over to her. 'Go and sort this one out. Take her outside for a bit of fresh air and see if it brings her around.'

Jess came back to the table and clocked Sonny straight away. She winked at Gina and helped Lola to her feet. 'Come on, pissy-arse, let's get you sorted. I knew you were a lightweight, told you not to start drinking as early as you did.'

Lola lifted her head and she looked green. She covered her mouth with her hand and pushed past Jess, heading straight for the toilets. Jess moved out of the way and held her hands up to protect herself, her outfit. This was a Gucci dress, not some cheap shit from the market.

Gina shook her head and looked over at Sonny. 'Bleeding hell, she's not usually like this. I think we all needed to let our hair down after – well, you know'

Sonny looked at Gina a lot longer than he should have. 'You deserve so much more, not all this shit you've been going through. All the shit Scott has brought you into.'

She was embarrassed, not sure of how to handle this kind of attention from a man. Her life had always been straightforward, no man had ever dared speak to her while she was on the arm of her husband and that was just the way he liked it. Now she was smelling freedom for the first time in her life, tasting it and enjoying this new feeling. 'Give over, Sonny, I'm a married woman. I stay faithful, loyal. You won't hear me bad-mouthing my man.'

Sonny clocked her empty glass. 'Are you having another one?'

Gina looked around her. When word got back to Scott, she could tell him Sonny was an old friend. What was the harm in that? 'Go on then, I'll have a pink gin and lemonade. It looks like I'll be on my tod for a while, judging by the state of Lola.'

Sonny stood up and walked towards the bar. He kept looking back at her and smiling.

Jess stood outside the club with Lola. The poor girl was spewing her ring up at the side of the door. Jess was holding her hair back and rubbing her back. 'Come on, get it all up. I'm like this when I've drank too fast. Once I've been sick, I can drink again.'

Lola was mumbling under her breath. 'Take me home to my kids. I want to go home.'

Jess stood back and looked down the street. She could see a taxi pulling up. She ran towards it and opened the door. 'Can you take my friend home? I'll give you the address.'

The taxi driver looked at the figure approaching, wobbling from side to side and declined the fare. There was no way he wanted someone in that state in his fresh clean whip. 'No, love, I'm not taking her when she's like that.'

'Come on, mate, I'll give you an extra tenner. She only lives up the road.'

'No, sorry,' he said and wound up the window.

Jess spun on her heel. She was fuming. If she was stuck looking after Lola, her night was ruined. Jess went back over to Lola and started to walk her up and down, hoping the crisp cold night air would sober her up. Anyone could see Jess was fed up and, if this had been any other friend, she would have left her on her jacks and gone back inside the club.

Gina took a mouthful of her drink and spotted the dealer Jess had bought from again. She elbowed Sonny and whispered in his ear. 'Who does he work for, do you know?'

Sonny nodded over at Carl Clarkson and his boys. 'Clarkson and his lads run the shit round here. Scott and his boys have never been able to take it over. Carl is a force not to be messed with and he's one of the ones who'll be rubbing his hands now Scott's doing time. He's a fucking prick, full of himself, if you ask me. I've not had any dealings with him, but I know a few guys who have and he's on another level. Nutter.'

Gina studied Carl and his boys and asked more questions. 'So, he runs the town centre? I thought Zac Mannion had a patch round here before he got done.'

Sonny didn't like having this kind of conversation and changed it very quickly. 'I'm not interested in those clowns, Gina; I'm just enjoying catching up with you.'

She knew when to back off, but she kept her eye on Carl Clarkson and his clan. Sonny moved in closer, and she moved away, didn't feel comfortable anymore. She was looking for her friends now. Sonny realised maybe he'd stepped too far into her personal space and backed off. He started to talk about people they both knew and how their lives were going. They were laughing and relaxed with each other again. Jess was back now and looked flustered. 'We'll have to get her home, Gi, she's not in a good place. We've gone from being sick to her going on about how much she loves us both and is missing Mike. She is crying her eyes out.'

Gina lifted her drink and necked it in one. She grabbed her coat. 'Sonny, it's been nice catching up. Take care, love, and look after yourself.'

Sonny was gutted and Gina could tell by his face he didn't want her to go. 'What if I get a taxi for her?'

Jess held her hands up and shook her head. 'I've just tried. They refused to take her because she's pissed.'

Gina moved out from her seat. 'It's fine, Sonny, I'm ready for my bed anyway, plus, Scott will be ringing me soon and I want to speak to him.'

'No worries. Lovely seeing you too, Gina. Maybe we can go for food one night, if you're not busy.'

Gina shook her head, looked over at Jess and then at Sonny. 'I don't think so. My Scott would shit a brick if he knew I was going out gallivanting with you.'

Sonny nodded. 'Yeah, he would do just that. He'd have a hit on me before the night was out.'

Jess joined in now and started laughing. 'He'd do more than a clean hit, pal, he'd have your bollocks chopped off.'

Jess and Gina held Lola up as they waited for a taxi. She seemed a little bit better than before, though she was still sobbing. 'My Mike is not here with me. He knows what to do when I'm like this. Who's going to look after me now?'

'Sssh, Lola. You'll be fine. You've just had too much to drink, that's all. Have a good sleep and in the morning everything will be better,' Gina said.

'It won't, it will never be better until he's home. My kids are heartbroken, and I feel an emptiness in my heart that won't leave me alone.'

'You and me both,' Gina said. 'Tonight is about enjoying ourselves again. Course we are all sad, but we can't be sad for the whole time our men are away. We have to put a smile on our faces and stand tall. Nobody has died, have they? At least we can go and see them, speak to them daily. Think about all those women who have lost their partners and how they feel. Plenty of men die young in this game. There is always someone who is worse off than us.'

'It's alright for you, Gina. Let me cry for my man. You're tough, you'll cope.'

Gina bridled. Who the hell did she think she was talking to? Pissed or not, she was getting told. 'Everyone deals with the shit that lands on them differently. I'm hurting just as bad as you, but crying and moping about won't change anything, will it? You have your children to think about so what good is it to them seeing you upset every day? Put a face on and get on with it.'

Gina flagged a taxi down and they managed to conceal the state of Lola as they got in. Jess sat in the front and kept the driver talking, flirting, showing him a bit of leg.

Bethany opened the front door and her eyes widened when Lola stumbled past her. She giggled and stood with her back against the wall. 'Wow, what's she been drinking? She's steaming.'

Her friend Hayley was at Bethany's side now and they were both laughing. Jess stood at the gate and watched everything that was going on. 'Girls, I'm getting off. I've got another party to go to. If you're coming, Gina, hurry up.'

Gina waved her hand in the air. 'No, love, I'll sort her out and get a taxi home with Beth.'

Jess didn't need telling twice. She got back in the taxi, and she was gone. Gina took Lola straight up the stairs. She lay her on the bed, yanked her shoes off and threw the duvet over her. This was the best she could do and already she was fed up with nursing her. She turned the light off in the bedroom and closed the door. That was Lola out for the count, for sure. Gina headed down the stairs and went into the living room. The place was a state – toys all over the place, wet washing on the radiator, unwashed dishes. It was not what she was expecting to see. Lola was finding it hard and, looking around this front room, she could tell even cleaning up had become a chore for her friend. 'Do you want to stay here tonight, Beth, and make sure she's alright in the morning? You can give her a hand with the kids too and help clean up.'

Bethany was good like that, and she never mentioned that she'd already started to clean up. If her mother had seen it before she come in, she would have had kittens. Gina was house-proud and cleaning was on the top of her daily list. 'Yes, we'll stay over but you owe me, Mother,' she chuckled. 'The kids have not been long in bed, and they don't listen to a word you say to them. Cheeky, they are.'

Gina rolled her eyes and rang for a taxi. She stood next to the window so she could see when her taxi arrived. An alert on her mobile phone: a friend request from Sonny Lawson. She rammed her phone into her coat pocket and stared out into the night sky. Bethany was behind her now. 'Was it a good night out, Mam? Did you try the new club what I told you about?'

'Yes, love. I'll tell you what, my legs will be done in tomorrow, I was dancing all night. I've not danced like that for years.'

Bethany smiled and went to sit back down. Gina was telling the truth when she said she'd not danced like that for years. Why, she asked herself now, why had she only ever been involved in her husband's life? Why had she not concentrated on her own? Life was passing her by and seeing how Sonny had turned his life around had made her realise it wasn't too late to make something of herself, find out what she liked, what she was good at, instead of thinking about everyone else all the time. Yes, she was a mother and a wife, but she was still a woman, a person, an individual who wanted to make her own footprint on this earth, not walk in someone else's. The taxi lights were outside, and it honked its horn a few times. Gina gave her daughter a kiss and headed towards the front door. 'See you tomorrow, love. Don't forget, Lola will have a banging head in the morning – please help her with the kids and that. I'll make it up to you, don't worry.'

'Night, Mam. Ring me when you get home, so I know you are safe.'

'I'm always safe, Bethany, always,' she said as she walked out of the front door.

———

Gina pulled up outside her house and paid the taxi fare. She could see a car parked opposite her garden and a few men sat inside it. Slowly she approached her front path. Was it her son sat in the passenger side? She wasn't sure. She opened the gate and closed it behind her, still trying to get a better look. Her eyes were playing up tonight – she didn't know if she needed to go and get them tested or if it was just the gin. She went inside the house and closed the front door behind her. There was no place like home, for sure. Inside these walls she had always felt safe and secure, but that feeling had left her now: she was vulnerable and alone. Maybe she'd been too quick to ask Beth to stay at Lola's. She walked slowly into her beautiful front room, the decor, the curtains, the furniture. It was all going to be lost. Everything she loved was slowly disappearing.

Upstairs, Gina looked at her phone and went to call Scott but stared at the friend request again. What would the harm be in speaking to an old friend? Maybe he could help her out, give her some advice on earning a quid or two. She pressed the button and accepted Sonny's friend request. Placing her phone on the side, she got into bed and picked up her book, anything to take her mind off the car outside. Whoever was in it, she couldn't let them know that Gina Gilbert was afraid.

Chapter Eight

Scott Gilbert lay on his bed with his hands looped behind his head. He looked over at Tommy, who was sat opposite. 'The Mrs didn't phone me back. I wonder what time she rolled in. On my life, she better not start fucking about with my head while I'm in here. She knows how my head works when I'm stressed out.'

Tommy let out a laboured breath and replied as he folded the newspaper on his lap. 'Welcome to my world, pal. Jess is always out, even before I got sent down; tells me she doesn't have to explain to me where she is all the time. And she wonders why I am paranoid. I've got a gut feeling she'll cart me in a few weeks. I suppose it's my own fault for getting with her in the first place. Everyone told me she was a gold-digger, only out for what she could get from me, but I never listened. In all fairness, I would have done anything to have her by my side. The woman is fucking stunning and she's a top shag. Kinky she is, not shy of trying out new things.'

Scott rolled on his side, ready to listen to anything to take his mind from his own troubles. 'Jess is trouble, mate, but you never listened to any of us when you hooked up with her.'

'Love is blind and all that, Scott. I knew she was danger but you only live once – and when have I ever minded a bit of danger?'

'You should have stayed with that Mandy. She loved the bones of you, do anything for you. She wasn't as bling as Jess but still her heart was in the right place.'

Tommy sat up straight. 'Nah, mate, she was too much. On my life she was always on the blower asking me for a handout. Plus, she had three kids. I want a relaxed life I do, mate, like you, not running about after some other fella's kids.'

Scott lay thinking. 'Yeah, I'm lucky with my Gina. She ticks all the boxes, cooks, cleans up, gave me two gorgeous kids and is decent in the bedroom.'

Tommy stared over at Scott and smirked. 'But shagging the same woman for all these years, doesn't it get boring?'

Scott tapped his finger against his nose and changed the subject. There was no way he was discussing his love life in detail with Tommy. He got up and went to stand near the window to inhale the cold air coming in from outside. 'Today we find that prick and deal with him. Zac Manion needs knocking down before he comes and looks for us.'

'Defo, mate. I'll tell you now, he'll be already plotting to take you down, so we need to be quick.'

'When Mike comes in, we'll round up our troops and come up with a plan. Mike's been a bit quiet lately, don't you think? He seems distant. We'll have to have a chat with him and make sure he's alright. His mental health has been shite recently, so let's keep a close eye on him.'

Tommy sucked hard on his gums. 'Yeah, I was thinking the same thing. He's missing Lola alright. But look, Zac's on the next wing so I'll word that screw up who's already on our books and make sure it's sweet.'

Scott nodded and got down on the floor to do some press-ups. His head was in the zone now and the large vein at the side of his neck was pumping. It was game on.

The prison was noisy when the cell doors opened on Scott's landing. He stepped outside his door and held a tight grip on the cold metal rail, looking down at the other inmates. Mike was stood next to him now and Tommy came and stood at the other side of him. 'It's going down today, Mike. Zac's leaving here in a body bag. You go ahead with a few of the others and give me a nod when the coast is clear. Get me everything I need.'

Mike nodded, no other words needed; he knew his role and he disappeared. Tommy was edgy; he always got like this before something went down.

'Tom, don't forget we have to speak to the firm at home today and see what's what. We need to keep an eye on the ball while we are all in here. You know as much as me that the fucking scavengers will be eager to take our patch once they know us three are banged up. Don't get me wrong, we have a good team left out there, even though it's not the numbers I'd like, but will they fight to the death to protect our work while we're in here?'

Tommy scratched his head. 'I'm all over it, Scott. I thought your lad was going to step up. Have you spoke to him?'

'I'm not sure yet. He's not like me, Tom. Don't get me wrong, he's got balls, the lad, but he knows fuck all about the real secrets of grafting the area. He's already told me he has a few lads on board, but if I can I want to keep him out of the really messy stuff. He should only be picking the cash up, making sure Gina gets her cut. I want him as the money man, not the one with the blade.'

'Yep, that's the last thing you need is your boy getting stabbed up, isn't it?' Tommy walked off in the opposite direction. He had things to do now, busy making sure their empire was not falling down while they waited for Mike to give them the all-clear to hit Manion.

Scott headed towards the stairs. The wing had fallen under an eerie silence, and everyone seemed to disappear. Scott walked down the first stairs. He was about to look over his shoulder when the first blow struck. Scott stumbled down the stairs, each pounding into his body. He never stood a chance after that. Three men, identities covered, all kicking ten bells out of him. The silver blade dug deep into his abdomen, once, twice, three times, blood spurting from the open wounds. The prison sirens started blaring as an officer on the other side of the landing saw the commotion. The three attackers were on their toes and gone before the officer got to Scott. He screamed at the top of his voice trying to alert his colleagues. He bent down and quickly examined Scott Gilbert, panic setting in. Thick red claret was pumping from Scott's stomach, blood seeping from the side of his head, his eyes flickering.

Tommy roared like a lion from the top landing as he clocked the crowd forming on the stairs. He sprinted to the top, but the officers, out in force now, blocked his path, three of them gripping him and leading him back to his cell.

'I'll kill them. On my life, each one of you lads who did this will be six feet under when I get my hands on you,' he roared. The prison was on lockdown now and all the doors were slamming as everyone got herded back into their cells.

Scott's eyes looked up at the officers and his mouth was moving but no words came out. His breathing was laboured. The guards called for a stretcher.

Tommy stormed about his cell. He booted the door time and time again. He was like a caged lion. 'Manion, I'm coming for you, I'm coming for all of you.' His words echoed throughout the wing. But now Scott was down they were all vulnerable. He was a sitting duck and he knew it.

Chapter Nine

Gina lay on the bed. The light from outside burned her eyes. Dry mouth, head banging. Never again. The hangover from hell had set in. If Scott had been here, he would have handed her two paracetamols, got her a drink of water, and told her stay in bed. He'd have looked after her. But she was alone. Jenkins had gone out about an hour ago and she hadn't moved since. She remembered him popping his head into her bedroom early this morning and laughing when she tried to raise her head up from her pillow. Gina rolled on her side and licked her lips, wishing she had brought a drink up with her last night. She reached for her mobile phone and checked if Scott had rung her while she was asleep. Nothing. She shot a look at the clock and phoned her mother. She always rang her in the morning and had a quick chinwag. She needed to be honest with her, tell her she might be moving back in with her if the worst came to the worst.

Gina spent at least twenty minutes on the phone with her mam, asking the normal questions: had she had her medication, had she had breakfast? Bev, her neighbour, was a good soul and for over a year now she had gone into Mildred's in the morning and made sure she had everything she needed. Gina bunged her a few quid for her troubles and always told her how much she appreciated her help. Now it looked like she'd be moving in and taking that on herself – but she couldn't bring herself to tell her mum today. Gina ended the call and lay staring into space. Her eyes settled on the pile of papers in the corner of the room. She'd promised herself she was going to read through them all, but she'd been putting it off. Balls to it, she got out of bed, picked up the depositions, walked back to her bed and snuggled under the duvet. The cleaning could wait. What did she have to get up for anyway? Absolutely nothing. She scooped her hair back and tied it with a black bobble. One by one, she read each piece of paper. Her eyes were wide as she digested every movement her husband and his boys had made while they were being investigated by the police. She had set out to look for a loophole, something to help get Scott off or his sentence cut. But this was interesting stuff. She found she was more intrigued about the details of his empire – how had she not paid attention to all this stuff before now?

It was mid-afternoon, and Gina was still reading the police evidence her husband had been given before he was up in court. She had a blue pen and a note pad in hand and was circling notes on the pages. She stared at the piece of paper in her hand for a moment then started to search for previous pages she'd already read. She was confused. It had taken her a while to piece everything together but now she was sure something was wrong. Her blood ran cold as a terrible suspicion formed in her mind. But before she could even think about her next move, her mobile started ringing, the screen flashing with her husband's number. She tossed the paperwork aside. She didn't want Scott to ask what she'd been doing.

'Bloody hell, I've been waiting for you to ring, I thought you was having a lie in or something,' she said.

Then a pause as she realised this was not the voice of her husband, but Tommy. The colour drained from her face as she listened to the voice at the other end of the phone. 'What the fuck! I need to see him, Tommy. Where have they taken him, why have the prison not informed me? Oh my God, Tommy, how the hell has this happened, where were you and Mike?'

The voice was desperate at the other end of the phone and Gina was trying her best not to lose it. The call ended and Gina lay in bed frozen, just staring at the wall. A single fat tear rolled from her eye. She crossed herself and pressed her two palms tightly together. 'Please Lord, please let my Scott be alright. Our family is falling apart right now, and we need your help.'

Then she dived out of the bed and started to get ready.

Gina rushed into the hospital and found the ward her husband was on. She'd finally got a call from the prison staff who told her he'd been moved there as soon as the injuries were looked at by the doctor on-site. Too serious for him to handle. Gina opened the double door on the ward and already the police presence was easily felt. She could practically smell the misery behind these doors:, sickness, sadness, it was all lingering in the air. And added to that, the coppers. She didn't know if they were protecting her husband or waiting to question him. There were two police officers manning the door, stood tall, chests expanded fully. 'I've come to see my husband, Scott Gilbert.'

'I need to see your ID first, love. As you know, your husband has been moved from HMP temporarily and we must do our security checks exactly like we would at the prison.'

Gina dug her hand in her bag and pulled out her purse to show her driving licence. She shoved it in the officer's face. 'Here, have a look, and now let me go and see my husband.'

The constable examined her driving licence and looked at her. 'He's in the room on the left. You can't stay long, doctor's orders, not mine.'

Gina ignored him and walked through the double doors, mumbling under her breath, 'Bleeding jobsworth.'

Every second could count and she needed to set eyes on Scott to know how bad it was. She flinched as she rounded the corner: more officers on the corridor, watching her every movement like she was about to go on a rampage. 'Scott Gilbert,' she hissed at them. She could hear whispering as she passed them, probably calling her names. Gina took a deep breath and opened the side room door. There were two screws at Scott's bedside, and she eyeballed them. 'I'm here to see my husband. Can you give us some time alone, please?'

One officer shook his head. 'Sorry, love, this is twenty-four-seven security. It's for him as much as anything. We need to be at his side around the clock until we're clear what went on.'

Gina rolled her eyes. She dragged a chair over and sat down next to the bed. There were tubes in her husband's arms, his stomach, and he was wired up to a heart monitor. The sound of his heartbeat at least brought her some comfort, knowing he was still fighting. She pretended the two screws were not there, her head falling onto the bed as she spoke. 'Scott, what the hell have they done to you, what the fuck?' she sobbed. Then she gathered her thoughts, lifted her head and shot a look at the screw. 'I want to see the doctor as soon as possible. I want to know what the damage is, what his chances are, and you can bet I am going to find out what happened to him. He was meant to be safe on your watch and I want to make sure whoever has done this to my husband is hung, drawn, and bleeding quartered.'

'Mrs Gilbert,' the officer said in a quiet voice. 'The doctor will be here soon. In terms of the incident, we take prison security very seriously. We will have to wait for the report from the prison to see what has happened. At the moment our priority is making sure your husband recovers. As you can see, he is not a well man. The next twenty-four hours will be crucial, so let everyone do their job and give your husband the best treatment possible.'

Gina needed to calm down. After all, these men were protecting him. She spoke in a calmer tone. 'I'm sorry. My head is all over the place. As you can imagine, I'm heartbroken. Sorry if I'm coming across as rude, I'm just stressed out. This is a lot for me to take in.'

The officer nodded. 'He's in the best place he can be. But I can tell you I heard the doctor saying the blade missed any major organs.'

Gina lifted her husband's hand and held his cold fingers. 'I'm here now, baby, I'm here with you. You have to get better because we need to talk. Don't you dare go dying on me.'

Daytime turned into night and the officer tapped Gina softly on the shoulder. 'It's time to go now. Go home and get some rest and something to eat. If there is any change in your husband, we will let you know straight away.'

Gina slowly turned to face the officer. 'Will I be able to come back later on tonight, stay with him?'

'I'm sorry. The rules say one visit a day. Definitely no overnights at this point. I've let you stay a lot longer than you should have. Go home, have a good sleep and come back tomorrow. Hopefully, they will be able to tell you more about his condition.'

Gina stood and picked her handbag up. She bent over her husband and kissed his cheek softly. 'I'm going now, baby. I'll be back tomorrow. I love you. Be strong.' Then she whispered in his ear, 'I'll make sure these bastards pay for this, Scott, cross my heart.' Gina left the ward and, as she walked past the officers, she eyeballed each of them. A look that told them she was a woman on a mission. Heads were going to roll.

Gina sat in the car in the car park and rested her head on the cold leather steering wheel. She let herself sob until the tears finally slowed and her breathing settled. She searched her handbag for her mobile phone. She sent the same text message to both Beth and Jenkins, trying to make it sound less serious than it was, then another to Jess and Lola.

Come to my house as soon as possible. Scott is in hospital.

She pressed the send button, flicked the engine over and headed towards the main road.

She was talking to Tommy on the phone when she pulled up at her house. 'Tommy, where the hell was you and Mike? You know the score in the jail and you more than anyone have been shouting it from the rooftops that Zac Manion needed sorting out. He's seen you are weak now, seen Scott go down. It's only a matter of time before he comes for you and Mike. Sort your shit out and make sure you don't leave yourself open again. For crying out loud, it's not bleeding rocket science, is it? Never be alone unless the doors are locked, don't trust anyone you don't know inside out, and always watch your fucking back.'

She ended the call and looked at herself in the rear-view mirror. Reading the evidence pack this morning then seeing Scott at death's door this afternoon had changed everything. No one was coming to her rescue. This was on her and she would show them she was more than just a wife, cooking and cleaning and ironing, more than a bird on a bad guy's arm. She would show them all.

Gina walked into her house, placed her car keys on the table and kicked off her shoes. She sat down on the sofa and pressed the remote to turn the TV on. She hated sitting in silence, hated being alone. A car pulled up on the driveway. She looked out of the window and saw her son rushing inside the house with a look on his face that told her he was furious. She'd kept it from him until now that his dad was in the hospital. She kicked her legs up behind her and waited for him to come inside.

The door swung open, and Jenkins rushed in, face bright red. 'Mam, that message, it almost killed me. Is he OK? Has he come round? I got straight on the phone to find what the word is. Those Manion tossers have shanked him. I swear to you, each and every one of them rats involved will be taken down. Watch this space, Mam, just fucking watch.'

She patted the spot at the side of her, inviting him to sit down. She needed to calm him. She used her inside voice. 'I know, son. There'll be more blood spilt before this is settled. But your dad is doing OK. They're keeping him sedated for now. It's rest he needs, but he will get through this. He's strong inside and out.'

Jenkins sat beside her and dropped his head low. 'Mam, I swear down if anything happens to my dad I will go to jail for those bastards. What the hell is happening? Dad knew he was a target, why has he left himself open? How many times has he told me, when you have beef, you never leave anything to chance, and there he is, lying in hospital. What the fuck have Mike and Tommy had to say about this? Where were they?'

'I've asked the same question, son. I'll know more when I speak to Tommy again later.'

Jenkins let out a laboured breath and lifted his eyes up before he spoke. 'I've been to see the firm, Mam. I know what you're going to say, but Dad needs us more than ever now, so I will be his eyes and ears while he's in there. We need to be on the ball, act fast if anything happens. I just hope Tommy and Mike get these pricks and show them what's what. They need to make an example out of them and show everyone what our name means.' Jenkins hugged her and kissed the top of her head. 'It's going to be fine, Mam. It's all going to work out.'

Jenkins could feel the pressure rising and he knew it was only a matter of time before the Gilberts' empire was over if he didn't act soon. They were going to have hit back fast – and hit hard.

Chapter Ten

Jess paced the front room with a glass of red wine in her hand. She'd had quite a few glasses already. Lola was sat on the sofa, watching her. 'He'll be alright, Gi. Scott is a fighter. He'll pull through, trust me. Look when Mike was in hospital that time we all thought it was the end for him. He pulled through, didn't he?'

Gina nodded slowly. Jess came to stand by her friend, hooked her arm around her and squeezed her. 'The lads will make sure these twats are put on their arses. Tommy rang me before and he was livid. You should have heard what he was saying to me, some sick twisted stuff.'

'It's all words, though. You both know the same as me they can strike at any time. I don't want Scott in that world anymore. This is a wake-up call for all of us. Look at us now, we've got nothing. I'm losing the house and then I'll be back at my mam's, back to bleeding square one. The fellas say they do what they do for a better life for us all, but come on, girls, they do it for themselves, for the greed, for power. None of us are our own person, really. They set the rules, we follow. When I was younger, I had dreams, but where did they go, eh? When did I fade away and become some kind of background noise? Yes, I'm Scott Gilbert's wife, but I should have been a lot more. I should have been a person respected in her own right. I'm more than a handbag-holder.'

Jess swallowed hard and shot a look over at Lola. 'Gina, you're upset. You've loved being Scott's wife, don't forget that. Our boys look after us, there is no denying that. The nice cars, the latest perfume, the winter sunshine. I don't want for nothing when Tommy is here.'

Gina was right back at her. 'But he's not here now, is he? None of us have stood on our own feet, we've depended on our men for everything. I could kick myself.'

Lola swigged a large mouthful of her drink and reached in her handbag for her fags. 'I'm going in the garden for a ciggie, anyone coming with me?'

Gina didn't need asking twice. She stood up and followed Lola into the garden. Maybe a cigarette would calm her down. She was raging inside and nothing they were saying was changing her mind. Lola side-eyed Gina. Jess came out too and sparked a cig up which wasn't her usual style – usually she was surrounded by a cloud of sickly-sweet vape mist. Gina looked up at the night sky and sighed. 'Sorry, girls, I'm not saying you did anything I didn't do. I'm gutted I never took control of our finances, bunged money away for rainy days. I know Scott has got a stash, but I should have had a plan B.'

Lola nodded. 'We've been stupid, all three of us. We took for granted that the boys would be with us all the time. I never in a million years thought they would get slammed. That's what the foot soldiers are for – doing time to keep the top dogs in the clear. And,' she paused, 'fucking ten years on my tod is not what I bargained for.'

Jess piped in, eager to get her words out. 'I've been thinking about salons since we had our chat, Gi. We should have opened our own business.'

Lola nodded in agreement. 'Cudda, wudda, shudda. Too late now, isn't it?'

Gina sucked hard on her cigarette. 'Is it? Maybe now's the right time because we won't be playing – start a business now and we'll run it like our lives depend on it. Because they do. Be a success and buy your own dress, that's what my mam always said to me, and I ignored her – thought getting a ring on my finger was an easier life – but, you know, she was right.'

Bethany, back from her latest rehearsals, popped her head outside. 'Bloody hell, it's freezing out here. I could feel the draught as soon as I walked in. Mam, how's my dad?'

Gina walked back inside the house. 'The doctor phoned me before and said he's stable. His injuries are bad, sure, but he has had a scan and there is no cause for concern.'

Nonetheless, Bethany's eyes filled with tears. Gina led her into the front room and sat her down next to her. 'Sssh now. I've told you he's going to be alright. Your dad is strong and, you know more than me, give him a few days and he'll back on his feet shouting the odds out again.'

'That's what I'm worried about,' said Bethany. 'When he's back in the nick, he'll be out for revenge, and then what?'

She was still drying her eyes when Jess and Lola walked back into the room. Jess changed the subject straight away. 'So Beth, fill us in on your love life. We won't be getting any for years now so we will have to listen to someone who is.'

Gina went beetroot. 'Wow, Jess, I am sat here, you know. My princess is my baby, remember that.'

Jess rolled her eyes and chuckled. 'Oh, relax, I'm only teasing.'

Bethany smiled: Jess had done the job of cheering her up. 'Mam, all the lads want me on their arm. You should see all Jenkins's mates trying to graft me when I'm out. Honest, I'm never short of attention. Reece Manion is always in my DMs trying to take me on a date.' Bethany cringed after the words had left her mouth, knowing her mother would be straight on her back about him.

'Zac Manion has put your father in hospital and you're getting messages from his son? Tell him to piss off. Your dad would shit a brick if he knew that.'

Bethany came straight back at her. 'Mam, my dad has beef with most families around here. Reece is an OK guy.'

'The apple never falls far from the tree, Bethany. That lad is nothing but trouble. You can't polish a turd.'

Jess and Lola sniggered. Bethany managed to crack a smile too. 'Forget him, I've got some good news, Mam. I've only gone and bagged a lead role as Ronnie Kray in our next show.'

Gina looked confused. 'What, you're playing a man again? Bleeding hell, when are they going to start casting you as a woman?'

Bethany chuckled. 'It's this husky voice I've inherited from my dad. I'm better at speaking as a man than I am a woman. I'm not bothered though, Mam. For me to play Ronnie Kray is amazing. I've got enough information how a gangster lives, haven't I?'

They all looked at each other. Gina knew her girl was right. If anyone knew about dodgy characters and crime, it was Bethany, despite what she had tried to protect them from growing up. It had been harder to keep the truth from them as the kids got older. She thought how quick she'd been to dismiss Reece Manion, and realised anyone else would say the same about Beth and Jenks. It hadn't mattered while Scott was here to protect them all, but now they were like sitting ducks. Every whisper about them could be a death sentence.

Chapter Eleven

Jenkins sat with the boys as he listened to some of the older men talking. Why didn't they shut up waffling and get to the point? He was eager to speak, sat on the edge of his seat cracking his knuckles. He glanced over at Jim McClean, his dad's deputy, and shook his head; he had heard enough. 'Nah, Jimbo, this shit just got real and sitting here talking about it for days is not going to get us anywhere. You know as much as me how things work and if we don't strike now then we're fucked. Carl Clarkson has got a shipment coming down from Leeds and we can tax it before it gets to him. We're talking a good raise here, not pennies. We need to be grafting as many patches as we can now and showing these runts we mean business. He's running the Cobra club in town. Why are we sat here watching him rake it in?'

Jim looked like he'd sucked on a lemon. Who the hell did this kid think he was? This wasn't his first rodeo, and he knew what he was talking about. So what, it was Scott's son. He didn't give a flying fuck, this was his shout, nobody else's. He eyeballed him, that hard look held deep in his eyes. 'Your old man left me in charge, lad, and I say when and where. You know fuck all about what we do and how we roll, so sit down and keep your mouth shut.'

Jenkins went bright red, his nostrils flaring, his ears pinning back. He could feel all eyes on him. His mates Rob and Lee were waiting for his comeback. Come on, lad, don't just sit there, defend yourself, he told himself. He bolted up from his seat, walking one way then the other, ragging his fingers through his hair. 'My dad has given me power too, Jim, so wind your neck in and listen to what I have to say. I need to look out for my family and doing that means making business decisions. We take Clarkson down and then move onto Zac Manion's boys. There is enough of us, so what's your beef? That's your problem, Jim, you sit about watching the world go by. It's happening now, not in two fucking weeks when you decide to get up from your arse.'

Jim was as cool as a cucumber. This kid didn't rattle his cage one little bit. He'd chew him up and spit him back out in an instant. His voice was firm: he hadn't risen this far up the ranks of Scott's empire without having to put a few upstarts in their place. 'My problem is you know fuck all about your ops, pal. You have only just stepped into this world and think you know it all when in fact you know fuck all. Have you even fired a gun, stabbed someone up?' He held Jenkins's eye and, when there was no reply, said, 'So, go back to watching fucking *Billy Elliot* or something, and leave the real men to crack on with this.'

Jenkins froze on the spot, all eyes on him, cheeks going redder by the second. 'I would stab someone, if I had to.'

Jim was right back at him. 'I didn't ask that, I said have you ever stabbed or shot somebody.'

Alex and Ray nodded at Jim. They were old timers in Jenkins's eyes, but they had all used a shooter before.

'I rest my case, enough said,' Jim sneered.

Jenkins made his way back to his seat and plonked down next to Mickey, Rob and Lee. 'Fucking wanker,' he whispered under his breath.

Jim was calling the shots now. The plan was to protect what they had rather than make a move, no mention of taking Clarkson down whatsoever. Jenkins was brooding. He had plans too, and the moment this bunch of fossils left, he would put them into action. He was going to make his dad proud, prove that he was made in the same mould. He would show them all there was a new sheriff in town and his name was Jenkins Gilbert.

Jenkins sat huddled close with his boys after the old guard left. He licked his lips and said, 'Rob, you round up our team and we'll take Clarkson down. Jim McClean's a pussy. He'll sit pretty and let us all lose everything. He doesn't have the passion like we do. He's an old-timer and he should hang his pants up and get a fucking job at Asda or something.'

Rob started laughing but Alex looked serious. He had always been the overthinker of the group. 'We don't have shooters, though. I'd stab someone up, yes, but I've never even fired a gun. Have any of you two?'

Rob bounced about pretending he had a gun in his hand, waving it about in the air. 'Can't be that hard, can it? We'll get one and do a few practice shots in the park or something.'

Jenkins was buzzing from the thought of it. 'I'll get one from Tate. He's the man for it, everyone gets them from him. We need some cash to get it sorted. I'll go and see him later and see what the script is.'

Jenkins sat in his black Golf GTI and watched as the figure approached him in the car park. He could feel his heart racing. He'd never have admitted it, but he was a fish out of water. He had to pull himself together and quick. He was a Gilbert and proud of it: fear wasn't an option anymore. He pulled his shoulders back and nodded slightly. Rob was in the passenger seat, the smell of weed lingering in the air between them. They all smoked most nights, sometimes to take the edge off things, more often just for something to do. The back door opened on the car and in jumped Tate Gavin. The guy was a unit, a tank of a man and he nearly filled the whole back seat. There was no way you would ever want to meet this guy on a dark night, for sure. Tate got straight down to business, no messing about. 'It's five grand for a Glock Nine, or I've got a basic revolver, a bit battered but it still does the job, for three grand.'

Jenkins was glad he wasn't sitting right next to the guy. He waited a moment, then turned round and spoke with his best poker face. 'Nice, that revolver sounds sweet. How long can you wait on the cash, bro?'

Tate ran his teeth over his gums and his eyes widened. 'What, you think I run some kind of try before you buy? If you want it on bail, then the price goes up.'

Jenkins was caught up in it now and he tried to keep his cool. Imagining in his head he was a big man, a man who could get anything he wanted if he put his mind to it, he steadied his voice. 'Yes, goes without saying that you get a drink on top of the price if you're waiting about for the money.'

Tate looked out of the window. The dibble was always on his case, and he didn't like to stay in one place for long in case someone tipped the filth off. 'Bell me tomorrow about two and I'll have it ready for you. You owe me three bags of sand and one on top for waiting for my till.'

Jenkins reached out and shook Tate's hot hand. 'Deal done, speak to you tomorrow.' And that's how easy it was to get a gun. Jenkins Gilbert had bought his first firearm.

Alex was still quiet when Rob and Jenkins got back. He'd not long got out of the nick and looked unwilling to put his neck on the line to help Jenkins start a war. 'Yo, bro, you know I've got your back if anyone comes for you. But starting beef? I'm not sure of this. Clarkson is no muppet and, if he finds out it's us who had him over, he will chop the fucking lot of us up. It's serious shit when he is involved. We're not on his level. We sell bits of weed on the estate, sure, but nothing like him. He'd be straight through my front door dragging me out of bed. Did you hear what he did to Wally Ward?'

Jenkins hunched his shoulders, waiting on him to continue.

'He battered his mam and his dad in front of him before he done him in. I'm not about involving my family in my shit. I'm all for earning a few quid here and there but I'm not willing to deal with the likes of Clarkson. He's proper dangerous and he wouldn't think twice about popping a cap in your arse.'

Rob dropped his head, spooked by this story. His mam was old and frail, always ill. Imagining anyone dragging her out of bed and subjecting her to violence made him feel ill. No, he wasn't down for it, either. 'Jenkins, you know me and Alex are solid, but we are not your dad and his boys. Not yet, anyway. We know nothing about big-time grafting and to jump into this without doing any homework, we could all end up brown bread.'

Jenkins's eyes narrowed. 'My dad is lying in hossy, almost dead. Are you two muppets forgetting that? Our house is likely getting took from us and you two who I call my mates are flapping at the first hurdle. Yes, we need to see what the crack is, but I'm going to do this with or without you two.'

Alex replied in a sarcastic voice. 'So, you're willing to put your mam and sister in danger then?'

Jenkins clenched his jaw and took a few seconds to reply. 'They already are in danger. So I'll do what I have to.'

Chapter Twelve

Gina lay on the bed and peered at the address in her hand. Something was not adding up. 15 Burnside Road, New Moston. This was the address that kept popping up in her husband's depositions. Scott had called at this address frequently in the months of May, June and July, just before he was nicked. Gina carried on reading through the evidence. She'd even made a huge chart to keep track of it all, like something the police would have on TV. There were names on yellow Post-it notes placed all about the board, and blue ones underneath them with locations of where to find those people. Gina had spent hours looking at it. She had the names of the drug suppliers, couriers, locations, the lot. But, still, something wasn't sitting right with her and it felt like time was running out.

Scott was still in hospital for now, where she felt he was safe, but the doctors said that in the next few days he would be moved back to Strangeways. His stay at the hospital was costing the tax-payer too much money for him to stay a moment longer than strictly necessary. Plus Scott wasn't playing ball with the investigation – he had been interviewed time and time again and he kept to the same story every time. Gina had been outside the room at the hospital on one visit and heard his line. He'd fallen, he told them, no one attacked him. Gina knew he kept the code of silence, made sure he never grassed. It was street law, and he had to abide to it, now more than ever.

Suddenly a thought hit her. She grabbed her coat and rushed down the stairs. She clutched her car-keys and ran straight to the car. It was chucking it down outside. The heavens had opened, fat drops of rain hammering down on her windscreen. She placed the white piece of paper on the passenger seat and put the address in her sat nav. She was a woman on a mission, for sure. There was no music in the car today, nothing to stop her concentrating.

Gina pulled up on a side street and looked at the address again. Yep, this was the right place. What now? At first, she simply sat there watching the property, eyes never leaving the house. Finally, she relaxed enough to light up a cigarette and opened the window slightly. But the nicotine didn't do its usual trick and she was still on edge. A message alert bleeped on her phone. She dug her hand in her handbag and quickly scrolled to the Facebook messages:

Hi there, how are you. Fancy a few drinks tonight? Sonny xx

She blushed but didn't reply. She'd type something later when she was thinking straight – at the moment her head was spinning with questions. She threw her phone back into her bag and sat in deep thought until movement outside the property brought her back to her watch. She slid down in her seat and kept her head low. This could be the answer she'd been looking for.

Gina got home and immediately called a meeting with the girls. She was curtain-twitching, waiting for Jess and Lola to arrive. Finally, she saw them park up across the road. She paced the floor until the moment she heard them knocking. Then she rushed to open the front door and stood with one hand placed firmly on her hip.

'Bleeding hell, it's a good job I'm not dying here. I said I needed you both as soon as possible. I've seen slugs move faster than you two.

'You're lucky I'm here,' Jess opened. 'I was about to have a nice soak in the bath. I got myself one of them bath bombs and I've been dying to use it.'

Gina was eager to get them both inside. 'Bleeding bath bombs,' she growled. 'The last time I had one of them in my bath, it was a knock-off and I had thrush for weeks, itching all the bloody time I was – so I've saved you from that.'

Lola giggled and raised her eyebrows. 'I hope you're not going to be long. My mam is going off her head, me dumping the kids on her all the time. On my life, you should have heard her having a go at me, reading me the riot act. She said I had to sort my head out and stop relying on her all the time.'

Jess headed into the front room and sighed. 'And that's exactly the reason I don't have any sprogs. I couldn't think of anything worse than being sat looking after kids all day. No relaxing baths, no chill days in bed. No, no way am I ever having any children. I like my freedom too much.'

Gina practically dragged Lola into the front room and watched as she and Jess both sat down. The stage was Gina's and they looked at her to enlighten them on what was so urgent. Gina inhaled deeply and pulled out her board with the Post-it notes almost covering it. Jess looked at it and eyeballed Lola, baffled. Gina sat down on the chair facing them. 'I'm asking you both to just listen before you start putting the dampers on this.'

Lola sat back in her seat and checked her wristwatch, aware of the time ticking away. She would have much rather been at home, pjs on and getting ready to watch a film on Netflix with a gob full of chocolate.

Gina began. 'I've been doing a lot of thinking during these last few weeks and my heart is breaking at the thought of us losing our house. And you're both having to think where the next quid is coming from. I've racked my brains trying to come up with a solution to my problems, *our* problems,' she stressed. 'Anyway, it's took some time and I have read through every bit of evidence in Scott's case. Who was involved, how it all worked, everything down from the generals to the foot soldiers.'

Jess fanned her nails out examining her cuticles. Gina could see she was losing their attention so blurted it all out like bullets being fired from a gun. 'I started reading this to see if I could get Scott off, or out sooner. But it turns out this is good as a handbook on how to do it ourselves. We can do it all, girls, we don't need the men to rely on.' Excitement had taken over Gina and she stood up now pointing at the board. 'Now Scott and the boys are down, Carl Clarkson is the kingpin who is running everything in this neck of the woods. Zac Manion's boys run some of the area too, so what's wrong with us taking a piece of the pie? We can start off small and build it up.'

Jess burst out laughing. She nudged Lola in the waist, and she started laughing too. 'Gina, are you for real, woman, do you realise what you have just said? These men you are talking about taking down are ruthless. We know jack shit about the world they live in, and we would be eaten alive. Imagine them finding out three women are threatening their thrones. Come on, Gi, you're talking out of your arse.'

Gina was straight back at her. 'But how will they know it's us if we keep under the radar? Like you said, we've been invisible until now. They'd never guess we'd have the nerve to do something like this. Sure, we will have to be two steps in front of them and one behind all at the same time – but listen to Lola just now – us mums are bloomin' used to multitasking. And you? Well Carl Clarkson is a womaniser and I thought you could charm him with those come-to-bed eyes of yours, Jess. A couple of dates with you and you'll have him eating from your hand. He'll tell you everything.'

'So, I'm as good as a brass now. Bleeding hell, Gina, it's not as easy as that to get a guy to trust you, especially in this day and age, they're all paranoid about telling anyone what they are up to.'

Lola chirped in. 'And where do you see me in this? I'm not sleeping with any Tom, Dick or Harry. Mike would go ballistic.'

Gina grinned. 'That's the easy part. We don't tell the fellas nothing. This is our call, nothing to do with them. We have everything to gain and nothing to lose. Obviously, we need to plan stuff, work out where and when deals are taking place and make sure we are on the ball.' Gina shot a look at Jess and then Lola. She could see she would have to sell the dream to them both, make it worth their while. 'Jess, you like money, right? And I'm not even bothering asking you, Lola, because I know you're on the bones of your arse, just like me. And none of us are waiting til the men are out to get some, are we? Sure, they might be able to send us bits while they're inside, but nothing like what we're used to, what we need. This way, we can earn big money, girls; all we need to do is learn the craft and know our shit inside and out. You both need to watch *Top Boy* on the TV. Honest, it's not that different to what goes on round here. I reckon you'd be surprised by how much you know already.'

Jess tilted her head. 'So, you seriously think we could pull this off and earn some decent money? Not just another dream like the salon?'

'I wouldn't have even mentioned it if I didn't think so. We have no power at the moment but I'm going to use some of the little of Scott's money I've still got left to start us off. Money talks and without it we're goosed.'

Jess nodded and she blushed slightly. 'So, don't judge me, but if we're putting our cards on the table, I've got a bit of a confession to make.' She covered her face with both hands and opened her fingers slightly as she began to speak. 'I've sort of been sleeping with Carl Clarkson already. It started a while back. You know what me and Tommy are like, and he was a shoulder to cry on one night when I was upset.'

Gina's jaw dropped. At any other time, she would have opened both barrels on her friend. Told her she was out of order, that she was dicing with death, but not tonight, she kept schtum.

Lola shook her head and whispered something under her breath.

Gina was relieved Jess didn't hear whatever the dig was, as she knew the two of them would have been scratching each other's eyes out given half a reason. Gina stood tall, pulled her shoulders back and exhaled. 'Then that's something else in our favour, Jess. That and the fact that our Bethany said Zac Manion's boy is always badgering her to go on a date, so, we could have a lead there too. Us women are going to surprise them all. I want this only us. We speak to nobody else about what we are planning, and we keep it properly on the down-low. I know what you're like, loose lips, so I'm making myself clear from the off, Lola, do you understand me?'

Lola shrugged. 'Like I'm the one you should be worried about. Jess is the gossiper. You have a short memory, you do, Gina. Remember when we told her about Joanne Taylor down the road sleeping with Johnny? Go on, who was the one who let the cat out of the bag then? It certainly wasn't me, was it?'

Jess brushed the comment off and spoke in a calm manner. 'Joanne Taylor was a dirty slapper and she deserved to be found out. Are you forgetting when she spread that rumour about me having the clap, or what?'

Gina stopped this conversation before it got heated. Her tone was softer as she sat back down. 'We needed a plan, and this is what I've come up with. Our lads have taught us well, even without realising, and, if we are clever, we can outsmart these men anytime we want to. So, Jess, it starts with you. Get that money-maker of yours working and find out all you can from Carl Clarkson: who his contacts are, where he goes and who he gets his shit from. I will start shifting money about and try and get a few deals sorted.'

'I'll be seeing Carl later on tonight. Gina, I just need to know if you are fully aware of what we are getting ourselves into. When I started seeing him, it was an insurance policy – someone to take care of me if Tommy got taken down. But I've found out since the kind of guy he is. We are talking knives, battering guns, they're all in a day's work for Carl. And if we aren't worrying about him killing us if he finds out, we'd still be talking big jail time if we get caught by the dibble. And imagine your Scott if he found out what you were up to?'

Gina's expression changed. 'Leave Scott to me. He left his family vulnerable and it's up to me to fix that.' She was angry, and the way she was cracking her knuckles told them she was a woman on a mission. 'I'll work out soon exactly how it's going to play out. Firstly, I need to get my hands on Scott's money and make sure we are ready to play ball. Money talks and, even better, it can hide most things so nobody knows we are behind anything. We don't have to be like the guys, always showing off and squaring up. No, I'll only involve people on a need-to-know basis.'

'Like who?' Lola asked with concern. 'Because we're not only trusting them with our money, we're trusting them with our lives.'

Gina tapped the side of her nose and smirked. 'Leave that to me. If there's one thing I've learned reading the court papers, the key to this life isn't just what you know, but who you know.'

Chapter Thirteen

Bethany curled her hair with her new Dyson Airwrap, a gift from her dad before he was arrested. Perfect curls, like she'd just stepped out of the salon. If this didn't work, she certainly wouldn't be dropping cash at the hairdressers again anytime soon.

Gina knocked and came into her room, perching on the edge of her bed with an apprehensive look. 'Remember, I don't want you to put yourself in any danger. We need names, times, locations of anything that is going on in the Manion household or anything to do with their business.'

Bethany looked at her mother through the mirror and smiled. 'It will be like taking candy from a baby, Mam. I was shocked when you told me your plan, but it's had time to sink in now and you're right, it's about time us women took things into our own hands. Although I don't know what Jenks would say if he knew what we were up to.' Bethany smirked. Jenkins thought he was the dog's bollocks and, whenever she added to a conversation, he always shot her down like she was a nobody. Well, watch this space, brother, she thought, this girl is going to show you just what she is all about. It was one of things she loved about the theatre: people did listen when she spoke. Maybe there were other ways she could make herself heard.

Gina glared, eyes fixed on her daughter. 'You tell Jenkins nothing, do you hear me, bloody nothing. If he got wind of this, he would be straight on the blower to your father. I'm trusting you with this, Bethany, don't let me down. We keep this close, mouth shut, say nothing to nobody.'

Beth flicked her bouncy curls over her shoulder. 'My lips are sealed, Mam, and I promise you I will do my best to get what I can out of Reece. I'm going to his house later to meet his mum too, so she'll be like putty in my hands when she gets to know me.'

'Just be careful when you're speaking to his mother. I've had dealings with Sadie in the past and she's a mouthy bitch. The mission is to fact-find so we can start to get some money behind us. I can't let your dad know what I'm up to, so I'll have to do my homework to find out if he moved the emergency fund. If the police have already got to Tall Paul, we're screwed. And it's not like I can ask your dad on a visit with all the screws listening.'

'It shouldn't be a problem, Mam. You'll work out what he's done with it. My dad has no secrets from you, does he?'

Gina turned her face away and quickly stood up from the bed. 'I want you to send your location to my iPhone.

I need to know where you are all the time. Tonight is your first job. Do me proud, girl.'

'Always, Mother, always.'

───────

Reece Manion picked Bethany up at the end of her street in his dark grey Mercedes. There was no way she was letting him pull up outside her gaff. Imagine Jenkins's face if he clocked him outside; he would have something to say about it. He was always the protective brother, and it was embarrassing sometimes how far he would go to prove a point. He'd punched her last boyfriend right in the face when he heard the way he'd spoken to his sister and deemed it a piss-take. He'd only said he didn't want her to go clubbing with her friends and Jenkins had overheard him and stepped in. He pinned him up against the wall and went nose to nose asking him who the hell did he think he was speaking to, telling his sister what she could and could not do. The guy never got chance to reply. Jenkins headbutted him then skull-dragged him down the stairs and flung him outside the front door. The poor lad was trying to scramble to his feet and explain that he would never disrespect Bethany, but he couldn't get a word in edgeways. Jenkins booted him up the arse and launched him outside the front gate, giving him ten seconds to move his arse from the property. Needless to say, Bethany had never been out with Taddy since. He was an alright lad too, a bit gobby and full of himself but, hey, who didn't have a big gob in this day and age? She still saw him around town – wondered if she should have pushed back with Jenks. Bethany had always been attracted to the bad boys. Her mother didn't know the half of it and thought when she went to stay at her friend Hayley's they had a girlie night in with face packs and foot treatments. As if that ever happened., They were both out on the piss, nightclubs and after-parties until the early hours. Bethany was in no way whiter than white. But what her parents didn't know wouldn't hurt, would it? In her eyes, she had an image to fulfil with her parents and, as long as they still thought she was an angel, then it was job done, wasn't it?

Reece inhaled deeply as Bethany got into the car. His nostrils flared at the smell of her perfume. She'd chosen something clean and fresh with a spicy lower note, and made sure not to just to dab it on her wrists but down her cleavage as well.

'You smell mint, babes, and you look stunning, Beth.'

'Thank you, and you look like you've had a wash and brush-up too,' she joked.

'Yep, my mam would kill me if I brought a girl home to meet her and didn't look like I'd made an effort. She's look-ing forward to me bringing you back later. You know I'm a bit of a mummy's boy and she's kind of like that with me. She wants to see if you have potential as a keeper. Honest, if you don't get the thumbs up from my mam then it's pointless, I can't even see you again. She's a nutter when it comes to me dating girls. On my life, I brought a girl home once and I'd already been seeing her for a good three months, so I thought the time was right to introduce her to my ma. My mum only spoke to her for like five minutes tops and she followed me out of the room with a face of a thousand cuts telling me to cart her. She said she had a gut feeling about her and it wasn't good. On my life, I think I stayed with her for a few more days after that, and it's funny because then I could sort of see what my mum was saying about her. She's always right about girls and she gets a vibe that I trust with my heart. My mum says she has gypsy blood running through her veins, and she has some kind of gift that lets her read people's auras. So you better be careful: she'll be able to see right through you if you're stringing me along or have got other guys on the go.'

Bethany didn't know if he was kidding with her or not, but she'd already decided that, when she met Sadie Manion, one thing was for sure – she was getting her best performance ever. She was determined Zac's mum would not see through her and uncover her real reasons for being with her son. She could pull the wool over her eyes for sure, she was convinced of it. Her nerves started to turn to excitement. She was so used to acting – and now it was showtime.

Reece had booked a lovely Italian meal for them both. Bethany could tell he was out to impress. Money didn't seem to be a problem and he never flinched when she ordered the dearest meal on the menu. She hadn't done it on purpose, she simply had an expensive palate, she supposed. By anyone's standard, this was romantic – candlelit dinner, soft music playing in the background – what more could a girl ask for? Cold hard information, thought Bethany.

'So, tell me more about your family, Reece. You seem very tight-knit, similar to how my family is.'

Reece glowed with pride talking about his family. Although he tried to keep his nose cleaner than his dad, he knew the way of the world and how his family earned their money. He wasn't blind, was he? 'So, you've probably heard, my dad's in the chokey like yours and he's not back home anytime soon. My uncle Albert is the one looking after things while he's away and he's a couple of butties short of a picnic. My mam can't stand him, and she only puts up with him because of my dad. He's too much, in all honesty, too violent, wants to make a name for himself.'

'Everyone wants to make a name for themselves nowadays, don't they? It's all about greed and power, I think.'

'Eh, don't think I'm from that mould. You can't pick your family, can you? I was born into this mayhem. But I guess you know what that's like.'

Bethany lifted her big blue eyes, sending him all the right signals.

'Beth, you know how I've felt about you for time and I'm buzzing you finally said yes to a proper date with me. I've been dying to get you on your own for ages now. I love spending time with you. I feel relaxed. You just chill me out. No other girls know what it's like when your dad's the big man, but you do. Everyone else is after what they think I can give them, but you and me, well, we're on the same level, yeah?'

Bethany wanted to get back to talking about what he might or might not know. She didn't want a deep and meaningful. She twisted some pasta onto her fork and reached across the table to feed him, knowing he'd get an eyeful as she leaned towards him. His mouth was wide open as she slid the silver fork into his mouth. 'So, tell me about your dad. Do you miss him, do you visit much?'

Reece sat back and began fidgeting. 'I can level with you, can't I? He's not really a nice person, shall we say, and in the past we've had our fights. He has a horrible attitude and thinks he can speak to people like shit. I've told him time and time again that we are his family, and he should leave the world he lives in. His mouth is rancid, though. He thinks we're like his lackeys. There's no respect. He's so used to bossing his boys around that he speaks to us all like we are some kind of muppets. My mum gets the brunt of it and, I'm not going to lie, she has had her work cut out with him over the years. She's caught him messing about loads of times, yet he always talks her around and she gives him another chance. I've asked her why she puts up with him and she never really tells me the reason. I reckon she's scared of being alone, alone and broke. Even now when he's locked away, she does not settle until she has spoken to him. Old habits die hard, I suppose. They've been together a lot of years and she doesn't know any other life. Saying that, though, she did try and leave him once and you should have seen him melt. I've never seen that side of my old man before, but his world fell apart and he was on bended knee begging her not to leave him. We all got taken on holiday then, gifts galore. New motor for my mardukes, so at least she benefitted from his love affair.'

Bethany gawped. She could never in a million years imagine her mother forgiving her dad for being unfaithful. No, her mother had pride. She would kick his arse to the kerb, shred his clothes, name and shame him to anyone who would listen. Bethany felt she'd had her suspicions confirmed: Reece's dad was a full-time dickhead and, if she ever met him in the future, she would remember that. One day she would even tell him that. She hated men who had no respect for women and Zac Manion sounded like a prize prick. 'Bleeding hell, I hope you don't turn out like him. You're not a chip off the old block, are you?'

Reece was up in arms, backing himself. 'Not an earthly. I have my own dreams, my own goals, and they don't involve all that shit my old man gets up to. I want to be a sparky, there's good money in that when I'm qualified. Set up my own little business, proper kosher. You see, me Beth, I like nice things in life, but I value my freedom more than anything. My dad has done a lot of jail time already and, in reality, he's missed us all growing up. It was my mam who held us all together when he was in the slammer. Anyway, I don't have to tell you about the life a criminal leads, do I?'

Bethany hated that he was comparing his old man to hers and, even though he had a point, she went on the defensive. 'My dad is a nice person at home. I'm not saying he's a saint when he's grafting, but he's never once disrespected my mam or any of us.'

Reece could see her back was up and backtracked. 'I suppose even in that life, they're all different, aren't they?'

Bethany saw her chance and played dumb. 'You're dead right. I know in my dad's set-up there are all kind of characters – different folks for different jobs. I'm curious, is it the same with the way your dad runs things? I don't pay attention to that world so I don't even know if your dad does the same thing as mine really – I just know it's all hard graft.'

Reece swallowed and checked around him to make sure nobody was listening. But then again, everybody round here knew his old man and what he got up to, so it wasn't like he was speaking out of court, was it? 'I bet it's not too different to what your dad got sent down for. He sells drugs, like most of players round here, but not bits, he does the big amounts. He gets it shipped in and then divides it up and gets it on the streets. A piece of piss, really, easy money.'

'I've never been brave enough to ask my dad how he fits into the chain. How do they know where to buy the gear from? I mean in serious amounts, not the wraps and baggies we all see the foot soldiers dealing in the Square.'

'You have to be in the know.' He tapped the side of his nose and winked at her before he continued. 'There is a darker side to Manchester than anyone sees and in the late-night hours and the shadows of the night you can see how many people are out to earn a few quid. It's like a food chain – everyone takes a bite.'

'So does your uncle have to do it all now – you're not dragged into it, are you?'

Reece was deep into the conversation, and he was singing like a budgie, clearly delighted to have Bethany hanging off his every word. 'Yes, he meets the guys, cracks a deal and the rest is history. My dad thinks he's been having him over, though. The count has been down a few times and he's sure he's creaming off a few grand here and a few grand there for himself.'

'Wow, it's a mad world, isn't it? I'm playing Ronnie Kray in our next show and I'd love to see some real-life deals and that. It would help me with my character-building and my performance. I'd ask my brother but he's way too protective to let me.'

Reece burst out laughing. 'Bloody hell, girls usually want to go away for a spa weekend, and you want to watch a drug deal. A cheap date you are, for sure.'

Beth blushed. 'Is it weird? Oh, I'm sorry. This could be life-changing for me if I smash this part. Honest, I've been waiting for this break forever. They say there's a talent scout coming to watch the show.'

'I like weird. Makes a change from the other girls I date that only want me to buy them the latest clobber. I like that you've got a passion. Leave it with me and I'll see if I can sort something out for you. This is our secret, though. Say nothing to nobody.'

She sat back in her seat. Reece checked his watch and Bethany chuckled. 'Let's get the bill and go and meet this mother of yours. Pointless me coming on to you, isn't it, if she doesn't like me.'

Reece necked the last bit of his drink, and he didn't need asking twice.

Sadie Manion sat up straight when Reece walked into the living room. Wow, what a gaff this was, thought Bethany, top notch: silver and grey décor, classy but not afraid to show it cost serious dough. Bethany edged in through the door and smiled softly. Sadie was already assessing every inch of her.

'Oh, come and sit down, lovely, instead of being stood there. I don't bite, despite what they say. Reece has already told me all about you and it's great to finally meet you.'

Bethany sat down facing Sadie – it felt like a job interview, except she didn't know what she was interviewing for – girlfriend or secret agent. 'I'm glad we have met too. Reece has been telling me all about you.'

Sadie raised her eyebrows at her boy, and Bethany could see she was wondering exactly what he had told her.

Reece came and sat down next to Bethany. 'Eh, Mam, Beth's into all that criminology like you are. She's just bagged a lead role in some play she's doing, and, get this, she's playing Ronnie Kray.'

Bethany gulped: criminology, she had never said that, just that she was interested in how people in that world ticked.

'Honest, Beth, when my mam watches all these TV dramas she always tells me from day one who's done it. Vera, I call her, you know that old woman detective on the telly.'

'Wow, less of the *old*, son. I'm not in a box yet and there is plenty of mileage left on me. I'm not far behind that Vera in age, you know, but I look well better than she does.'

They all started laughing, but Bethany could still feel Sadie's eyes all over her. 'So, tell me about yourself, then. I always think it's better when it comes straight from the horse's mouth.' It was clear this woman didn't mess about, straight to the point. Beth flicked her hair back over her shoulder and was ready to impress. 'I love acting first and foremost. I have done since I was a kid, and I left school to try to make a go of it. But if I'd stayed and gone to college then, yes, I'd have loved to do criminology. I guess I just love getting inside someone's head – whether it's on stage or in a case. I love working things out, just like you. When it comes to solving a crime, you have to treat the suspects like characters in a play.' Bethany was really getting into her stride, believing her own words 'Not everything is what it seems on the surface and to uncover the truth you have to pull it back layer by layer and you will always find the answer.'

Sadie seemed impressed and her eyes opened wide as she gave her son a quick look. Reece was as proud as punch and watched every move his mother made. 'Your dad is Scott Gilbert, right? I bet you still can't work him out, can you? I'm like that with Reece's dad. I know every-one's got their opinions of Zac, just like I bet they do with your dad. But no one can really work out how they've got where they have, can they? Just when I think I've worked him out he goes and does something different.'

Bethany hadn't expected Sadie to be so open. She didn't know how to reply in case she was walking into a trap. But the older woman seemed to take her silence as licence to continue. 'So, you only have one brother?'

'Yes, he's nothing like me, though. He thinks he's the next Don Corleone.' Too late, Bethany realised she should button it about Jenks. She didn't want her words landing him in the crosshairs of the Manions.

'Tell me about it, love. When they come from families like ours, it's easy to get pulled in. It's almost expected of them to step up to the mark and follow in their father's footsteps. It's a cruel world out there and...' She looked up at the large photo of a young man above Bethany's head and swallowed hard, her flat palm covering her heart. 'Our Ralph would have been nearly thirty years old if he was alive today, but they took him from me, left a massive void in our lives. Zac's still not over it. He misses his son every single day that goes by but won't talk about it, the night our son was knocked down by a speeding car. He would never admit that it was something to do with the life he leads and not a hit-and-run driver like the police said it was. Nothing made sense, a car mounting the pavements, driving off and never coming back. No, it was a warning to his father, a message that he wasn't untouchable like he thinks he is.'

Reece looked pained, then he pulled himself together. 'Mam, it was never proved that it wasn't a hit-and-run driver. You do your own head in overthinking things. We all miss our kid but we have to move forwards. You can't live in the past.'

Sadie still stared at the photograph of her firstborn. 'He was bloody handsome, though, wasn't he?'

Reece turned and looked at his older brother. 'Yep, a good-looking fella he was. You don't have ugly kids, do you, Mam?' He tried to lift the mood. 'Well, our Norm is not the best looker, and he does have a look of Uncle Albert more than Dad, if I'm being honest.'

Bethany half-expected Reece's mum to give him a clip round the ear but instead Sadie burst out laughing. 'Quit that, sunshine, before you pick a fight you can't win.'

Reece nudged Bethany. 'We always wind her up about Uncle Albert. We say he must have sneaked in her bed one night when she was sleeping and gave her our Norman.' He turned back to his mother. 'I'm joking with you, Mam, come on, like you would ever go near Uncle Albert.'

'Well, you can go and make a drink to make up for your lip. I'll have a nice white wine. It's in the fridge. Get Beth one too.'

Reece left the front room and Bethany made conversation. 'Your home is gorgeous, I love the colours you have used, it's so calming and comfortable.'

'I love a nice home; I'm always messing about with colours and changing things when I get bored of them. I mean, with Zac being in jail all the bleeding time, I have to keep myself occupied, don't I?'

'It must be hard. As you know, my dad is away too and I don't have a clue how my mam copes with him being gone. It's like her life has ended and she sits about every day waiting on him coming home. But he got sent down for ten years. That's a lot of waiting to do, isn't it, even if they let him out early if he keeps his nose clean?'

Sadie flicked her chestnut brown hair. 'We do what we do because we love our men. Don't get me wrong, I have my down days, but you just have to carry on, don't you?'

'Do you have any hobbies to keep you occupied?' Bethany cursed inwardly at how clumsy her question had sounded – but she had to find out how Sadie filled her time. She hoped she'd only sounded curious rather than a snoop.

Sadie paused for a few seconds before she answered the question. 'I don't think anyone's ever asked me that before. I mean, when the kids were small, I didn't have a moment to myself and, since they grew up, I guess Zac has got me used to the good life – shopping, eating out, nothing you'd call a hobby. I mean I've often thought of learning how to play the guitar but, when I mentioned it to Zac, he put me off by laughing. I've wrote a few songs over the years. I've never told anyone that. I feel a bit of a sad case, you know, geeky, writing songs I can't even play.'

Bethany leaned in. 'It's not one bit geeky. It's creative. Book some lessons and sing your own songs. Omg, you could even record them. Go on *X-Factor* or *The Voice*.'

Sadie shook her head, aware she'd let her secret out of the bag. 'I don't have the confidence for anything like that. I'm too old. I'd be a laughing stock.'

Bethany could see sadness in this woman's eyes and knew there were many different layers to her. Her voice was softer now, the one she used with her mum when she found her upset. 'You only get one life, Sadie, and sometimes you have to be a bit selfish and do something for yourself. If you're anything like my own mother, you probably worry about everyone else first and when it comes to doing things for yourself you have no energy left or time. I'm not going to pretend I don't know that me mam and you have had words, but you two are more alike than you might think. You should meet up, I think you would get on great.'

Sadie scoffed. But Reece walked back into the room before she could say anything to break the trust between the two women. He'd stalled in the kitchen for a few more minutes, giving his mother time to talk to Beth.

'Here you go, ladies, two white wines. I'll grab a can of lager in a minute. I don't know how you drink that crap. It tastes like vinegar.'

'It's nearly thirty pound a bottle, that wine is. Kate over the road drinks that one from Aldi and it smells like paint stripper. I know my wines, son, and when it comes to me having a little tipple I'm not tightening the purse strings. Anyway, hurry up and get your drink, I've got something to tell you.'

Reece hurried back into the kitchen and come back holding his can of Foster's. He plonked down on the sofa and looked over at his mother. 'Go on then, spill the beans, what's the news.'

Sadie smiled over at Bethany and sat up straight in her chair. 'I'm going to learn how to play the guitar. Beth here has given me the push that I needed and as from tomorrow I will be taking some lessons. I've wrote songs about our Ralph, about how much we all miss him.'

Reece nodded. 'Go on, Mam, about time you stepped out of your comfort zone rather than spending your days waiting on phone calls from the nick. I mean I've heard you belt out a good tune at karaoke a couple of times, but I never really knew you had an interest in stuff like that.'

'Well, nobody has ever asked me what I do and don't like, that's why. I'm always a second thought but maybe it takes another woman to recognise I'm overdue something for myself.'

Bethany sat back sipping on her wine. She'd smashed it here tonight and was more than sure she'd got her boyfriend's mother's seal of approval. Job well done.

Sadie dragged deeply on her drink, tipsy now, and Bethany wondered how many she'd had before her and Reece got there.

'I would like to meet your mam. At the end of the day, we are in the same boat, and both have men in prison. If I see her at the prison, I'll make conversation with her. Your dad is in Strangeways too, isn't he? They didn't sling him into one of those nicks at the other end of the country?'

Beth dropped her head, a wave of nausea hitting her as she remembered that this woman's husband was likely the one who had ordered the hit on her dad, whether he'd actually done the deed or not. 'Yes, he is,' she replied, a sudden fear that maybe she wasn't as great an actress as she'd felt a moment ago. What if Sadie had seen right through her? What if she was playing her at her own game?

———

Reece pulled up near Bethany's house and he looked around the area before he turned the engine off. 'You were a hit with my mam. I've never seen her like that with any girl I've brought home. You've inspired her to learn how to play the guitar and I'm buzzing for her. I just hope he doesn't put the dampeners on it.'

'Who?' she asked, knowing full well what Reece would say.

'My dad. Once he gets wind of her doing something – anything – out of the ordinary, he sees his arse. Mark my words, once she tells him he'll kick up a fuss and she won't end up doing it. He's always had some mad hold over her and to say she's locked in chains by him is an understatement. He won't sleep until he knows she decided against it.'

'That's selfish, if you ask me. What does he want her to do, sit looking at four walls all day? Times have changed and long gone are them days when women stayed at home cooking and cleaning all day.'

'Well, someone needs to tell my old man that,' he sniggered. Bethany looked down the street and squinted as she spotted a car with its lights on. Jenkins was due in about now and if he knew she wasn't in yet then more than likely he would be belling her phone out anytime soon looking for her. She didn't have long. She looked over at Reece and sensed he was planning his next move. He was going to go in for a kiss. She could tell he was fidgeting about in his seat trying to pick the moment. And here it came. His warm lips pressed against hers and Bethany let herself relax into it but only for a few seconds, never one to give too much away on a first date. Plus, if her brother drove past and he could see some guy's tongue stuck down the back of her throat he'd go ballistic. If he saw it was a Manion, there'd be blood on the street.

'Thanks for a lovely night, Reece. I've enjoyed it and loved meeting your mam too.'

'So, can I call you tomorrow and we can go out again?'

There were no flies on this lad, thought Bethany, he was straight in for the next date. She sat thinking, not sure if two nights in a row were too much too soon. She usually made her men wait at least three or four days before she saw them again – but she knew her mum would be pumping her for information.

Reece clearly felt he needed to bring out something else to persuade her. 'I reckon I can take you to watch a bit of a drug deal if you really think it'll help your acting. Well, I'll have to double-check when it's happening, but we can park up and you can do some research for your character and all that, then we can go on somewhere nice.'

Now he had her attention, but she pretended to be looking for something in her bag – she didn't want to seem too eager.

'Ring me tomorrow. I'm not sure what I've got on but maybe we can go out again.' She was as cool as a cucumber when she got out of the car. She dipped her head and smiled at Reece. 'Goodnight, speak soon.' She slammed the door shut and her heels clipped along the pavement as she made her way home.

Gina was pacing the front room when Bethany got in. As soon as she walked through the front door, she was all over her like a rash. 'Bleeding hell, I've been pulling my hair out. I thought you would only have been a few hours, not all bloody night. You could have texted.'

Bethany kicked her shoes off and threw her coat on the back of the chair. 'We went for food, and I ended up going back to his house to meet his mam. She was nice, you know, nothing like I thought she would be. She even said she would like to meet you, put the past behind you.'

Gina looked like she'd bitten a wasp. 'Sadie Manion is a crank. I've met her a few times over the years in some club or other and she's always thought she was above everyone. Up her own arse she was, acting like royalty. Why would she want to make me her friend after all these years, anyway?'

'Well, she's not like that now. In fact, I felt sorry for her. She's ruled by Zac Manion and he's led her a dog's life, from what I've heard.'

Gina sat down and folded her arms tightly. 'Why, what's up with her?'

'Nothing really, just that she has no life, runs around for everyone else. Her husband has cheated on her and he's a bully, always telling her what she can and can't do, even now he's on the inside.'

'Sounds like me, doesn't she?' Gina admitted.

'Mam, did you know she had a son who died? A hit-and-run it was, but Sadie seems to think it was something else. A vendetta against her husband. It spooked me out, freaky shit that these gang killings can even pick on the kids rather than the kingpins. Imagine if it had been me or Jenks.'

Gina closed her eyes, trying to remember the story from years ago. 'Yes, yes. I remember now, it was all over the news. They had a massive funeral for him. Everyone on the estate was talking about it. Horrible it was – you know I've got no time for that family as a rule, but kiddies are kiddies. Who does that?'

'And was it a hit-and-run driver?' Gina hunched her shoulders, thinking. 'There were lots of stories going about back then. But who knows what the truth is? Zac had beef with that many people it could have been to do with him. The family put up a big reward for the arrest of the driver, but nobody had seen anything, zilch.'

'She has a big photograph of him in the front room and Reece said she sits and talks to him when she's had a few glasses of wine each night. It freaked me out, if I'm being honest.'

'Poor cow. I could only imagine what she is going through. To lose a child must be the worst feeling ever.' Gina rubbed her arms as the tiny blonde hairs stood on end.

Bethany swapped the subject. 'Where is Jenkins? There was a car outside. I thought it was him.'

'He's still out. He popped in earlier, but he was straight in and out.'

Bethany glanced at the door in case he was about to walk in. 'So, tonight was a success in more ways than one. I've only managed to get Reece to take me to watch a drug deal soon. I've blagged it and said I wanted to see one for my character research.'

'What's that when it's at home?' Gina looked baffled. 'And he bought your story about you being a wannabe Oscar-winner? Bloody hell, is he thick or what?'

'Mam, it wasn't like that. We were talking and I told him how much I cared about my acting, so I wasn't lying to him exactly. Anyway, he's taking me tomorrow night, if it goes ahead. You can track me on my phone and know where it all goes down.'

Gina had lost some of her usual spark. Was she even ready to step into this world? Had she bitten off more than she could chew, sending her only daughter into a drug deal? 'I'll chat with the girls. Jess is on the job tonight and with any luck she will have something to report. If she's found out enough from Carl, then you won't have to go anywhere dodgy.'

'I'm actually enjoying it now, you know. I want to go. But what's your next plan? I mean, if this all goes to plan and you find out everything you need to, then what? Sure, we could get some gear, but if we take someone's patch, these men won't take it lying down. And who is going to take these men down if and when they come for us? Because, correct me if I'm wrong, four women are no match for the kind of guys that work these streets. We'll be eaten alive.'

Gina was thoughtful – she could get some cash, she could get the intel. But what about the manpower? 'Lesson one,' she said to her daughter. 'We walk before we can run.'

Chapter Fourteen

Jess rolled over onto her side and ran a long, manicured fingernail down Carl Clarkson's chest hair. He pulled her in closer and kissed the top of her head. 'You're mint in the sack, you know, you really make me work. I like that in a woman.'

She purred, 'Only the best for you, darling.'

He snuggled into her. 'So, what about coming to this party tonight with me? I'll give you some money to go and get a new dress and get your hair done. You have to look the bomb if you're on my arm.'

Jess rolled away from him and stared at the ceiling. 'I'm with Tommy, as far as most people know, I can't just walk about with you in public like he doesn't exist. And, more to the point, what about your girlfriend?'

Carl's voice snapped, 'The man's in the fucking slammer. He can't expect you to wait ten years, can he?'

'And what about your girlfriend, or whatever she is? I'm sure she wouldn't be too happy when it's reported back to her that you have me on your arm.'

'Like I'm arsed about what she has to say. You see the thing with me, Jess, is that I will do what I want to do. If she doesn't like it, then she can fuck off. She's not my proper bird, just a sack emptier. Women are ten a penny and she needs to remember that. Otherwise, she can say goodbye and do one.'

Jess squirmed and turned her face away from him. What an absolute arsehole this guy was, no shame about slagging off women in front of her. But if he wanted to play the game then she would too. This wasn't her first rodeo with someone who was in a relationship, and she knew how to ride it out like the best of them. 'Alright then, but my dresses are not cheap. I'm not a Primark bird, you know.'

'I'll give you five ton to get a dress and your hair done. Is that enough – to get yourself something nice and to stop worrying what Tommy fucking Seymour will say if you're out with me?'

She placed her tanned arm over his body and gently kissed his chest. 'Yes, and I'll make it worth your while later.' She let her hand stray back down to his waist.

Carl's phone started ringing and he jumped up and made his way into the bathroom. She sat up too. 'Yo, man like Roddy, what you saying, bro?'

Jess screwed her face up, hating that Carl had changed the way he was speaking when he was on the blower. She crept out of bed and edged towards the door so she could hear more. 'Yes bro, got six boxes of Cali being dropped tonight at Nookie's.'

The name rang a bell with Jess, and she ran back to the bed and grabbed her mobile phone to search Facebook. She had heard mention of a guy called Nookie – after all it wasn't a name you forgot. In fact, she was sure he had messaged her in the past. Loads of Tommy's friends and enemies had tried their luck at one time or another, and normally she ignored them until she was feeling lonely or like she needed to get her own back. She concentrated on the screen and scrolled through her DMs. Bingo! There, Nookie was looking straight at her. Not a bad-looking guy. She was sure he was from the Collyhurst area. Quickly, she shoved her mobile phone back in her bag and lay flat on the bed as Carl came back into the bedroom.

'I could go again if you can handle it,' he joked.

Jess smiled at him, fluttering her long black eyelashes. 'I'll take whatever you've got to give, Carl.' And there it was, he needed no more encouragement. She wondered if he'd had a little blue pill as he got right down to it. No foreplay, nothing more than a grope of her tits, and then he drove right into her. His arse was like a fiddler's elbow, and he was going for gold. Jess knew what a man wanted in the bedroom and her lying back and thinking of what dress would look best wasn't going to cut it. She flipped him over on his back. This was her show now. She slowed it all down, teased him, bit his tanned chest softly. Yes, that was better. She would never be just a bang. She made love to her men, made sure they were keen to come back for more, even if she was already moving on. She moaned now as she made sure he hit the spot – no harm having some fun on the job, was there?

———

Carl had been gone for over an hour and Jess was still in bed. All these late nights were catching up with her and she'd promised herself an early night at the next opportunity she got. But, tonight, she was on the arm of Carl Clarkson. She shot a look at the silver clock on the wall and sighed. She had to make a move, get her slap on and get ready. She saw the stack of money at the side of the bed and smiled. There was no way she was buying a new dress or even paying to have her hair done. She could do her hair better than anybody else – and dresses, she had rails of them in her wardrobe. No, she was stashing her cash, saving it. The last few weeks had proved she needed to have a nest egg. Jess picked her mobile up and found Gina's number.

'Hi, babes. I'm on task so don't be going on that I've not answered my phone. Carl's taking me out tonight and I've heard he's got boxes of weed being dropped off at Nookies tonight.'

Jess listened to the voice at the other end of the phone. 'I'll send you Nookie's address, and you and Lola can stake it out or whatever it is they do on telly. Right, I've got to go. I have to get bloody ready. I'm dead on my feet, you know. I could have done with a chill night.'

Jess laughed out loud at whatever Gina said to her. It was game on now; all the pieces of the jigsaw were fitting together nicely. She got out of bed and picked up the wad of notes. Forget diamonds, sometimes cold hard cash was a girl's best friend.

Chapter Fifteen

Lola jumped into the car, stressed. 'I'm not sure if I'm cut out for all this crap. I'm a mother, Gina. What would happen if anything happened to me? My kids, my home, I'd lose it all. Fucking hell, I could go to jail. What then, eh?'

Gina gritted her teeth and started the engine up. 'If you want out, then get out of the bloody car and stop wasting my time. You need to chill out, breathe, woman, and decide what you really want.'

Lola stared out into the night sky and let out a laboured breath. Her emotions were all over the place. Her voice was softer now. 'I'm struggling with everything at the moment, Gina, the kids, money, the house. My mental health is through the floor, I don't know what to do for the best. I feel like I'm in a deep dark hole and I can't get out of it.'

'We're all in the same boat, Lola. But this is do-or-die time for me. Scott has left me high and dry and, no matter how much he tells me everything will be alright, it won't, will it, if I just sit back and wait for someone else to save the day?' Her eyes clouded over as she bit down hard on her bottom lip. 'Just because you don't see me falling apart on the outside, it doesn't mean that, on the inside, I'm alright. I'm not like you. I've never been good at showing any emotions. I had a tough upbringing and tears were for the weak, or so my mam told me.'

Lola patted a comforting hand on Gina's shoulder. 'You seem like you hold it together all the time. You know what to say and do, whereas me, I'm all over the bleeding show. Look at when Mike was boning that scrubber from Ancoats, I wanted to go around there and skull-drag her out of the house and tell everyone what she had been doing, and you were the one who kept me sane. You made me sit back and wait, told me exactly what to do. I would have been banged up now for GBH if you hadn't stopped me. And,' she stressed, 'I wanted to hurt that woman and make her feel pain just like I did in my heart.'

Gina was blunt, straight to the point. 'Yes, you didn't go round and deck her when I told you to back off and think about your options. But you had him back, even though I'd told you to kerb him and cash out. Time and time again you had him back. All he had to do was book a holiday, buy you some gifts and you were back in the big bed with him. You never learned.'

Lola was on the defensive. 'Oh, come on, Gi, he begged me for weeks to have him back, virtually slept on my doorstep, crying every bloody night. I have kids: did you want me to cart him and break their hearts too?'

Gina realised she was going in on her friend and backed off. 'Love conquers all, or so they say. So, if you are really meant to be together, then it will happen, but we've still got to look after each other until the boys get out.'

Lola twisted her white-gold ring around on her finger and lifted a gentle smile. 'At the end of the day, Mikey and I, we do love each other and somehow I think we will always have our ups and downs. Plus, we all have our secrets, don't we, Gi? I mean come on, if it's good enough for the goose, it's good enough for the gander.'

Gina shook her head as she pulled out from the street. 'This is an important job, Lola. I need to know you're all in. If Scott's stash is where I think it is, it'll give us the funds to really do this. I'm going into the house, and you are the one keeping watch. Tall Paul should be down the boozer at this time, and he usually falls out of there around midnight. I know where the cash is so I'm straight in and out. I've got my phone so ring me if you see anyone coming. Once we have finished there, we can head over to Nookie's and see what's what with Jess's info.'

Lola had picked almost all the old red nail polish from each finger. 'Be careful in there, love. Be as fast as you can. I'm shitting myself already and you've not gone anywhere yet, but if we're going to do this thing, put your foot down and let's get it done.'

The journey took over fifteen minutes and when Gina pulled up in a dark alleyway, Lola's eyes took time to adjust to the gloom. The headlights were turned off and there was an eerie silence. Gina placed her black bobby hat and gloves on and pulled her scarf up high over her nose, as if it was normal for her to wear this kind of get-up. She knew where the spare key to the stash house was. She'd been here before with Scott and seen where it was kept, but she could feel her heart thumping fit to burst. If she knew where the key was, how many others of Scott's gang did too? Who was to say she was the first there?

Gina was moving fast now. Once she got to the house, she lifted the grey flowerpot and there it was, like she expected. Her hands shook as she slid the silver key into the door. She was inside. She sprinted up the stairs and into the spare bedroom. She knew exactly where the cash was. Her husband had told her a hundred times before, she'd just forgot. She dragged the white high-gloss wardrobe door open and pushed all the clothes on the rail to one side. Where the hell was it? Gina was more or less inside the wardrobe now. She exhaled as she felt something under her hand. She flung the clothes from it and dragged the sports bag onto the bed. 'Please be in here, please, please,' she whispered under her breath. Bingo! As she pulled the zip open, she could see wads of cash, lots and lots of money, the answer to at least some of her problems. For a few seconds, she held the money in her hand and sat thinking. The she started to neatly place back the clothes she'd messed up. She froze as she felt another bag. Probably just shoes. She yanked at it – it was too heavy to be clothes. She heaved it out, placed it on the floor at her feet and peered inside. Now you were talking. This must have been the last shipment of cocaine Paul received before her husband got arrested. This was music to her ears. There was enough sniff here to really place her on the map. Money was power and all she wanted now was the power to change her life, the power to deal with anyone who crossed her path. Money talked, she knew that. Quickly, she folded the clothes back in place and hooked the two large bags over her shoulder. She was sweating and she could feel the vein at the side of her neck pulsing. Gina headed down the stairs, hoping she didn't have a heart attack before getting back to her car. She dropped the bags near her feet, lifted the plant pot and slid the key back under it.

Gina was still struggling to breathe as she opened the back door of the car and flung the two bags across the seat. She jumped into the driver's seat and turned the ignition with haste, looking as white as a ghost in the rear-view. She rummaged in her jacket pocket and dialled a number. 'I'm on my way. Open the garage door ready for when I get there.' She rang off.

Lola turned to look at the bags on the back seat. 'Did you get it? Is that the money?'

They sped out onto the open road, Gina constantly checking in her rear-view mirror. 'I got it and a little bit more than I bargained for. We need to go somewhere safe and stash this.'

Lola had a puzzled look. They'd not even spoken about where they were going to stash the money, so who the hell had been on the other end of the phone? The call ended and Lola turned to face Gina. 'So, are you going to tell me where we are going, or this another one of your guessing games?'

'Somewhere safe, somewhere nobody knows. When this gets out, all the grafters in the area will be under the spotlight. I needed someone nobody would suspect.'

'And that person is?' She delved deeper, waiting on an answer, but Gina blanked her and carried on driving.

———

The two women had been driving for well over twenty minutes when Gina took a sharp left fork in the road and drove to the top of an avenue. A light came on in the house facing them and a silhouette was highlighted in the window. Gina turned the engine off and walked over to the house. Lola was trying her best to make out who this person was, but their identity was hidden.

Gina stashed the cash and got back into the car. She was flustered and sweat was beading on her forehead. How often did Paul check the stash? If it had just been the cash, perhaps she'd have had a few days' head start. But that much sniff? You didn't leave that in the bottom of a wardrobe without checking on it morning and night. The shit was going to hit the fan for sure when Scott knew every penny he had, had gone walkies. Would he tell her? Or would he keep it from her? And if he did bell her about it – what would she say? One wrong word and he'd know she was involved.

Gina checked the time and turned to face Lola. 'Let's get to the other address now. Jess said some drugs are getting dropped at that guy, Nookie's, tonight. It's not far from here so we can take a butcher's and see what we can see. If there's a drop tonight at his gaff, then we know where to hit next time, don't we?'

'What, me and you? Nicking your husband's own money I think we handled – but you tell me, Gi, how are we nicking a motherload of gear from a Clarkson stash-house? I know we're tough, but I'm not the bleeding Terminator.'

Gina tapped her fingers rapidly on the steering wheel as the traffic came to a halt. 'Not us, people who we put on the job. I know my limits and I also know what a bit of cash can buy.'

Lola sighed. There was a fine line between being kept in the dark and learning something wish you hadn't asked.

Chapter Sixteen

Mickey and Lee watched with eager eyes as Jenkins paced the floor, ragging his hands through his thick locks. 'What the fuck am I going to do now? Alex is a complete tool; he's made me fuck up and miss out on money that would have put us on the map. His arse fell out, for sure.'

Mickey swallowed hard as he rolled a spliff. 'Alex is the least of your worries. You owe Tate four bags of sand and, I'll tell you now, he's not the sort of man who waits around for his money. You've heard the stories, pal, the guy is a nutter.'

'Shut the fuck up, Mickey, don't you think I know that? If we had Clarkson's drop, then we would have been laughing all the way to the bank. It's Alex's fault, fucking prick.'

Lee coughed to clear his throat. 'Maybe go back to the elders and tell them you've messed up. Jim is all bark and no bite, and I'm sure he will fix this shit for you.'

Jenkins was in uproar. 'Like I'll ever let that cock know I've messed up. I can see him now loving every minute of it. Nah, the less he knows the better. I'm a grown man with a big set of balls and I'll sort this out.'

Lee sucked hard on his gums. 'It's either tell McClean, phone your dad or go back to Tate and tell him the pot is empty for now but for the extra time he's waited you'll have to bung him another few hundred quid.'

Jenkins looked desperate; he was listening. He plonked down next to Mickey and grabbed the zoot out of his hands. 'Give me a few blasts of that, my head is in bits, I need to calm down.'

Mickey patted his shoulder. 'Lee could be onto something, you know. You could take the bull by the horns and go and see Tate. Just tell him straight how it is and see what he's saying. He'll either have it or put a cap in your arse.'

Jenkins's face dropped. 'Fuck off, Mickey, you seen the guy – he's a fucking unit. I can have a fight like the next man, but he's scary. Honest, just the way he looks at you is enough to put the fear of God in you, never mind anything else.'

'So, then it's option one or two: speak to the elders or your dad.'

Jenkins dropped his head. There was no way he could ever tell his dad he'd failed and let him down. And going to Jim and the boys would be more or less the same as speaking to his dad. The moment he told Jim, he would be straight on the blower to his old man. He was back where he started. There was only one option left: face Tate.

Chapter Seventeen

Scott Gibert's face creased with pain as he rolled onto his side. The doctors had told him he was a very lucky man and the knife that had dug deep into his torso had just missed his heart. He was back on the hospital wing in Strangeways but there had been no sign of Mike or Tommy. But Tommy had sent messages over to Scott and the wing cleaners would be dropping an iPhone off with him later that night, to replace the one hidden in his cell. Scott wanted revenge; he wanted every single one of Manion's men on stretchers before the week was out, but he knew time might not be on his side. No doubt his transfer paperwork would be on the governor's desk now and they could class him as at-risk and ship him out for the sake of his safety and a peaceful wing. He had to strike back and strike back fast.

A screw came into the room and stood at Scott's side. Dave Planer sneered, 'My, how the mighty have fallen. Nobody is big in here, pal. It comes to us all. I've seen it a hundred times over and, no matter how big you think you are, there is always someone bigger and better than you behind prison walls.'

Scott fidgeted on the bed. 'Fuck off, you prick. Piss off out of the room. Why are you even here? This is the hospital wing, for sick people might I add.'

The officer nodded slowly. 'I'd keep that big mouth of yours closed if I was you. It would be so easy to let a few of your rivals in here and let them finish you off.' He let out a menacing laugh.

Scott spoke to him through clenched teeth. 'Like I said, do one, wanker.' Scott wasn't biting. If he lost his rag this scumbag would raise the alarm and he would be flung down the block, ill or not.

Planer smirked. 'I could make your life a lot more comfortable in here, you know. Maybe you scratch my back and I'll scratch yours?'

Scott sat up in his bed: he was listening. He already had a nice little list of staff who were on the take, but it was usually the cleaners or the desk boys. To have a screw on side behind prison walls was priceless. Dave Planer was right, he could make Scott's life more comfortable, but the big question was, at what cost?

Dave was waiting on an answer. He jerked his head once. 'So, big man, is that a yes?'

What a bent bastard the officer was, out to line his pockets, make his bank balance bigger. But Scott wasn't wet behind the ears. 'So how do I know you're not saying the same to Manion? I wasn't born yesterday, and I know how you fuckers roll.'

Planer pulled his shoulders back and chuckled sarcastically. 'The way I see it is you don't have any other options. I can walk away now, and we'll never speak about this again. But this offer is only on the table while I'm stood here. I've not got time to be pissing about. I'll go for a slash and come back and see what you're saying. Have a good think about it while I'm gone. It's a one-time offer.' The screw turned around and walked out of the side ward.

What a crafty bastard. Scott knew Dave had him by the short and curlies. Sure, he might be in Manion's pocket, but Scott wasn't in a position to negotiate. He could feel his stitches straining as he pulled himself straighter in the bed ready for Planer to return.

Dave Planer strolled back into the room, checking behind him. He lifted his cuff and checked his wristwatch. 'So, are you in or out? Simple, really. I want five hundred quid a week and I'll get you everything that you need. Your time here at Hotel Strangeways will be a doddle.'

Scott was used to making the best out of a bad situation. He was backed into a corner and knew it, so it might mean splashing a bit of cash to sort it. But he had to test Dave first, make sure this clown was for real. 'You get Tommy and Mike over here to see me for half an hour and you've got a deal. I mean, the proof is in the pudding, isn't it?'

Dave kept his voice low, double-checking behind him. 'No problem. I'll have them over in the next hour. But, once I've kept to my side of the bargain, the first payment goes in my bank, no fucking about. I'll give you some bank details, then every week you can fly some cash over to my account.'

Scott shrugged. 'Yeah, I can do that. Like I said, get my boys over here pronto and we've got a deal.'

Dave nodded like he'd never expected Scott to say anything else, pleased that he was on another good earner behind these prison walls.

Scott knew his wages would be crap for what he put up with: long hours, stressful days, constant risk of it all kicking off. He needed a back-hander the same as the next person round here. And, like Scott always said, everybody had a price.

———

Scott had his mobile phone now and he couldn't wait to talk to his Mrs. He kept an eye out for anyone walking past the door and made the call. 'Hello, lovely, I'm missing you so much today.' He paused as his wife showered him with questions about his health.

'Is it tomorrow you've got a visit booked for, or the next day? Honest, Gi, I don't even know what day it is in here. My head has been sent west.' The sound of his wife's voice calmed his racing heartbeat down. She could always make him feel relaxed. It was the tone of her voice, the knowing she would always be there for him no matter what. She was his happy place. The call lasted over fifteen minutes and Scott had to end it when he heard voices outside the room. 'I'll phone you later, baby, someone's here, love you,' he whispered.

Scott shoved the mobile phone down the front of his boxers and froze as he listened carefully, footsteps getting louder, keys jangling outside his door. He was alert and sat up. Tommy walked in first followed closely by Mike. He tried not to stare. Tommy was as thin as a rake. He'd definitely lost weight he couldn't afford to lose. His cheeks looked sunken, his once broad chest deflated.

'How are you doing, pal? On my life, I've been doing everything to get over here to see you. How have you managed it?' Tommy looked relieved to have finally set eyes on Scott.

Planer stood at the door. 'I'll give you three half an hour, like we said.' He closed the door behind him.

Mike rolled his eyes over at Scott. The screw was gone. 'What's the crack with that wanker? He was as nice as pie when he brought us over here.'

Scott growled, 'He's bent, that's why. He's on our books now so count your blessings he's not on our backs anymore. Five ton a week he wants. Pennies to us, isn't it, if the lads outside are keeping trade going.'

Mike looked behind him to make sure the officer had gone. 'I wouldn't trust him as far as I could throw him.'

Tommy stopped him dead in his tracks. 'What options do we have? Because, as I see it, we need all the help that we can get in taking Manion down. That's still the plan, isn't it, Scott?'

Mike sat forward, hanging on his every word.

'Of course, that prick is going to suffer for what he's done to me. I want him hurt, and badly; he'll never walk again after I've finished with him.' Scott's face was a picture of vengeance.

Tommy was fuming too, cracking his knuckles. 'Never walk again?' he questioned. 'He should be in a fucking body bag. Why would you let that twat still breathe?'

'Because I want to see him suffer. Every day to feel pain, to never be the same again. Death's too quick for that Manion.'

Scott eyeballed Mike next. 'So where were you when they took me down, Mike? Tommy said you was nowhere to be seen. You knew the script, but you were missing in action. Talk to me, tell me where the fuck you were, because at the moment all kinds of shit is running through my head.'

Mike dropped his head into his hands. 'I fucked up. I only went to the toilets for a dump and, before I knew it, you'd been done in.'

Tommy didn't buy this story and Scott could tell by his reaction that he was going to go in on him. 'Nah, mate. I seen you on the landing. You weren't on the shitter at all. I've gone over it time and time again in my head and you were watching from the top of the other stairs. I can't be one hundred percent sure because, if I was, I would have kicked fuck out of you by now.'

It was getting heated, and Scott knew Mike would dive on him any second now and kick ten bags of shit out of him. He raised his voice and slammed his flat palm on the bed. 'Shut up, the pair of you. As it stands, we need to get back on our feet in here. Arguing between ourselves will only make us weaker. You two sort your heads out and round the troops up. Strength in numbers, remember that.'

Tommy still had a bee in his bonnet and his neck was bright red; he was on the verge of blowing. You could see he was trying to calm down, sucking in deep breaths, chest rising. 'I'll sort it, pal. We need you back on the landing as soon as possible. It will show them twats you're back and they won't know how you want to play it.'

'I'm playing it cool. Let them think I'm licking my wounds and then Boom! We'll take him fucking down. Going to try my best not to get shipped out too. I'll be fucked if they move me, but we've got to be prepared for that as an option, so we need to move fast.'

Tommy was moving from foot to foot, eyes darting everywhere. He had a mission in life now, no more moping about in the jail, spending hours behind his door. 'I'm ready. Let's show them all not to fuck with us.'

Mike lifted his eyes to Scott and nodded. 'Count me in too. I'll make sure I have your back this time. Sorry, Scott. Gutted I let you down. My head's all over the place. Got some tablets from the doctor. Hopefully they will sort me out.'

Tommy reached over to Scott and shook his hand. 'It's on, pal. The clock is ticking. Manion is living on borrowed time.'

Mike shook hands with Scott too but, before they could say another word, the door opened and the screw stood there with a smug look on his face. 'Right, lads, let's get you back over to the main jail.'

They left the room and Scott was alone again.

Chapter Eighteen

Jenkins sat in the car with Mickey at his side. He was gnawing at the skin on his thumb. Tate was making his way towards them, and they could tell he didn't look too happy. Tate gripped the car door handle and nearly took it from its hinges as he jumped into the back of the car. This wasn't going to be a friendly chit-chat.

Tate leaned forwards and gripped the back of Jenkins's seat. Jenkins's skin prickled as he felt the big guy only inches from the back of his head. 'Yo, bro, I've not received any cash yet. You knew the score, you knew the amount, so don't fuck with my head telling me you've not got it, because, as you know, I don't fuck about.' He pulled a pistol from his jacket pocket and shoved the cold metal barrel into the side of Jenkins's head, pressing it firmly.

Mickey pushed Tate's hand back on instinct. 'Fuck me, bro, just listen to him first before you start pulling fucking shooters out on him. Chill out and let him speak. For fuck's sake, we're in the middle of the estate, someone might see you.'

Jenkins was as white as a ghost as the pistol was slowly removed from his head. His breathing had doubled, and he took a few seconds before he could speak. He turned around and faced Tate, his voice shaky. 'The job fell through. I'll bung you a couple of hundred quid on as interest when this next job comes off.'

Tate voice was quiet which somehow made it worse. 'Do you think this is some sort of fucking joke? This isn't fucking Brighthouse, you know, making payments every month. I let you have the shooter on bail, you give me a date to pay and now you've fucked up. Now the price has gone up by a grand and will go up every week by another grand so, if I was you, I'd get grafting and pay me my fucking money. The next time I see you, you better have the green otherwise I'll make an example out of you and show everyone that you can't take the piss out of me.'

Jenkins was trying to calm him down, his voice desperate. 'My dad is Scott Gilbert. I'm not just some muppet from the estate, you know.' And there it was, the same as always when he got in deep shit, throwing his father's name about.

Tate laughed. He knew Scott and knew he was a main head, but still it didn't take away the fact that this prick owed him money. 'Your dad's not around to protect you, so you're playing with the real men now. Or maybe you should get on the blower to your old man and tell him you're not actually ready for the big bad world yet and hopefully Daddy can fix it, little boy.'

'I don't need anyone to fix my shit. Man can sort his own shit out.'

Tate held his head back and chuckled again, his hand already on the car door handle to leave. 'Fix it, bro, don't make me come looking for you because, if I have to come and find you, my little friend in my pocket will be out to play.'

Tate was gone and Mickey dropped his head low. Jenkins filled his lungs with air and started the car up straight away: he wanted out of here. 'The guy is a tosser. I swear I was ready to snatch that gun out of his hands and shove it down the back of his throat.'

Mickey frowned. This guy was chatting pure shit and he'd never seen his mate look so frightened in all his life. 'Mate, you need a fucking lifeline and fast. That man is serious when he says he will come looking for you. He'll be at your gaff, and what then?'

Jenkins pulled out onto the road and didn't really have a clue where he was going as long as it was away from here. 'Then I need to take Clarkson down, have his food away. I'll do my homework and hopefully he's got another drop or a grow.'

Mickey looked out of the window. 'Not sure if I'm up for it, Jenk, to be honest. This is not like taxing a few kids on the park, this is heavy shit. Lives can be lost, families put in danger.'

'Sssh, Mickey. If we plan it right, then it will go smoothly. And I saw you just then – pushing Tate's shooter away – you were hard as nails. Don't tell me you're fucking bailing on me now?'

Mickey rustled about in his seat and opened the window slightly, feeling the cold brisk air from outside. 'I'll always have your back, but sometimes I have to tell you when you're making a big mistake. If you want to have a crack at him, then I'll have your back, but just be mindful of who we are dealing with.'

'Clarkson is a wannabe. My dad would eat him for dinner and spit the bones back out.'

'That's your dad, though, Jenks. Not us.'

There was silence as they drove along the main road. Jenkins turned the radio on and pulled up at the Spice Cabin on Tavistock Square in Harpurhey. If you needed to find anyone, get information about who was doing what in the area, then this was the place to be. The square held everyone's secrets and in the shadows of the night this place changed and become one of the dangerous places to be in Manchester. You entered it at your own risk.

Jenkins parked up and slid his car seat back, stretching his legs. 'Skin up, then, bro,' he said to Mickey. The square was busy today and shoppers were out in full force, all trying to get what they needed before night fell. 'We'll pitch up here for a few hours and see what's what. Clarkson's grafters work on here and we can see where they go to after they've sold their weed.'

Mickey sighed deeper than he would have liked. 'Yeah, safe, bro,' he replied.

The day turned into night and two youths on motorbikes were skidding about the square. Young teenagers gathered in each corner, drinking, smoking, doing the things they hid away from their parents. Jenkins sat up straight and leaned forwards slightly. He nudged Mickey. 'Eyes to the left, quick, it's Boe and Pudding. They graft for Clarkson, it's a well-known fact. Let's sit tight and see what they're up to.'

Mickey pulled his baseball cap down over his eyes and slumped down further in his seat.

Jenkins was relieved to finally have a decent lead, a couple of lads everyone knew, and he was watching their every movement. Boe, real name Brian Fielding, and Pudding, who was Phil Cooper on his birth certificate, were around twenty-two years of age. Both of them had already done time in jail and both had a reputation as a couple of hard nuts. Clarkson was like that: he always recruited ambitious young grafters with similar backgrounds. He sold them the dream of earning big money when in fact he was the only one getting richer from these drugs they were selling. These numpties earned pennies compared to the top man.

Jenkins sucked on the spliff, watching how smooth the deals were done. Youths riding about on mountain bikes were grabbing something from Boe, then off they went once the money had been handed over. Where was the police presence? Where were the adults telling this lot that they could get arrested, flung into jail. Maybe, they all thought it was much safer to turn a blind eye. A grass was the lowest of the low in the area and if you were seen talking to the dibble then your windows would have gone in, for sure. Still, most of the older folk in the neighbourhood were sick of this kind of behaviour and there was always a petition on the shop counters for anybody to sign who wanted changes in the area too. Anyone who'd lived here for long enough would say how this used to be a nice neighbourhood before these dead-legs took it over. Hardworking people, families with good morals, people who wanted to live in a nice area, they were still here, just all locked away behind their doors come nightfall.

The lads had been sat in the car for well over two hours. Watching, taking notes of anything that happened. Boe was on his phone, and he walked over to a silver BMW as it pulled up. Jenkins eyes were wide open, alert. 'That's fucking Clarkson's right hand man, Dominic Flynn. He's collecting the cash, for sure. As soon as that geezer moves, we're all over him like a rash.'

Mickey nodded slowly, aware he was in this now and there was no way out.

After a package, larger than the ones the kids on bikes were moving, was handed over, Jenkins motored down Rochdale Road, the silver BMW never far from his sight. 'Come to Daddy,' Jenkins chuckled as he drove along the road. 'He's either taking the money to Clarkson, or going somewhere else we need to know about. This is class.'

Mickey didn't look so chuffed. 'Just make sure he doesn't see us and keep your distance.'

Jenkins was sticking to the game plan; he kept a good distance from Dominic. They followed him for around twenty minutes, and watched as he pulled up at a house in Ancoats. Jenkins parked up a little way back and turned his headlights off quickly. He rubbed his hands together and playfully punched Mickey in the arm. 'It's a fucking grow, for sure. Why else would he be down these ends?'

'He might be visiting someone or dropping something off.'

'Well, we're staying here now until we see what or who is in that house.'

Mickey huffed. 'Jesus, mate, I've got a shag booked tonight with Naomi. She'll blank me if I don't turn up. I let her down the other night too. Fucking hours we've been doing this.'

Jenkins mind was in the game now and he wasn't listening to a word Mickey was saying. All the answers to his prayers could be behind that door and he wasn't walking away anytime soon. 'Watch the fucker like a hawk, He's walking down the garden path. Let's see who opens that door.'

Dominic Flynn kept checking over his shoulder. He looked edgy as he knocked on the front door. Jenkins knuckles turned white as he gripped the steering wheel.

'Fucking Bobby Norris,' he hissed as the door opened. 'I know that guy, he's a gardener for Clarkson. Nudge knows him and wherever he is there is definitely a grow.'

Mickey nodded. 'Yep, defo a grow in there. Now we know where it is, can we get going? We can come back with more hands if you really think we can tax it.'

'Leave already? You and me both know it will be a big one if Bobby is involved in it. It must be ready to go, drying out. Bobby only comes in at the end to cut it all down and box it up.' Jenkins looked like he'd won the lotto.

'True. There must be a few rooms full in there, maybe all the house.' Even Mikey was looking happier at the thought of what they could get their hands on. 'We need to get our shit together and fast and get the team organised if we are having this away. We're talking big cash, enough to put us on the map anyway.'

Jenkins rubbed his hands together and chuckled. 'You've changed your fucking tune. Do I ever let you down, bro? I can smell a good graft a mile away.'

Mickey was in the moment and all he could see was pound signs. They sat outside the house for a further twenty minutes and kept a low profile as Dominic got back into his car. This was the sting that could change their lives.

Chapter Nineteen

Jess sat with Gina and Lola and Bethany. Jess had spent a few nights with Carl Clarkson now and already she had the knowledge where lots of his money was stashed. She'd even helped him out a bit. She'd been twisted, both of them fuelled with cocaine one night when he took her to a posh house and got some money to take with them. A lovely house it was, set in a quiet area in Todmorden. He said it was a house he stayed at some times when he was stressed out, probably a rental. Jess had reported everything back to Gina and more Post-its had gone on her board. But the more info they found out, the closer it brought them to disaster.

Gina was pacing the floor. 'Scott will be phoning me anytime soon and he will know that his money has gone by now. Girls, I feel like I'm going to have a heart attack. Say he knows it's me? What if we were seen, Lola? What the hell will he do to me?'

Bethany was calm and sat her mother down on the sofa. 'Mam, why the hell would he think it's anything to do with you? You're doing this for us, saving the house, saving the family, so sort your head out and relax.'

Jess looked rough. After nights on the tiles, the lack of sleep was showing in her face. 'Gina, we have what we need now to set us up. You promised we would all have enough money to look after ourselves. You are the brains behind this, told us it was child's play, so pull yourself together and let's finish what we started.'

Lola agreed. 'Gina, you're just having a panic attack. I have them all the time. Breathe, deep breaths, breathe.'

Gina's mobile phone rang. They all looked at each other as Gina held the phone up to see the caller's ID. 'It's bloody Scott, girls. Look at me. I'm shaking from top to bottom at my own husband calling me.'

Bethany spoke softly. 'Answer it and speak to him. You got this.'

Gina pressed the green button to answer the call, her voice low. 'Hiya, babes, how are you?'

They could all hear his voice, shouting, screaming, down the other end of the phone.

Gina opened her eyes wide. 'Scott, just calm down and tell me what the hell has happened. I don't understand a word you are saying when you're yelling at me.' There it was, her calm voice, calming her husband down. She walked out of the room with the phone held tightly to her ear and sat on the stairs talking to him. She was there at least fifteen minutes before she came back.

'Phew, he defo thinks it's Clarkson. He's raging and threatening to have people sent through his front door, kidnap his mam, his wife, the fucking lot of them.'

'At least he's not pointing the finger at us,' Bethany said. 'But Jess, you'd better watch yourself more than ever. And Mam, are you feeling calmer now? We need your head in the game.'

Gina inhaled deeply and sighed. 'I just had a moment before, girls. It won't happen again. We need to get our ships in order now and take on Clarkson. We need heads, though, someone to front us.'

Bethany sat thinking. 'I've already told you my ex, Taddy, would be in with us at the drop of a hat. He can run the jobs and I know he will never open his mouth as long as he's earning.'

Gina sat down and listened again to what her daughter had to say.

'I'll ring him, tell him some guy is looking for grafters and it's good money, he wants him to run his shit for a good wage. He won't be arsed who's behind it all as long as he's getting money.'

Gina didn't yet look convinced. 'But, can we trust him?'

'You don't need to trust him, Mam. I'll be the one who deals with him. I'll tell him it's some big name from London who I've met and he's got work with good money. I can be the middleman, even put on my stage voice and speak to him down the phone.' Bethany started talking like a man and Gina was in shock: she really sounded the part.

Jess burst out laughing along with Lola. 'Oh my god, Beth, where did that come from?'

She spoke again in a male's voice. 'All the acting classes my mam and dad paid for. I knew they would come in useful one day. It's my Ronnie Kray voice.'

The corners of Gina's mouth started to lift. 'So, we're all agreed. Bethany will sort the grafters out and we'll give them the location of where the money is. Once we take what Clarkson has, then we will have a bigger voice than any of them pricks out there. Money talks, remember, and with it we can buy anything that we want. Beth, you will be the voice of the main man, too. Taddy never meets anyone ever. Tell him the big man doesn't do meetings, make something up, because I never want you putting yourself in any danger. You sit with us when you talk to anyone, so I know exactly what is being said.'

Lola reached down to the side of her and pulled out a bottle of red wine. 'Let's crack this open. Girl Power.'

Gina reached over and grabbed an empty glass. She looked deadly serious as she spoke. 'We take it all, do you hear me, everything we can get our hands on. Then they can take this house and I will find another one, one that will never be jeopardised again.'

Jess filled her glass and raised it. 'Ladies, this is it. I need money and fast. Once I get it, I'm straight on a plane heading to the sunshine. My life will begin when I land there. Gina, you should come with me, start again. We can buy a bar, a business.'

Lola pulled a sour face. 'And, what about me, eh? Yeah, just forget about me, why don't you?'

Jess shot a look over at her. 'You have to stay here, don't you? The kids, the school, their friends, Mike?'

Lola thought about it and lowered her head before she replied. 'I guess you're right. My life is here for now, but it's not to say in a few years I can't join you.'

Gina stopped the conversation before it got heated. 'I never thought we would pull any of this off. But the more we get into this the more I realise it's not that hard. We just have to keep our mouths shut. This is the circle of trust. We take this to the grave.' They all raised their glasses high and said in unison: 'To the grave!'

Chapter Twenty

S cott was back on the main wing now, feeling more confident with each day that his transfer wasn't happening and the bent screw had done all he said he would. It was only a matter of time before Manion was taken down and Scott's reign of Strangeways would begin.

Scott was on one, ranting at Tommy. 'I want Clarkson's door booming in, a gun shoved down his throat. I want my fucking money back. Make the calls, see who's spending, who's talking. I'll put each and every one of them on a lie detector test. I'll find out who's had me over and, when I do, I'll make sure they never breathe again.'

Tommy sat on the edge of his bed. 'Cheeky bastards. No respect. Greedy shites they are. We'll get to the bottom of it, don't you worry. Jimmy Mac and the boys are already all over it and we should have a name before the end of play today.'

Scott walked to the window and struck his head against the cold metal bars. His eyes shot up towards the grey sky and his mouth was moving soundlessly. Perhaps he was praying to the big man in the sky, Tommy thought, asking him to bring his money back because, without it, he was a nobody. Money gave him the power, gave him the respect of all who knew him. Money gave him control.

Tommy whispered to Scott as he heard the keys jangling outside the cell door. The door opened slightly, and Dave Planer shoved his head inside. 'Your shout, lads. You've got about twenty minutes, cameras are off.'

Scott was ready, his nostrils flaring, his chest expanding, his ears pinned back. Tommy picked up the iron bar the screw had left for him at the door and gripped the claw hammer, passing it to Scott.

'Let's do this cunt,' Tommy growled as they motored out of the cell door along the landing. Planer had explained the route to Manion's cell over and over again. Once they got to his landing all they had to do was push his door open. Dave had left it unlocked. Scott was breathing heavily, remembering all the pain he felt when he was attacked, when he thought his number was up. His temper raged in the pit of his stomach, his scars pulsing.

Manion was in a single cell and, once they were in there, they both knew what they had to do. Tommy opened the door slowly and ran straight to the bed. He grabbed the pillow and shoved it over Zac's mouth. The claw hammer swung and swung at his legs, his ankles, his toes, and then his arms. Scott kept on swinging, his face red with effort at first and then with the spray of blood. Tommy removed the pillow from Zac's face, and Scott went nose to nose with him. 'Told you I would be back.' He let out a menacing laugh and hooked the claw hammer over his shoulder. Tommy then searched the cell – they'd had a tip off that Zac had drugs stashed there – and it wasn't long before he located a large bag of white powder shoved deep into the pipes at the back of the room.

Scott and Tommy ran back down the landing, listening to the retreating screams of Zac Manion.

As they left, Planer appeared and locked the door after them, then hurried back to their landing to make sure they got back in their cell. All he had to do now was make sure the cameras were switched back on. He'd done this before and knew this security system like the back of his hand. It was always freezing, always on the blink. This was a nice extra butty for him, extra money to go in his bank, to go on holiday.

Dave was back in the office and put his feet up on the table as the cameras started rolling again. Another screw come running down the landing in distress. 'Mate, where is the screaming coming from?'

Dave jumped up and looked oblivious. He ran with the other officer towards the noise. They opened Zac Manion's cell door and stared at the inmate lying on the bed covered in blood. The other officer raised the alarm, and all hands were on suddenly deck. This was yet another attack in Strangeways that no doubt nobody had seen. Planer stood outside the door as the medical team rushed inside, unbothered as they carried Zac Manion out on a stretcher. The inmates were all shouting behind their doors, banging and kicking at them. Any alarm or attack sent the mood on the wing wild. The prisoners could not only smell blood in the air – they could smell change. That's how quickly things changed behind prison walls. This was a new day, a new dawn, a new leader.

Chapter Twenty-One

Carl Clarkson cowered in the corner of his bedroom as a masked man shoved the barrel of a gun down his throat. 'Money, where is the fucking money? You had Scott Gilbert over and we want it all back, every fucking single penny.'

Carl was shaking from head to toe. 'I don't know what you're talking about. I've touched nobody's money.'

A teenage lad was dragged into the bedroom and flung up against the wall. His bottom lip was pumping with blood and Carl tried to get to his feet to shield him. Jim McClean went nose to nose with Clarkson again. 'One last chance before your boy is going to get a good fucking kicking. Can you let that happen? Ask yourself, is the money and drugs more important than your own flesh and blood?'

Carl knew the game was over. 'I don't have Gilbert's money, but you can have all that I have. Let my boy go and I'll give you what I have in the house.'

Jim knew Clarkson as well as the next man. He couldn't be trusted. 'Tell me where it is and one of my boys will get it.'

Carl sobbed as he looked over at his boy. His eyes told him he was sorry for ever putting him through this. 'There's a safe in the cellar, under the rug, code is one, five, one, nine, two. I swear on my son's life that's all I have. I've had nobody's dough.'

The young lad was a mess, crying to his father, 'Dad, dad, make them stop.'

Jim gave the nod to one of the men stood at the door, and he was gone. Jim was immune to tears. In fact, if they were still snivelling, it was a sure sign they were OK. It was when they went quiet you had to watch it. He'd been in this game long enough to know you never let anything get to you. That's what gave him his reputation. Jimmy looked down at Clarkson and booted his legs. 'Did you think we would never find out it was you?'

'I'll take a lie detector test. I'll prove it was fuck all to do with me.'

'You'll be coming with us, lad, and doing just that. And,' he paused, 'if you fail, it's Goodnight Vienna for you.'

'I'll do one, I'll do as many as he wants. If I'd had him over, I would own my shit and say so. You know I'm no liar. If I have someone over, I make sure people know. You're barking up the wrong tree here with me. And, if anything happens to my boy, I'll make sure every single one of you pays for it, on my life. Leave the kid out of it.'

The money was out of the safe now and Clarkson was dragged from the floor to his feet. He tried saying something to his son, but it was too late, he was dragged down the stairs, out down the garden path and rammed in the boot of a car. He kicked and screamed from the car, but as soon as the engine was flicked over the screaming stopped. Carl Clarkson had realised today that, no matter who you were, everyone had a jugular and, once your opponents got their teeth into it, you were no longer the strong, powerful man you thought you were.

Not more than half an hour later, Carl Clarkson sat in the chair with grey bands strapped around his stomach and his arm and gadgets clipped on his fingers. A man was facing him with his identity hidden. He held a white piece of paper in his hands and his voice was soft. 'I'm here to help you. I'm going to ask you some questions and all you have to do is answer them truthfully.'

Carl clenched his teeth together tightly and growled , 'Get this fucking over with. I'm telling the truth and I've got fuck all to hide.'

The man started by asking Carl some true questions like 'is your name Carl Clarkson?' He went on to ask several more questions that he knew were true. Now it was time for the biggies. 'Do you know anything about Scott Gilbert's money going missing?' Carl was dripping in sweat, balls of it rolling down his forehead into his eyes. 'No, I know fuck all, like I told those goons.'

The man looked down at his graph and scribbled something down with his black biro. The questions were being fired out now and Carl Clarkson maintained he knew nothing about the hit.

Jimmy stood outside the room when the man came out. He pulled his mask off and shook his head. 'Sorry. The guy is telling the truth, he knows nothing. Look at his graph, fuck all on there to suggest he's lying.'

Jimmy looked over at his boys and let out a laboured breath. 'So, he stays here until we speak to Scott, then. We'll see what he wants to do with him, but one thing is for sure, that twat stays with us until this is sorted. Given the chance, he'll have his boys on us, for sure. Let's be smart and keep him as long as we can. With him off the streets, it gives us more scope to do what we have to.'

Jimmy pulled his phone out of his pocket and made the call to Scott. He'd been a good friend to Scott for a lot of years – boys' holidays, nights out together, and many a time he'd been to Gina's house having food with them. Their wives were good friends and often spent hours on the phone putting the world to rights. Stepping up to fill his boots was something he took pride in – he was going to find out who'd nicked the stash, come hell or high water.

'Mate, he passed the lie detector test. On my life, every question, top marks. Maybe it wasn't him after all.'

Scott was saying something back to Jimmy and whatever he was saying was serious.

'It's all in order, boss. I'll speak with everyone else in the area and see what is on the grapevine. When we get

182

these pricks, Scott, we'll show them good, we'll show them real good.'

The call ended and Jim gave the nod to his boys. 'You two stay here with that rat and the rest come with me. We have work to do.'

Chapter Twenty-Two

Taddy sat looking over at Bethany, love-struck eyes. 'So, who's this hot-shot from London, and how come you know him?'

This lad was on the ball and this work that Beth was bringing to him seemed to be too good to be true. She fluttered her eyelashes at him. 'Taddy, like I said, my mate's been seeing him, and he wants to break into Manchester. He wanted somebody who knew their shit and, well, wasn't scared of stepping on anyone's toes.' She moved in closer to him. 'And who wanted to make some decent money. I know you, Taddy, and you have quite a few heads with you. It was just a thought and, if you don't want the work, then fine. I'll forget we even had this conversation.'

He wanted to know more. 'And what's in it for you? Why haven't you asked your brother?'

This was getting uncomfortable. Bethany smiled and sighed. 'If I'm being honest, I don't think Jenks is ready to step up now Dad's doing a stretch. I liked you a lot when we were seeing each other and, well, if it wasn't for our Jenkins, who knows what would have happened? I always thought you had potential. But forget I even mentioned this. You're right, I should have spoken to someone else. I just thought, if I asked you, maybe I could have earned a bit of money myself. I can't ask my dad, can I, he would go sick. I'm his baby girl, aren't I?'

Taddy smirked and sat back in his seat smiling at her, remembering their time together. 'Yeah, I was well into you. Your brother is a prick, and on my life, I was going to come back to your gaff and do him in. It's only out of respect for you that I took it on the chin. If that would have been anybody else, I would have ended him. I was a kid back then anyway. I would like to see him try something now. I'd snap his jaw.'

Bethany nodded. 'Our kid is a hot-head. I can't be arsed with him anymore. He thinks he's a name around here now since my dad got slammed, and he's doing my head in – like I said, he's not ready to fill Dad's shoes yet. Anyway, if you're up for this graft, Ronnie will ring you later and sort out what he wants.'

He nodded slowly and sat playing with his fingers. 'No harm in listening, is there. Yeah, tell him to give me a bell. If its big dough, I'm in. I don't graft for pennies anymore. I'm up for the big dollars.'

Bethany looked relieved. 'But, manpower: do you have a team ready to go? This isn't kids on street corners stuff.'

He burst out laughing and moved in closer to her. 'I've got heads, love, big enough and bad enough to do whatever he wants.' Taddy stared at her, and she could tell he was eager to get something out. 'So, you said you was into me. Does that still stand?' he probed.

Bethany knew how to play the game. 'I don't know, depends, doesn't it?'

'On what?'

'On you and what you can bring to the table. I'm not dating guys who have about ten girls on the go. I want to be exclusive and treated right.'

Taddy jumped up and stood in front of her. 'Oi, I'm not a cheater. I stay loyal to my women.'

Bethany opened her eyes wide and stood up too. 'Yeah, whatever. I'm just saying I don't stand for any crap from guys. Play your cards right and who knows what will happen?'

Taddy smirked. He liked her cheek. 'So, it's a maybe. I can live with that.'

They both walked towards the door, and he patted her shoulder. 'This could be a good partnership, Beth, earning money together and the chance of a shag,' he giggled.

She turned on the spot and playfully punched him in the arm. 'Oi, cheeky bollocks, keep your skanky remarks to yourself. I'm a class bird, me, not one of them slappers from the estate.'

'Wow, wind your neck in, I was only joking. I respect you; I always have.' This was a good day after all, a shot at Bethany Gilbert again and a chance to earn some big money. What more could he ask for?

Back at home, Bethany rubbed her hands together and shot a look at her mother. 'Mam, you're a mastermind. I never thought in a million years you would pull this off. And I told you my acting lessons would pay off one day.'

Gina smiled and looked at Jess. 'I'm not sure if we can count on Lola, you know. Her head's all over the place and, if I'm honest, do we really need her?'

Jess nodded. 'Exactly what I was thinking. She would be getting a cut of the money and for what? She brings nothing to the table.'

'We can't just bin her off, though. We have to treat her with kid gloves. The last thing we need is her turning Jeckyll on us. We have to keep her sweet to make sure she keeps her big trap shut. You're forgetting what she's like when she's upset. She doesn't think before she puts her mouth in gear.'

'So, tell her we will help her out and she doesn't need to be involved. She'll be happy with that.'

Gina sat thinking, sucking at her lips. 'Leave her with me for now. I need to think it over.'

Bethany waited to jump back into the conversation. 'So, we're on for tonight, then. Taddy can take Clarkson's grow and we can start the ball rolling.'

Jess checked her mobile again. 'I've heard nothing from him for a few days now. I'm not ringing him, because that makes me look desperate, but I thought he was well into me. I hope I'm not losing my touch.' Jess jumped from her seat to look into the mirror, pulling at her skin, puckering her lips. 'They say your looks fade after a certain age, don't they? I'm going to book in for a facial with Jodie and maybe she can top my lips up. Honest, I need to start look-ing after myself and stop burning the candle at both ends.'

Gina grabbed her fags from the table and headed to the back garden. Jess followed. It was nice, the sun was beam-ing down in the garden, birds tweeting in the nearby trees and a nice gentle breeze. They looked like a couple of women enjoying the weather – not planning a gangland hit. 'That's funny that he's not rang you. I thought you said you had him eating out of your hand?' Gina was twitchy.

'Me too. I'll play it by ear. We have enough information from him anyway and, if the wanker thinks he can blank me now, so be it. I'm not begging for it.' Jess shrugged.

Gina's mobile started ringing. She was flustered as she grabbed it out of her pocket. 'I've been dreading this call. Bleeding hell, I need to breathe.' It seemed like forever before she answered the call. She lit her cigarette and started to walk up and down. 'Hiya, babes,' she said in a soft voice. She quickly turned on the spot and open her eyes wide as she looked at Jess. 'What do you mean, Clarkson hasn't got the money?'

Jess sat down on the garden chair and sparked a ciga-rette up too. She was hanging on Gina's every word. 'What are we going to do, Scott? I have nothing, no savings, no nothing. I thought you said he was the prime suspect. If it's not him, then who the hell is it?' Gina listened to her husband. 'Scott, I may as well pack the house up and move out now. I've had piles of letters saying they are taking the house from us so what's the point in delaying it? On my days, you couldn't write my life at the moment. It's like a soap. We're fucked, basically, aren't we?'

Maybe Bethany got her acting skills from her mother because she was giving a performance that any leading lady would have been proud of. The call ended and Gina sucked hard on her cig, then let the smoke wreathe out. 'He thought it was Clarkson who had him over. Apparently, he's got him locked up somewhere, said he's denying it. They've taken Zac Manion down too. He got what he deserved, if you ask me, bleeding snake.'

Jess rubbed her hands together with excitement. 'So, he doesn't have a clue about what we're up to, does he?'

'I know Scott in and out and he won't rest until he finds out who's had him over. We need to be careful, never leave ourselves open, make sure we cover our tracks.'

Jess wafted her hand in front of her face. 'I knew Clarkson didn't bin me. Phew, for a split second I thought I was losing my touch. I wonder where they have got him banged up.'

Gina sat down next to Jess. 'They won't be able to hold him forever and, when he's walking the streets again, do you think for one minute that any of us are safe? The man is sick in the head. He'll want revenge, and who are the people closest to Scott?' She stubbed her cigarette out in the ashtray on the table. 'Us.'

Back indoors, Bethany practised her male voice over and over again. She was good, sounded like an older man. 'Right, I need to get this over and ring Taddy with the details. Are all the addresses right on this piece of paper, Mam? I don't want to send him to the wrong house.' Gina doubled-checked the information she'd written down and passed the paper over to Jess. 'That's the right address, isn't it?'

'Yep, that's the one I give you.'

You could have heard a pin drop as Bethany made the call, a cold glass of water at her side. Her hands were sweating but she was used to curtain-up nerves.

Showtime: Bethany was on the blower to Taddy. Jess covered her face with both hands, unable to look. Bethany was on point, there was no doubt about it, she sounded like a man, a proper cockney gangster, and she knew her shit when it came to what they wanted doing, the cuts each of them were getting and how they would be paid. Gina started to relax; it was all going to plan. Bethany read the address out slowly, filled Taddy in on how many people could be in the house and what they were going for. The call ended and Bethany let out a whoop. She stared at them both. 'I did it! He never questioned me once. Mam, I pulled it off!'

Gina clutched her and kissed the top of her head. 'You sure did, my girl, you sure did.'

Jess punched her clenched fist into the air and jumped to her feet. 'All we need now is the money coming in and I'll be off – you two can clear out too. Follow your dreams instead of your fellas.'

Gina was quiet. Beth could tell something was wrong. 'Mam, what's up? Come on, don't worry. Everything will be fine.'

'It's the house, love. We're going to have to move out. I feel like I've let you and Jenkins down. Even if we pull this off, it won't be instant. We have two choices; we can go back home to my mam's or we can rent somewhere short-term until we are sorted.'

Bethany cringed. 'Mam, I can't go back to Harpurhey. I love my nana and all that, but we'd be a laughing stock. Let's rent somewhere instead.'

'Let me think about it. I've got the money we took from your dad, but we need that to get bigger, to get where we all need to be. So where would the extra money come from to rent?'

Bethany hung her head, thinking too much about how her dad would feel if he ever found out what they were up to. He'd been good to her, never let her down. He'd always provided for her and given her everything she'd ever wanted and here she was playing behind his back. 'Mam, if we need to go back to Harpurhey, so be it. It is what it is. I'll do what I have to. But there is no way Jenkins will, you know that, don't you? Not like I'm bothered.'

Jess sat looking her nails, fanning them out. 'Well, whatever you two decide, we've got to get tonight done first. Let's go out, Gina, food and a few cocktails. There is no point sitting about worrying, is there? Taddy and his boys will do what they have to do and plus we are out in public and no fingers will be pointed at us.'

Bethany agreed. 'Yes, get out in the mix and be seen. I've got a date with Reece tonight and hopefully he will give us some info, too. More info, more money. More money, more freedom.'

Chapter Twenty-Three

S cott Gilbert walked out onto the landing and shot a look around the jail. This place stank of misery, a black cloud of despair following him around wherever he went. He needed to sort his shit out and fast. Maybe, a trip to the gym, smash a circuit, make him feel better about himself, prove he was getting his strength back. Scott was padded up in one of the more cushy cells since he was back on the wing. The screw had sorted that out, anything to make sure he got a wage from this lot. Tommy came to join Scott and stood by his side, clocking the look in his eye that told the other inmates he meant business today. Fuck Zac Manion and his foot soldiers. This was his shout now and he was ready for anyone who thought they could take him down. Once bitten, twice shy.

Tommy stretched his arms over his head and spoke. 'I'll sort some stuff out today and get these drugs shifted around the wings. We need to start earning some money in here as well as what Jimmy and the boys are keeping running on the outside. More than ever, with you being had over at Tall Paul's gaff. Cheeky pricks they are, whoever has crossed the line with you, pal. Was that all of the money you had on the out?'

Scott clenched his teeth. 'All my money has gone, Tom. That was all I had to make sure my family were safe while I'm in this shit-hole. I need to find out who's on the take. I want my money back, every fucking last penny.'

Tommy patted Scott's arm and nodded, his eyes still fixed on anywhere his opps could be lurking. 'We'll find out. Jimmy and the boys are all over it. If Clarkson has passed the lie-detector test, where do we look now? He was our prime suspect.'

'Clarkson is going to be a problem. Our lads ran through his house, slapped his kid up. He'll want revenge.' Tommy felt a cold chill pass through his body. 'You better warn Gina, tell her to make sure all the doors are locked. Why don't you have a couple of the lads staying over with her? They could kip on the sofa, make sure they get any twat that's comes through the door.'

'I'm gonna give Jenkins the heads up and put him in the picture. He's green, sure, and I don't want him any deeper than he has to be, but he could handle this. He's got a few heads that chill with him. I will make sure they are all tooled up and ready to play ball.'

Tommy sighed. 'I'm not being funny or anything, Scott, but I don't think Jenkins will cut it if Clarkson and his boys come through your door. You've said yourself that you have tried to keep him out of this life, and I personally think he would fold if this shit got real.'

Scott turned to face Tommy, his ears pinned back and a look in his eye that told him he wasn't happy. 'My boy can tackle anything that is flung at him. Just because he's never fucking chopped anyone up or shot any bastard yet, it doesn't mean he wouldn't do it for his family. He's my lad and, no matter how you want to look at this, he needs to learn. This might give him the confidence to be a proper team member.'

Tommy raised his eyebrows and sucked on his cheek. 'If you think he can step up, who am I to disagree? Tell him to be ready.'

Scott hung his head. 'How the fuck have I ended up here? I thought I had it all mapped out, my future set in stone. I should have listened to Gi when she told me to leave this life behind, but I just couldn't do it, could I? Now I'm dragging my boy in.'

Tommy could see he was on the verge of having a meltdown. 'Let's get down to the gym and see what's what. Zac's been shipped out, I've heard. So, one less prick for us to worry about. Get on the blower to Jenkins and tell him the crack. You can't keep Clarkson down for long, you know. The clock is ticking.'

'I know, I know. I'll tell Jimmy to put Clarkson on the phone to me and see what he's saying, but the truth of the matter is I gave the order to run through his house. He won't let that go.'

Tommy started walking down the stairs and jerked his head back at his pad-mate. 'Give Mike a knock and see what's what with him. On my life, I'm sure he's on the rag or something. He's more miserable than you, and that's saying something. He's got a face like a smacked arse.'

Mike sat on the edge of his bed as Scott walked into his cell. 'Fucking hell, bro, I can't half smell sweaty feet in here.'

Mike smirked and lay on his bed with his hands looped behind his head. 'I've told Lola to bring me some more socks. It's these pillocks in the laundry in here. They don't wash your clothes properly. It's always damp.'

Scott sat down on the bed facing Mike and looked around the pad. He clocked a pile of books stacked neatly on a wooden table. 'Since when have you been a reader? I thought you told me you were dyslexic?' Mike blushed and laughed it off. 'Nah, I said I find it hard to concentrate when I'm reading, that's all. I've joined the library and, well,' he paused, 'I've started reading a few books. It calms me down and helps me relax. You should try it – best thing you can do in here.'

Scott screwed his face up. 'Me, reading? Give your head a shake, lad. I couldn't think of anything worse. I can only just about sit still to watch a bit of telly. Gina is always saying that I can't keep still for long and she's sure I've got ADHD.'

Mike smiled at her name. 'How's she been holding up? Hope she's not been like Lola has with me, fucking moaning every time I get on the phone to her. Last night she spent the first ten minutes chewing my ear off about how much shopping has gone up and what she used to get for fifty quid and what she gets now. Honest, I wanted to say to her, shut the fuck up, woman, like I'm arsed about how much a pint of bastard milk has gone up.'

Scott sat chewing on his fingernails. He never knew how much anything cost and he'd never been shopping with his wife in all the time he'd been married to her. He just bunged her some money and she sorted everything out. Gina paid the bills, bought his clothes, taxed the cars, booked the holidays. He did nothing on the domestic front. 'Yeah, my Gina is alright. 'I've told her the money has gone and she took it quite lightly, if you ask me. She probably knows I'll come up trumps and get some cash another way. The POCA team are still saying they're taking the house. They've given her a few weeks to move out. She cried her eyes out to me the other night, Mike. It broke my fucking heart. She loved that house, always told me it was her dream home. She loved cleaning it, decorating it, showing it off when we had guests.'

'That's proper crappy, pal. I'm so glad Lola kept her council house and we never bought one, otherwise I would be in the same boat as you. I'm gutted for you. Where is she going to go?'

Scott scratched his nuts and let out a laboured breath. 'Back to her mam's, I think. Mildred lives on her jacks so she's got two bedrooms spare at her gaff. It will only be for a few months, well, until we start earning in here and getting some decent money together. Jimmy is still working our patch but, come on, Mike, how long before someone comes along and starts having a pop at us? Some wannabe knows where I stashed my money, they must have been watching me when I was out. I bet they put a tracker on my motor. Fuck me, mate, why the hell didn't I get onto someone following me about, knowing every step I made. We've done it before, Mike, we've banged trackers on loads of cars when we know they are onto something big, so why did I think it would never ever happen to me? Mate, from now on I'm going to have my head screwed on and make sure I'm never in this boat again. I've only been in here two minutes and I got shanked. Usually, I'm two steps in front and one behind every fucker.' Scott bolted up from the bed like he'd had an awakening. He walked over to the window and sucked the crisp fresh air in from outside. 'Get your arse up, Mike. We're back in the gym. Fuck these losers in here. It's our jail now.'

Chapter Twenty-Four

Bethany quickly checked her wristwatch and pulled her sleeve back down. Reece smiled over at her aware she was edgy tonight. 'Do you have to be somewhere or something? That's the third time in the last ten minutes you have checked the time. Am I boring you?'

Sadie, Reece's mother, glanced over at Bethany and held her gaze, studying her. She was on her second bottle of wine tonight and, after hearing that her other half was in a bad way, the thought of learning to play the guitar had gone out of the window. Her man was her priority now, always would be. She topped her glass up again and sat running a single finger around the top of it, staring into space. She sucked hard on her lips before she spoke. 'They say it's all fair in love and war, but it isn't, is it? Zac could have died through those bastards who did him in and do you think they gave a second thought to what or how his family would feel? I'm sick to the bleeding back teeth of it all. Day in day out, I'm just sat about waiting for that knock on the door, the one that tells me my husband is dead.' She turned her head slightly to look at the photograph of her son hung on the wall. 'I know that feeling more than anyone, know how deep it cuts when you receive the news that one of your family is gone. Every day, I re-live that feeling, it never leaves me, ever.'

Reece went and sat next to his mother and put his arm around her, a gentle squeeze. 'My dad will be alright, Mam. He's had worse injuries. Look when he came off his motorbike and the priest was at his bedside giving him his last rights, he pulled through that, didn't he? He's as strong as an ox, my old man is.'

Sadie closed her eyes and lifted her glass up to her mouth. 'They're saying it was your dad, Bethany, who done this to Zac, do you know that?'

Reece's cheeks went beetroot, aware his mam was ready for laying into her. Sadie was like that when she'd had one too many, told the world and his wife what she thought about them. There was no stopping her. But there was no way she was having this conversation while his bird was here, how embarrassing. He piped up straight away. 'Mam, I've told you before that Dad doesn't know who messed him up, all names are being thrown about the jail. So until you get your facts right, keep your mouth shut. You can get people in trouble shouting your mouth off.' He shot a look over at Bethany, proud that he'd defended her. 'Sorry about that, Beth, she gets like this when she's had a skinful.'

Sadie moved his arm away from her, needed nobody to comfort her. 'The truth will come out and when it does, if your old man has had anything to do with it, then I feel sorry for him.'

Reece snapped again. 'Mam, I said clamp it. Fuck me, like you need to be having this conversation now. It could be any number of grafters out to get Dad. I've heard that Carl Clarkson's vanished – maybe he's in hiding after ordering Dad offed.'

Sadie sat back in her seat and lifted her legs onto the sofa. She flicked her hair over her shoulder and sat looking into her glass. 'Reece, run upstairs and get my crystal ball. I will see what is in store for Bethany, predict her future.'

'Mam, bloody hell, now's not the time to start doing your Romany bit. You can just about see in front of you, never mind look into the future. And Beth won't want her fortune told anyway. Isn't that right, Beth?'

Bethany was on the spot, caught between the two but aware she needed something to get Sadie to stop speaking about her dad. 'Actually, I like stuff like that, and it would be nice to know that I'm going to be alright.'

Reece was surprised. He didn't have her down as being into all this mumbo jumbo. Didn't really fit with her criminology, he thought. Whereas his mother was always looking into her crystal ball. 'In all fairness, Mum has been bang on the money with some stuff she's predicted. Look at the time she told old Percy Garside to watch himself when he was crossing the road. Two weeks later he was laid up in a hospital bed with a fractured leg and arm due to getting knocked down.'

'Go on, it will take you two minutes to go upstairs and grab it,' Sadie prompted. 'I work better when I've had a drink. It loosens me up.'

Reece eventually got up from his seat under protest. They were alone now, and Bethany hated the silence. She started speaking. 'So, have you dug out those old songs you wrote?'

Sadie frowned. 'You must have caught me at a low. This is what happens when I think about doing something for myself: my shit falls apart. I only mentioned it to Zac and he laughed his head off, asking me if I was on drugs or something. It was just a daft idea I had, a magic moment. I'm a family woman and they need me here with them, not pissing about learning some instrument and singing tunes. I don't know what I was thinking.'

Bethany knew she was wasting her breath even mentioning the subject again, so she decided to grab the bull by the horns. 'Have they said if Zac will be alright? When I heard Dad had been done over, it took ages to get news from the doctors.'

'It was touch and go at first. They said he's lucky to be alive. He's still in hospital but, as soon as he is fit to travel, they're shipping him out to HMP Haverigg. It's miles away. I don't know how he expects me to travel up there every bleeding fortnight.'

'At least he will be far away from whoever is out to get him, though, you have to think about that. I don't know if I'd rather my dad was nearby or somewhere where he's got a chance of getting his head down and keeping out of the firing line. I know my mam was out her mind with it all.'

Sadie's expression changed. She quickly glanced over her shoulder and made sure they were alone. 'Your mam should count herself lucky. From what I heard, there is a price on your dad's head and, if they can't reach him, she's next in line.'

Bethany was about to delve deeper when Reece came back into the room holding something covered by a red silk scarf. 'There you go, Mystic Meg. Do you want me to set the table up near you?' Reece knew the crack and pulled a small table from the side of the sofa. He placed the red silk over it and plonked the crystal ball down. 'All set up, Mother, ready when you are.'

Sadie gripped his arm as he tried to sit back down. 'Let me read your fortune too, son. Come on, it's been ages since you had a reading.'

Bethany joined in. 'Go on, Reece, you go first and show me how it's done.'

'Wow, how on earth have I got roped into this? But for you, Beth, I will.' Reece rolled his eyes.

Sadie swigged another mouthful of her wine and then placed her slim fingers on the glass ball. Her eyes were narrowed at first, and she looked like she was having difficulty seeing properly. Then her eyes focused on something that seemed deep inside the ball.

Reece was unnerved. He hated all this crap, and he was only doing this to impress Bethany.

Sadie started smiling. 'Oh, this looks nice, son. You have a big house in the countryside, and I can see horses in a field near you. There are two children running about in the field and I'm presuming they are running to you. A boy with ice-blonde hair and a little girl with bright red hair.'

Reece squirmed. 'What, I'm going to have a ginger kid? Sack that, Mam, I'm the worst for slagging ginger people off.'

'It looks like it, son. That's God paying you back. Maybe keep your mouth shut in the future.'

Reece smirked over at Beth before he asked his next question. 'Can you see my wife? Who's there with me, what's her name?'

Bethany was on the edge of her seat, and she was into this more than she was letting on. Sadie was holding the ball tighter now. 'Oh no, bloody hell, I hate it when this happens. I've lost the vision, son, but at least you have a nice home and a couple of children.'

Sadie wasted no time in getting Bethany into the seat next. Her eyes squeezed together for a moment then she looked deep inside the crystal ball. Bethany was hanging on every word, concentrating, impatient. 'Can you see anything yet?'

Sadie was quiet for a few seconds as she gazed deeper into the ball. 'Lies surround you at the moment. I can see you crying. Earthy fresh soil at your feet, flowers being placed on top of it.'

Bethany rubbed at her arms. 'What does that mean? What lies? Am I at someone's grave?'

Sadie lifted her head up slowly. She reached over and gripped her glass of wine. 'It's gone now, the vision has gone.'

'But, what about what you could see? Was it good, was it bad?'

Reece could see Bethany was distressed and urged his mother to answer. 'Mam, you can't just leave Beth like that. Look at her, she's turned white. You've shit her up. Tell her what you could see.'

Sadie sat back in her seat. 'It's nothing to worry about, lovey. It just means you've told a lie somewhere and it could come back to bite you on the arse, that's all.'

'And what about the soil, the flowers, does that mean someone is going to die?'

'I don't know, love, I just saw what I saw. It doesn't come with an instruction manual.'

Reece chirped in. 'Beth, it doesn't mean it's true. My mam has told lots of people different stuff and it's not all come true. She told me to buy a lottery ticket last year and I did, and I've never won a carrot, so take everything she's told you with a pinch of salt.'

But Bethany was spooked. She checked her watch again and turned around, looking for her coat. 'Reece, I have to be home in half an hour. My dad is ringing me, and I want to speak to him. I hate not talking to him before I go to bed.' She paused. 'Oh, I'm sorry, you must think I'm a right cow for talking about my dad when yours is lying on a ward. He'll be out soon, I bet. It was only the other day that I thought my dad's number was up. These guys are fighters, though. They pull through anything.'

Sadie smirked over at Bethany, and you could see she wanted to say something but chose to keep her mouth shut instead. Bethany felt she was starting to see more sides to Sadie and, although at her first meeting she thought she was a nice woman, she'd changed her mind. Perhaps her mother was right: this woman should have been given a wide berth, after all. Bethany stood up and started to put her coat on, eager to get out.

Reece was by her side and whispered in her ear, 'Ignore her, Beth, she's as pissed as a fart. Sure, some of her predictions are bang on, but she makes a lot of stuff up too. Ask anyone, she's well known for it. My dad's threatened to smash that crystal ball loads of times. Honest, she does everyone's head in with it.'

Bethany took a deep breath and forced a smile over at Sadie. 'Thanks for the reading. Hopefully I will see you soon. Well,' she smirked. 'That's if I'm still alive.'

Sadie was right back at her. 'I didn't say you were going to die, I said you will be at a funeral. Don't twist my words.'

'Mam, go and get in bed.' Reece hollered. 'Don't be staying up all night drinking. My dad told me to keep an eye on you and that's what I'm doing.' He repeated himself, eyes fixed on her. 'Go to bed.'

Sadie looked at the photograph of her dead son on the wall and raised her glass to him. 'Can you hear the way he is speaking to me, son; you wouldn't have allowed that if you were here, would you?' Sadie stared at the photograph on the wall as if she was waiting on a reply, but none came. She stood up, plonked her glass on the table and walked over to Bethany and Reece. She wobbled, the smell of booze hanging in the air. 'Goodnight, love. Make sure my boy isn't out all night.'

'Don't worry, Sadie,' she said with a sarcastic tone. 'He's only dropping me at home, and he'll be straight back here with you.'

Reece looked deflated; his mam was a right cock-block. He thought he might have had a bit of time with this beauty, maybe get his end away tonight. No such luck.

Bethany was quiet as they drove along the main road. It was Friday night, and she could see gangs of youths sat on the pub corners getting steaming drunk or huddled on benches with bottles of vodka in their hands. Bethany smiled as she went past. It wasn't that long ago that her and her best friend Hayley were just like them. Every Friday they would get someone to go into the corner shop for them and buy them a half bottle of vodka each. They were the days, the days when she didn't have to worry about anything. Days when her dad fixed anything she was worried about. She looked over at Reece and squirmed. He wasn't the guy for her and, after just a few dates with him, he'd served his purpose. Maybe she should be straight up with him and tell him she wasn't feeling it, there was just no spark, no chemistry between them, he was so vanilla. But could he help her any more, tell her things that would help her earn more money?

Reece pulled up at the roadside just down the road from her house. He turned the lights off straight away. 'My mam is a right dickhead sometimes, you know. Some days she's as nice as pie and the next I don't know if I'm coming or going with her. Mind you, she has got the worry of my dad on her head now. I don't know how she sleeps at night, what she's been through, losing a son and all that.'

Bethany reached over and patted his arm. 'Eh, you don't have to apologise to me. My mam can be a night-mare sometimes too. They get stressed out and don't know how to handle it. Married to the mob – sounds glamorous, but it's no fun if it lands your fella in intensive care, is it?'

'Yeah, but my ma is on another level, fucking head-the-ball she is. She worries me sometimes, says things that aren't normal.'

Bethany wasn't paying attention anymore. She was looking at her front door – the home she was going to have say goodbye to any day. She would miss this place, miss this house all her friends were jealous of, miss bringing Hayley here for girlie nights. Her nana's house was clean and tidy but not a patch on her home. Nana Mildred was old-fashioned and there was no way she was bringing any of her friends to that house, no way on this earth. But what would she tell them all? Tell them what the real reason was that she was back in Harpurhey where she started off? She could hear them whispering behind her back, coming up with all different scenarios why the Gilberts were back where they started from. They would love her downfall, love that she was no different from them anymore.

Reece leaned in, but Bethany pulled away and held her head away from him. 'Give us a kiss, then,' he said.

Beth bit the bullet. 'Reece, I think it's best if we just stay friends for now. My head is messed up with my dad being away and all that. I have my acting career to concentrate on. It's so stressful at the moment. I don't have time for a boyfriend. It wouldn't be fair on you because I'm always working or have something to do. Plus, let's face it, it's never going to be simple if our dads are at each other's throats.' Jess had got them enough info, hanging around with Reece until he got round to taking her to a deal could take forever. And now she had Taddy lined up, dating a Manion was just extra risk.

Reece sucked on his front teeth. 'It's not my dad, though, is it? It's my mam. I knew she'd messed things up for me. I'll have a word with her, she will be fine. Don't bin me off when we've only just started to date each other.'

Beth sighed; this wasn't going to be easy. Reece was a nice enough guy, but he wasn't her cup of tea. Their families were at war and he wasn't exactly Romeo. Bethany had some family loyalty left, she thought, as she bent down to pick up her handbag. In her eyes, this was done.

Reece gripped her shoulder and squeezed at it. 'So, that's it? I've been taking you out, bringing you home and you've led me on when all along you knew this was going nowhere.'

Beth backed off from him and already she had her hand on the door handle ready to get out. 'Reece, I've seen you a few times and we've been out on a couple of dates. If I'm not really feeling it, then I'm not forcing it.'

Reece looked cold. 'Fuck off then, you prick-teasing bitch. I don't even know what I saw in you anyway. I would have just fucked you then carted you anyway.

Because, let's face it, you're a Gilbert when all is said and done.'

Beth screwed her face up and hurried out of the car. She stood at the open door and bent her head low so she could see his face. 'Very nice, Reece, I knew you were a shady character. It's great that your true colours are coming out now and I can see you for the low-life prick you are. Once a Manion, always a Manion, eh.' She slammed the car door and hurried down the road, looking over her shoulder with every step she took. Reece couldn't be trusted, for sure. If he found out the whole story, she'd be dead meat.

Beth walked quickly down the garden path and felt relief as she slid her key into the front door. Her hands shook as she twisted the lock to get in. Once she was inside, she stood with her back against the door and closed her eyes, digesting everything that had happened. One thing was for sure, she'd made an enemy today of Reece Manion. Maybe she was her father's daughter in more ways than one.

Chapter Twenty-Five

Taddy and his boys were in position and waiting on the nod to boom the front door down on this gaff. Each of these men looked as hard as nails, scars and grimaces on what little you could see of their faces, tooled up, ready for action and more than ready to take down anyone who stood in their way. They were hungry for money, needed a decent graft so they could live the life they were accustomed to, and hungry for the fight too.

Taddy held his head back then gave a sharp nod, all he needed to give the signal for the door to come off its hinges. 'Showtime. Take the fucking door down,' he sneered.

It happened so fast. Banging, grunting, kicking. The boys were in. Taddy ran into the front room followed by his boys. His eyes were all over and he made his way to the biggest man in the room. Bobby Norris ran to the corner and covered his head with his shaking hands. He'd been in this situation a few times before and knew being a hero would only get him butchered. The last time he tried to fight for any drugs, he was macheted across his hand and nearly lost it. No, he would give them whatever they wanted. There was no time to think, no time for chats. Taddy was here for two things and two things only: the drugs and the money. He gripped Bobby by the scruff of his neck and dragged him to his feet. His head swung back and he headbutted him. Blood was spraying about the room, Bobby wobbling, trying not to hit the deck.

Taddy saw his chance and punched the man to the floor, booting him for good measure. 'Money. Where is the fucking cash, you prick? We need the gear or the dough – or, if you've got both here, then you'd better spill.'

The living room door swung open, and another man was flung inside. Taddy watched as his boys dealt with him in the same way. 'Get them fucking tied up and out of the way. Boys, get every bit of weed, don't leave fuck all behind.'

The men split up and each of them knew what their role was. The two men were being tied up and Taddy stood over them. 'How many boxes are we talking, lads? Before you answer, think carefully, because if you have some stashed I will personally cut your balls off and shove them up your arse.'

Bobby's bottom jaw trembled. 'The money is in the black safe under the bed upstairs. Please, I'm only the bleedin' gardener. Take what you want, it doesn't belong to me. I'm just here earning a bit of money.'

Taddy smirked down at Bobby. 'Good lad, you know the crack, don't you.' He jerked his head over at his boys.

'Go and see if it's there. I hope for your sake you're not telling porkies because, mate, I'm in the mood to beat the living daylights out of you.'

'On my life, it's there. Go and see.' The other man tied up next to Bobby never moved, his head dropped low onto his chin, barely breathing.

The black safe stared at Taddy. There was no way he was trying to open it here. No, it could take hours to crack, and time wasn't on his side. 'Who does the grow belong to, who you grafting for?'

Bobby swallowed hard, aware that he was singing like a budgie. A few hundred quid was all he got paid to tend to this crop – definitely not danger money. 'Clarky, mate. He's lying low at the moment, but he'll have me and you for dead once he gets wind of this.'

Taddy's expression changed. This was not as cut and dried as he first thought. He knew of Clarkson, everyone did. Bethany hadn't said it was a main man he was hitting – he'd assumed it was a wannabe. This was a whole different ball game now. The stakes just got higher, and he knew, one way or another, Clarkson would do his investigations and sooner or later his name would be thrown into the mix. But he couldn't stop now and brood on it. He would deal with the knock on the door when it happened.

The weed was soon loaded up into the cars and the safe was carried by two men out of the house. Whoever

Bethany's contact was would be delighted with this haul. Taddy looked around the room one last time and edged back over to Bobby. He pulled the gun from his jacket pocket and rammed the cold barrel down Bobby's mouth. 'Listen up, sad sack, you keep your mouth shut, alright? All you know is you got had over, and that's it. If I hear one peep that you are telling stories, I will be around at your gaff and snapping jaws. You get me?'

Bobby nodded frantically, aware that his ordeal was nearly over. 'I'll say fuck all, pal. Seen nothing, I know nothing.'

'Keep it like that if you know what's good for you.' Taddy pulled the shooter out of Bobby's mouth and rammed it back inside his pocket.

Taddy and his boys were gone. The job was a good one.

In the shadows, Jenkins's eyes were wide as he watched Taddy and his firm leaving the house.

'What the fuck is happening? That's our graft, who the fuck are these muppets?' Lee sat forwards in his seat and scratched his head.

Jenkins shot a look at him and Mickey, and Snarled, 'Have any of you muppets been chatting our business, because how the fuck do these clowns know about this grow?'

Mickey spoke through clenched teeth. 'Have we fuck told anyone. You're the one with the big gob out of us, so look closer to home when you're pointing the finger.'

Ryan jumped into the conversation and all eyes were on the road facing them. 'Fucking hell, shut up waffling and let's get them followed. We can see where they stash it and then we're in there like rats up a drainpipe. Who knows, they might have done us a favour taking out Bobby. We can wait til they think they've got to their safe house and tax it there.'

Jenkins flicked the engine over. He was chomping on the bit, hungry for action. He couldn't keep Tate waiting any longer after tonight. 'Mickey, you keep your eyes on them, don't let them out of your sight. This grow is ours and god help anyone who tries to stop us.'

Chapter Twenty-Six

G ina studied Scott like she was painting his portrait, every line, every wrinkle looking deeper than ever. He looked older, the twinkle from his bright blue eyes dull and grey. She turned her head to Mike with Lola and smiled as she watched them all over each other. Wow, Lola had no shame whatsoever. Scott followed her eyes, then reached over and grabbed her hand. 'It's all fucked up, babes. You moving back to your mam's house makes me feel so guilty. I'm para.'

She pulled her hand away slowly. 'Do you even know what guilty looks like? I thought I did, but how wrong could I be?'

Scott wasn't sure what she was getting at. 'And what does that mean?'

Gina turned to look him straight in the eyes. 'Ignore me, Scott, I'm not feeling myself today. I've been packing all our stuff up last night and it's broke my heart. I thought that house was our happily ever after. You let me down,

Scott, let us all down. You should have protected us from this.'

Scott sneered, a face she was not used to seeing. He was on the turn. 'Whoah, don't throw this on my head. The money I had to look after you was nicked. Some toerag is out there laughing their bollocks off at me and there is fuck all I can do about it.'

'The money wouldn't have saved the house, Scott. You should have done things properly, made sure nobody could ever take our house from us. Got out when we first talked about going straight.'

'Sort your head out, woman. I've looked after you and the kids all your bleeding life and now you are throwing this on my toes like I don't have enough going on.' There was a few seconds' silence. Scott lowered his tone. 'For richer for poorer, remember. I'll fix it. I'll buy us another house, just give me time.'

She rolled her eyes. 'You do realise you are in jail, Scott, don't you?'

'And what does that matter? Already I'm earning cash in here, so the money will stack up and before you know it there will be enough for us to get a new gaff.'

'Save it, Scott, it is what it is. I'll stay at my mam's until I get sorted. I'll get a job and do things the way they should have been done. I've let myself down too – and the kids. I should have been more independent.'

Scott chuckled. 'What, you get a job? Are you having a laugh or what? You've not worked a day in your life.'

She snarled at the low blow. 'No, because I've been at your beck and call every bastard minute looking after your needs instead of my own. I should have gone to college, learned a trade instead of listening to you. Look at that time when I wanted to go on that accountancy course, and you talked me out of it. I'm good with figures and I would have been good at the job.'

Scott slammed his huge palm down on the table and leaned towards her, teeth clenched tightly together. 'What the fuck is up with you, woman? Are you on the rag or something? Because, like I've already said, I'll fucking sort it.'

A few of the other inmates were looking and a screw was already on his way over to the table. 'Is everything alright over here? Voices getting loud and all that?'

Gina smiled, tightly. 'Yeah, boss, nothing for you to worry your pretty head about.'

Scott could see Mike looking and nodded over at him. He made small talk with Gina, hoping this screw would leave them alone. 'So why hasn't Jess turned up for a visit, then? Tommy won't be best pleased.'

'I'm not her keeper, I've not seen her. What's Tommy saying, are they fell out or something?'

'He said he has a gut feeling she's binned him. She never answers her phone, always throws excuses about why she can't come and see him. I think she's found someone else.'

Gina hunched her shoulders. 'He doesn't own her and the sooner he realises that the better. In fact, none of you lot own any of us.'

Scott shook his head. 'Gina, whatever it is, spit it out and get it off your chest. You have been snide with me for months now. What's wrong? Come on, I know you, and something is definitely eating away at you.'

She stared deep into her husband's eyes, never blinking. 'Like I said, I'm pissed off. No husband, no home, no money. What do you expect me to be doing, bleeding cartwheels or something?'

Scott didn't like this version of his wife. He sat eating his butty in silence, but he had only a few bites then flung it back onto the table with disgust. 'I've got no bleeding appetite. See what you've done to me.'

Gina shook his comment off and changed the subject. 'The kids are asking after you.'

'Probably just looking for a handout. What's Jenkins been up to? He never answers his phone when I try and ring him.'

'I've not got a clue, but he's in and out of the house all night long. Honest, no sooner do I close my eyes and he's waking me up, slamming doors and up and down the bleeding stairs like nobody's business.'

'A young lad, isn't he, probably got a few birds on the go.' Scott laughed out loud, proud that his son was getting notches on his belt.

The officer nearby shouted that the visiting time was over. Maybe it was a blessing in disguise because whatever she was going to say still seemed stuck behind her front teeth.

Scott pulled his wife's hands to him and kissed her fingertips. 'Babes, I hate us arguing. We need to be strong and get through this together. Remember, the dream team we called ourselves.'

Gina lifted a half-hearted smile. Yes, they *were* the dream team, but that was then, and this was now. For the first time in her life, she was seeing her husband for the man he really was. But she played the part well enough. She kissed him goodbye and told him she loved him. That seemed enough for Scott, and he gave a sigh of relief when he heard the words whispered into his ear.

'Gina, please bear with me for a few months until I sort my shit out. I've got a few guys on who stole my money so hopefully we will have that back soon and you can go on a holiday for a nice break with the kids. Yeah, you can put your feet up and get pampered. What do you think about that?'

'I thought you said you didn't have a clue where the money was?'

'Yeah, but it's only a matter of time before someone hears something. And when I do, it's *sayonara* for whoever has fucked with me. Clarkson passed the lie-detector test, so it's fuck all to do with him, and I've had Manion done, but they've all got deputies who could be in frame, and there are always kids coming up looking to make a name. But you need to be extra careful for a bit because Jim and the lads ran through his house and gave his son a few slaps. I've spoken to Clarkson on the blower, and he said he understands why I gave the nod for the boys to go through his front door, but still, he's a shady bastard and he'll want his revenge. Tell Jenkins, too, to watch his back and make sure he never leaves himself a sitting target. I've already told him, but remind him again and again.'

But Gina was already standing and had one eye on the door. Lola followed and they walked down the stairs together.

'Bleeding hell, what was going on with you and Scott? I could hear raised voices from where I was sat. Mike was concerned. He was nearly coming over to make sure you were alright. You looked like you wanted to one-bomb Scott.'

Gina's voice was high-pitched. 'I'm fine. It was Scott who was having a dickie fit. He got told some home truths, that's all.'

Lola carried on walking and Gina thought it was the right time to have this conversation with her. 'Lola, I'm glad we're on our own. I needed a chat with you. I think all this we've got going on is going to be too much for you. We'll still bung you some cash and that, but I think it's for the best that you stay out of this. It's getting messy now – a price on some of our heads at this rate.'

Lola snapped, hurrying to get out of the prison to let rip. 'You can fuck right off. I've been there with the both of you, watching jobs, making phone calls and all that. No way are you telling me you don't need me anymore. I'm just like you and Jess. I need the money to keep my head above the water just like you do. Don't do this to me, Gina.' Lola stopped walking and placed a single hand on her hip. 'I bet Jess has been down your ear, hasn't she? The crafty bitch, it's got her stamp all over this, this has. A bigger share for her if she can cut me out. I bet that's her plan.'

'No, she hasn't. We both said your mental health is not that good at the moment, and you have the kids to look after too, don't you?'

'And I'll carry on looking after my children. Gina, don't do this. I'll sort my shit out and, whenever you need me, I'll be there. We started this thing together – we'll end it that way too.'

'It's going to get a lot tougher, Lola. What if the shit hits the fan, men rushing through your house and all that?'

Lola screwed her face up and her nostrils flared. 'Then I'll deal with it same as you and Jess. You're forgetting I've had shit at my door before, had men stood at the side of my bed looking for Mike, and I survived that, didn't I?'

'You did, but look at your nerves after it. You're scared of your own shadow sometimes.'

'But, like I said, I'm still here, aren't I. I'll take the good and the bad, like you will.'

Gina sparked a fag up once they were well away from the prison and stood looking back at the high walls. She held her head back and sucked in a large mouthful of air. 'Lola, you better pull your socks up, then. The weed from Clarkson was taken last night and you know heads will roll for this.'

Lola swallowed hard, reached over, took the cigarette from Gina's hand and sucked on it hard. 'Bleeding hell, not what you need, is it? Clarkson is one angry bastard and, when he has a score to settle, he's not one to sit about waiting, is he?'

'Nope, don't you think I know that? I'm moving back in with my mam tomorrow so at least nobody will know we are there for now. It should buy us some time and see what the script is. I just need the final word on how much Taddy cleared.'

Lola passed the ciggie back and placed her hand on Gina's shoulder. 'That's it, girl – think of the money.'

Gina smiled. 'Look, if you're definitely staying in on all this, are you free tonight? We need to plan ahead, see where we're shifting stuff and where the next lot of money is coming from. Now we've started this, there's no going back.'

Bethany was waiting for Gina when she walked inside the house. 'Mam, Taddy has got all the weed stashed and there was over one hundred grand in the safe. He's got a buyer for the weed if you want, or should I tell him you'll sort it?' She corrected herself,. 'Well, not you, I mean our mystery Londoner.' She put on her best Kray voice for the last part.

Gina took her coat off, flung it over the back of the chair and placed her car keys on the table, exhausted. She was thinking as she sat down. 'You may as well get him shifting it. The sooner it's sold the better. Tell him to get the best price for it and sooner rather than later. The longer we hold onto it the more chance there is of it going walkabouts. I've got money coming in later from the drugs I took from Tall Paul's. If I get what I'm promised, that'll be the best part of a deposit on a new house – round here or maybe somewhere new.'

Bethany sat down next to her mother and placed her warm hand on her knee. 'You see. We won't be at Nana's forever, Mam. We'll call it a stopover. It's only me and you anyway, because Jenkins said he will stay at Mickey's until we get sorted. He said he would rather eat shit than move back to Harpurhey. You know what he's like, posh boy.'

Gina pinched the bridge of her nose. 'I've done what I've done for us, Beth. Your dad left us vulnerable, and I'll left you two vulnerable. We're never going back to how we were. I've never admitted it before, but he's alright as long as I'm jumping through hoops for him. He has never wanted me to be a success. It's always been about him and his pissing big ego. To him, I'm just Scott Gilbert's wife, nothing more, nothing less.'

'Mam, don't be talking like that. You've been a great mam, a home-maker. You've kept this family together when everything was falling apart. My dad knows that too.'

'He knows where I am and what I'm doing every day because I sit here waiting for him to come home. I've not had a life. Yes, I've had holidays, nice cars, jewellery, but come on, he picks the holidays, the cars, and even what we have for tea. I should have been more independent and found my own path in life, not walking behind your dad in his shadow for all these years.'

Bethany studied her mother in more detail. There was a sadness in her eyes, a pain she had never seen before, a look that told her that maybe everything she had said was true. 'So, once we pull this off and get a new place sorted, you start a business yourself. You're a great cook. Open a café, a diner.'

'No, love. I've stood behind a stove for years and I'm certainly not doing that anymore. I have a few ideas. I'm thinking of opening a bed and breakfast abroad.'

Bethany laughed. 'You've been watching that programme again, haven't you? *A Place in the Sun'*.

Gina was on the defensive. 'So, what if I have? I can do anything I want to when I've got the money behind me. I'll be a success then in my own right.'

'And what about my dad? You think he'll just wave you off, or are you planning he'll join you on the Costa del Crime when he's done his time?'

Gina turned her head away and bit down on her bottom lip. 'That man was my everything for as long as I can remember. But he's left me with a whole lot of nothing,' she stressed.

'But we can get it all back again. You know what my dad is like, he's never down for long.' Beth could feel the cracks in her family getting wider by the second.

'Beth, I don't know if I want this life long-term, always waiting for the knock on the door, not knowing when it's all going to come crashing down again. This stuff now, it's a young man's game. Your dad has kept plenty from me, and don't get me wrong, I was happy to turn a blind eye. But from the moment I read those court papers, I knew everything had to change. And I know what I've read was just the tip of the iceberg, love. There are things he's kept secret. Things I should have known. The trust has gone between us, and I don't know if it will ever come back again.'

Bethany sat back in her chair and sighed. Bloody hell, were her mam and dad splitting up after all these years? Yes, there were times in the past when they'd had their moments, times when her mam had flung her dad out, but that was behind them. She'd thought they sorted that out a long time ago.

Gina checked the clock on the wall. 'I'm going out. I can't be sitting here waiting for the phone to ring. Come, if you want?'

Bethany picked up her script. 'No, Mam, I need to practise my lines. The show is nearly here, and I need to make sure I don't mess up.'

'So, what's happened with Reece now? Have you carted him?'

'Yes, more or less. We don't need him anymore, do we? He turned snide on me, you know. You should have heard the way he spoke to me when I told him I wasn't feeling it. He nearly bit my head off, weirdo.'

'Well, make sure you are nowhere near him on your own. I don't trust those Manions as far as I can throw them.'

'You don't have to worry over me. I'm kind of into Taddy at the moment anyway. He's always asking to take me here, there and everywhere. I'm going to phone him now and sort them deals out. I can carry on with this voice for a little bit longer but then we need to sort it out because he's not daft. Why would he graft for a guy he never sees? Plus, if I start seeing him, I can't be lying to him.'

Gina agreed. 'We'll get this money from him and then we have one last hit and then we should be sorted.'

Bethany was puzzled. 'You've not mentioned anything to me about another job.'

'Because I wasn't sure at first, but us girls can deal with this one on our own.'

'So, are you going to tell me about it or what?'

'Zac Manion has all his money transported every last day of the month. It's one man carrying it and he is nothing we can't deal with.'

Bethany scoffed in disbelief. 'Mam, the Manion team is strong. Is this something you have thought about properly?'

'Yes. It's one last hit to get us where we need to be, Beth. We can pack up and do one from around here, head for the sunshine. Or you could move to London – take your acting seriously.'

Bethany hesitated. 'And Dad?'

'I'll cross that bridge when I come to it. Right now, I need to make sure these next jobs go off smoothly and I need to keep packing these bloody crates. We are moving tomorrow, and I want this chapter done and dusted.'

Bethany watched her mother leave the living room and sat thinking. Her mum wanted a new life, but even at her age she'd already learned an important lesson – you can't always get what you want.

Chapter Twenty-Seven

S cott Gilbert sat on the cell chair cracking his knuckles, bored. The door opened, and Dave Planer stood there staring at him cockily.

'So, what's the crack, Scotty-boy? You've been wanting to speak to me all day. I've only just got a minute, so I came straight over to the wing as soon as I was free. Better be worth my while.'

Tommy was alert. This was news to him too; he was all ears.

Scott sniffed. 'Dave, this is a big ask, but the till for it will be big too, if you can pull it off.'

Tommy braced himself. He recognised that tone from years of audacious hits Scott had put together, but this one he'd clearly plotted in secret. He'd heard nothing about what his pad-mate was planning. 'What's going on, Scott? Don't you run things by me anymore or what?'

Scott shot a look over at Tommy. 'Listen, will you, and I'll explain. There is no point in telling you if it's not going to happen.'

Dave was listening now. More money was music to his ears.

'I've got a hospital scan coming up, haven't I?' Scott knew he was lucky to be alive and the doctors seemed equally surprised, given the beating he'd taken.

Dave nodded. 'Yeah, I've seen it on the prisoner transport list coming up.'

'Well, I'm not planning on coming back after my appointment. I want out of this place. I'll have my boys waiting at the hospital and they can get me the fuck out of there.'

Dave looked sceptical. This was a big ask and not something he could arrange easily. 'It won't just be me who's taking you, Scott. They will have a couple of us with you at all times. You're high-security, mate, they won't take their eyes from you for a second.'

'Twenty grand, mate, it's yours if you are up for it? You choose if or how you split it with whichever screw tags along. There must be one of your team you know wants a bit of wedge – or if not, pick one of the slower ones you could easily fool. Half of the screws couldn't catch a cold, they're so bleedin' dumb.'

Tommy was up in arms. No mention of his name, no nothing. He slammed his palm onto the bed. 'And, what about me? Are you going to leave me to rot in here? Sack that, I'm coming too. Make that another twenty grand for me to get out too.'

Dave was seeing pound signs now. He started to pace about the cell. 'Leave it with me and I'll see what I can do. It's been done before, and it can be done again. I might have to bring Steve in this with me. I know he takes back-handers, so he'll be sweet. But Tommy, I will struggle with you, pal, not going to lie.'

Tommy stood up and marched around the cell. 'Nah, you can sort it Davey-lad. We'll have to tell Mike, too. We can't leave him behind, it's shady.'

Scott growled, 'No, it's an escape run not a fucking coach trip to Rhyl. We leave him here, like he left me when I got stabbed. I don't trust him anymore.' He shot a look at the screw. 'Dave, it's just the two of us who want a bus ticket out of here. Go and see what you can do and come back to us. Remember, this is good money, life-changing.'

Planer rubbed his hands together. This money would pay for a lot of things in life and definitely take the pressure off his home life. The Mrs was a shopaholic and, no sooner had he bunged her a few quid, she was back for more. Plus he had a weakness for the horses – had a few betting debts this would settle. 'I'll sort it, lads. Bear with me for a few days, this needs careful planning, every detail needs covering.'

Scott smirked. 'And that's what we're paying you for. No fuck ups.'

The officer left the cell and closed the door behind him. There was silence for a few seconds, then Tommy spoke. 'So, come on, what's going on in that big daft head of yours?'

Scott was staring at the ceiling. 'Manion's done, we've settled that, and now I need to see what's really happening on the outside. Clarkson will be after my kids now unless they know I've got out of this place. Heads will roll when I get back on the streets. These piss-taking twats won't know what's hit them.'

'Well, I'm up for it. I thought I would adapt to the life behind bars but it's breaking me down day by day.' Tommy was already dreaming of getting out.

Scott nodded. 'Tell me about it. Gina is being a right bitch too. You should have heard her on the visit the other day. More or less blaming me for us losing the house and all that shit.'

Tommy chuckled and rolled on his side. 'She's probably been listening to that scrubber, Jess. Yeah, it's got her stamp all over it, fucking women's lib and all that.'

'After all I've given her.' Scott held a serious look in his eyes. 'Do you think she's thinking of carting me, trading me in and getting a new man? You hear about it, Tom. Women these days are fucking ruthless. No more listening to their husbands, they're all about being independent and wanting equal rights.'

'No way that would happen. Your Gina is a loyal woman. She's stood by you through thick and thin, plus, you would know if she was putting it about. The boys would tell you.'

Scott dropped his head. 'No Tom, something has changed, I have a gut feeling. That's why I need out of this shithole. We say nothing to nobody about this yet. We'll get a gaff to stay out of the way and sit pretty and watch from a distance. Imagine our opps when we bounce out of the woodwork.' Scott's eyes were dancing with madness, his fist curling into two balls. Luckily the buzzer sounded and broke the tension. It was social time now and the cell doors were open.

Mike appeared at their door, and he looked like Chief Blackcloud, misery written all over his face. He'd been going to the doctor a lot lately and he'd already told them both that he wasn't sleeping properly. 'You coming for some scran and a game of pool?'

Scott was up first, closely followed by Tommy. 'We sure are, Mike. Tom, can you make sure you pick up that money from B-Wing? Get it all sorted and get Planer to get it shipped out. He knows the crack.'

Mike scratched his nuts. 'And my cut is going to Lola, right?'

Tommy sneered at him and shot a look over at Scott, waiting on his reply. 'Mate, you've lay on your bed all week and not done a tap. Do you think we're paying you for fuck all?'

'I've been ill, not been able to keep my eyes open.'

'So what?' Tommy snapped. 'We work as a team and we all get our hands dirty. That's how it works in here, or have you forgot?'

Scott could see this was getting heated and walked to the door. 'Like Tom said, you work you get a cut, no work, no money, simple. Do yourself a favour, Mike, and fuck off out of my face. You know what the script is and, if you don't like it, you know what to do.'

Mike was weighing the odds up. The moment he made a move, these two could twist him up and hurt him bad. Those who turn and walk away live to fight another day, sprang to his mind. He backed off and let Scott pass. Tommy was right behind him and ready to one-bomb this dickhead if he gave any grief.

Mike plodded behind Scott and Tommy as they made their way down the stairs towards the canteen. His blood was boiling and with every step he took he was getting ever more angry. He suddenly darted to the side and snatched a pool cue from another inmate. He ran up behind Tommy and whacked the wooden cue right across the back of his head. It didn't take a moment before the inmates were cheering and shouting – watching a scrap was the favourite entertainment in this place.

Scott stood back. Tommy would take him down without his help. The blow had shocked him, but it hadn't floored big Tommy Seymour. He span round, fury in his eyes. He was like a gladiator now, running towards Mike. He gripped him in a choke-hold and took him to the floor, biting his arms, his cheek, any place he could sink his teeth into. Scott didn't flinch. Mike had overstepped the mark and now he was paying the price. He'd always let his men settle disputes the old-fashioned way. Who needed HR when you had a fist fight?

The two inmates were doing their best to hurt each other now. It was horrible to watch and hard to believe they would have called each other mates, if anyone had asked them that morning. The alarm was raised and the screws were running towards the fight. Scott smirked as Tommy headbutted Mike, causing blood to surge from the side of his mouth. 'Turn it in, for fuck's sake, you two,' an officer shouted. It took at least eight screws to pull the men apart. The cuffs were finally on them both and they were dragged down to the block.

'It's not over, you prick,' Tommy screamed at the top of his lungs.

Mike was in no condition to talk. He was dripping in blood, his eyes swelling with every second that passed.

Scott watched Tommy leave the corridor and carried on walking to the canteen. It was all in a day's work for him. But he'd noted how snide was Mike, taking Tommy down from behind, a shady move by anyone's standards. He should have asked him for a straightener, a one-on-one. Even without Tommy and Mike, Scott was still surrounded by men, walking to the canteen like a soldier returning from war. His army had grown for sure, more men behind him every day, more power to rule this jail like he wanted to. A few of Manion's boys were stood at the side of the canteen, watching Scott's every move. They knew what he was capable of now his team had doubled in size, and they knew it was only a matter of time before they were taken down too unless they were prepared to cross the floor and join him. It was a hard choice to make, but they all knew they had no option if they wanted an easy life in this prison.

Scott sat down, smiling over at them. A jerk of his head was all they needed to know they were living on borrowed time. Their main man was gone now and, if they didn't jump ships soon, they would leave this jail in body bags.

Chapter Twenty-Eight

Jenkins sat in the car with Mickey and Ryan, chonging on a spliff. He stared over at the house opposite. 'The weed is in that house, and all that stops us from a big pay out is them muppets inside. I'll fuck each and every one of them up, on my life, the way I'm feeling at the moment I'll go to town on anyone who steps in my way.' He patted his coat. 'I'm ready to go sick and if that means popping a cap in them clowns, then so be it. I've got fucking Tate on my case for the money I owe him, and I need to earn big to pay him back. What are you saying, lads?'

Mickey hunched his shoulders. A graft was a graft, in his eyes, and even if it wasn't personal for him he was as hungry for money as Jenkins was. Ryan pulled a machete out and waved it about in the air. He'd carried it for years, and tonight he might actually use it. 'So, is it on or what? I'm not sitting here all fucking night again watching the gaff. I need money, so I'm ready to go as soon as you say the word, Jenks.'

Jenkins pulled his hat down low and yanked his neck scarf up over his mouth. 'Let's do this. Straight in and out. We take anyone down who stands in our way,' he spat. With that, the three rushed out of the car and ran over to the house. Mickey waved his hand at a group of lads in another car and they ran towards the house too.

Taddy was stood in the living room as the front door was boomed down. The grafters sprinted straight into the living room. Jenkins pulled the shooter out and pointed it at Taddy with shaking hands. 'Get down on the fucking floor, hands over your head, keep your head down, don't fucking look at me. I swear if you lift that head up once, I'll fucking end you.'

Taddy was weighing up the odds. For crying out loud, his boys had just left to go and get food and he was left open, a sitting target.

Ryan and Mickey had already found the boxes of weed and started to load them up in the car that had been driven onto the drive.

'Hurry the fuck up,' Jenkins roared. 'Take the fucking lot.'

Taddy knew he was outnumbered but looked directly at Jenkins. 'Mate, we'll find out who you are and, when we do, you know there will be repercussions. I'll find out who you are, who your family are and anybody else you care about.'

Jenkins stormed over to Taddy and whacked the side of the gun across his head. 'You're a prick, you won't do nothing to nobody. Trust me, carry on with that gob of yours and I will end you now. Go on, one more word and you'll go and meet your maker.'

But this move had given Taddy his chance and he bolted up from the floor. Seeing Jenks up close had shown him this dickhead didn't have a clue about guns. Taddy could tell by the way he was holding it. Jenkins stumbled and Taddy was on top of him in an instant, knocking the life out of him. Mickey came back into the room, flew in, punching and kicking and tried wrestling Taddy to the floor. But Jenkins was still down and there was little movement in him, bright red blood seeping from the corner of his mouth. Mickey had always classed himself as a street fighter and soon he was getting the better of Taddy. He screamed, 'Ryan, get your arse in here, quick!'

Ryan and a few of the other lads abandoned the boxes they were shifting and jumped in. Together they made sure Taddy was going nowhere fast. Punching, kicking, grunting, Taddy was a hard fucker for sure but not strong enough to fight them all off. The weed was loaded up and all that was left now was to get the fuck out of there. Mickey dragged Jenkins up from the floor and made his way to the living room door. Taddy was scrambling to his feet, getting ready to steam in again.

'Ryan, get him to the car, start the engine.' Mickey cracked his neck and sprinted back over to Taddy. He curled his fist and hit hard again.

Mickey was gasping for breath as he stumbled to the car. 'Fucking drive, get me the hell away from here. He's a mental twat in there and he'll be out any second now. Quick, fucking drive!'

Ryan started the engine up and he skidded off the driveway, smashing into a fence, scraping parked cars.

Taddy was on his feet and standing in the doorway of the house, yelling after them. 'I will find you all, mark my words. Each and every one of you are dead men walking.' He set off down the street after them, swinging a silver claw hammer at any car unlucky enough to be parked on the street, smashing every window.

Mickey had had lots of fights in the past, but nothing like this. Taddy was on another level. Jenks lay across the back seat, his mouth moving slowly. 'Mam, get my mam,' he moaned.

Ryan kept his foot down, speeding down the road, weaving in and out of traffic. 'Where the fuck am I going, Mickey? Which way? For fuck's sake, speak to me, bro.'

Mickey was injured, blood pouring down the side of his face, hands shaking, still in shock. He stuttered. 'Go to Jenkins's house. We can hide the car away in the garage.'

Ryan parked up outside Jenkins's house. Gina had moved out a few days before and the place was dark. Jenks knew he could use this place as anything he wanted now until the POCA team had it boarded up or a repo note was stuck to the front door.

'Jenkins, give me the fucking key and I'll go inside and open the garage door. Come on, mate, let's get this car off the road and then we can sort you out. Do you need to go to the hossy or what?'

Jenkins lay on the floor in the living room, his body in shock, sweating. The room was bare, and any noise was amplified. Even his breathing seeming louder than ever. Ryan and Mickey sat down next to him and rolled him on his side so they could see the damage. Mickey cringed and covered his mouth with his hands. 'Fuck me, look at the gash on his head, defo needs stitches in that. Ryan, go and get something to put on it, stop the bleeding. It needs some pressure on it. We can have a closer look when it's cleaned up. I'm no doctor, but this is bad.'

Ryan motored into the kitchen and came back holding a tea-towel. 'It's all I could find, better than nothing.'

'Fling it over here then. Fuck me, I'd hate to see you on a big job, fucking tea-towel to stop the bleeding,' Mickey muttered.

Jenkins was trying his best to sit up. Mickey held him down with one hand. 'Stay put for now, bro. Let's stop the bleeding and then you can do what you want.' Mickey folded the blue and white striped tea towel in half and placed it on the cut with firm pressure.

Ryan was by his side now, a worried frown on his face. 'And, what now, eh? Taddy and his boys will find out it's us and money will be on our heads. You heard him yourself, he said our families, the people we love. Fuck that for a game of cards, I'm getting on a plane and never coming back. There is fuck all around these ends anyway. I'm too young to die for this shit.'

Mickey looked down at Jenkins. 'Mate, it's not what we bargained for. This needs sorting, and fast. The word will be out on the streets, and you know more than me that it's only a matter of time before we all get a knock.'

Jenkins dragged the tea-towel from his head and looked down at the blood, then pushed himself back up. His words were slurred. 'I'll sort it, just leave it with me.'

Mickey and Ryan looked at each other and shook their heads slightly. It didn't look like Jenkins could handle standing up, let alone finish Taddy. They were dead men walking and they knew it.

Chapter Twenty-Nine

Gina was singing her head off, swaying one way then the other, having the time of her life. She loved Karaoke and she was up next. Scott had always made sure she never got up singing when they were out. He had hated any attention being on her, hated her being in the limelight. But those days were done. Lola and Jess were by her side and could see Gina's mobile phone ringing on the table, even if Gina hadn't noticed. The noise was deafening in this bar tonight and they couldn't hear themselves think. It was a rough pub by anyone's standards, and Lola and Jess had only come here under protest. The customers were usually the dregs of society, the ones who didn't care about the shitty décor or the fact it stank of old people and everyone seemed to be living from hand to mouth. The few people who bothered to dress up wore cheap dresses, heavy make-up and enough jewellery to sink a battleship.

But Gina was living in Harpurhey now and she was settling right back in. Being here made her remember who she was before she moved away from this place, plus it was far from likely Scott's boys would spot her in here – they'd never believe a Gilbert would set foot in this kind of place. But Gina's mam Mildred used to always be in this boozer grabbing a bargain when she was growing up, anything the shoplifters brought in. It was mostly the usual: washing powders, air fresheners, and sometimes she got the good stuff, legs of lamb, or even the steak they could never afford at shop prices. Anything to save herself a few quid.

Gina stood up now and made her way to the stage. It had been moons since she belted a song out. Jess nudged Lola and shouted down her ear, 'Eh, Gina's really up for a laugh tonight, isn't she? Since when has she ever got up singing? She always said it wasn't for her.'

Lola nodded. 'She might even have a bump in the toilets with us later, a quick line with the girls to liven her up.'

They both roared laughing. 'I doubt that, Lola. She's only just started wearing a thong. She's been wearing granny knickers for years, so one day at a time with her, I think.'

Gina was up on the stage, the lights blinding her as she looked out at the audience. She narrowed her eyes and quickly clocked the locals. Deep breaths, a quick straighten of her dress and she was ready. The first bars of 'I didn't know my own strength' rang out. She'd always loved a bit of Whitney Houston. It was a song she'd often listen to when she needed a pick-me-up if she was feeling down, when life was getting the better of her. She stood holding the mic like her life depended on it and started to belt the song out, confidence growing as the music swelled. The crowd was behind her now, singing and swaying from side to side. Jess had never heard the song before, and she listened to the words with tears in her eyes. But Gina didn't need to look at the words, she was singing from the heart.

The song come to an end and Gina took a bow. She'd smashed it and, as she jumped down from the stage, she was patted on the shoulder by a few of the regulars. 'Well done, cock, you should sing more songs,' an older woman said. 'We do an open mic after bingo sometimes.'

Gina smiled and made her way back to the table. She wasn't ready for old folks' bingo yet – she had business to do. She reached for a swig of her vodka. 'Bleeding hell, look at my hand shaking. My heart was in my mouth up there. I thought I was going to mess it up.'

Jess beamed. 'You were amazing. You looked so confident, although you looked like you were tearing up at one point.'

'That song means so much to me, girls. Even more so now this shit got real for me. I'm not the woman I used to be. I'm much, more more. By the time we've finished with these toss-pots, we will all be very rich women. Come on, who thought we would pull this off when we first started out? I didn't,' she chuckled. 'But I kind of understand Scott now, because the more you get, the more you want. It's the power of knowing you don't have to depend on nobody else.'

Gina's phone started ringing again. Bethany's name was flashing on the screen. She answered the call and listened to the frantic voice on the other end of the line. 'Beth, calm down will you and speak slowly. I can't understand a word you are saying. Hold on, let me go outside so I can hear you properly.' Gina stood up and squeezed past Lola. 'Mind my seat while I see what's going on.'

A couple of minutes later Jess clocked Gina coming back to the table. 'Come on, let's get out of here. Taddy has been done over, they took the fucking lot.'

Jess and Lola eyeballed each other. Was this the truth or was this the start of Gina's quest to cut them out of their due?

Gina, Jess and Lola, stood waiting for a taxi, none of them speaking, paranoia setting in. The wind was picking up and they huddled together to keep warm. Finally, Gina broke the silence. 'So, how has this happened? Taddy has only just taken the weed from Clarkson so who knew he had it? Only us.'

A black taxi pulled up and the girls jumped inside. Gina gave her mother's address and prayed for empty roads. Lola was never one for holding her thoughts back and, despite being told to keep her big trap shut, she always said what was on her mind. 'I find it all hard to believe, if I'm being honest with you. Fucking someone's lying, because how on earth did someone get onto Taddy when he's only just grafted it?'

Gina turned her head quickly and was near enough nose to nose with Lola, hot breath spraying into her face.

'Say what you mean, Lola, don't beat around the bush. If you've got something to say, just bleeding say it.'

The taxi driver could hear the commotion in the back of the taxi and raised his voice. 'Ladies any more of this and I'll throw the lot of you out. I'm sick of picking up people from that boozer. Always the same, either fighting each other or spewing their guts up in the back of my taxi.'

Gina leaned forwards and gripped the back of his seat, fingers turning white. 'Just pull up on the next street, we'll walk from there, you miserable twat.'

He screeched the brakes as he parked up. 'That's a fiver.'

Gina flung the money onto the passenger seat and opened the door to leave. But before she left, she had to have the last word. 'You need to lose your attitude if you're picking up people who live around here. I've heard a few stories about taxi drivers getting their tyres slashed or worse for having too much to say, if you get my drift.'

The taxi driver was up in arms. 'Get out of my car, go on, piss off, and I'll make sure I report you three to the police. Who do you think you are making threats like that to me? The police will have you, trust me, I'll be reporting this.'

Gina was out of the taxi and stood looking at him. She lit a ciggie up and waited for Lola and Jess to get out before she replied to him. 'Do as you like, old man. Like I said, it's very easy to find you so do yourself a favour and fuck off before I chin you myself.' The old Gina would have never said boo to a goose, and here she was threatening to deck a cabbie.

The driver looked edgy as he pulled off, not sure if these were idle threats or the real thing. He wasn't waiting about to find out anyway. He pulled off and never looked back. Gina looked at Jess and Lola. 'Right, Lola, let's get this sorted before we go in my mam's because she'll be in bed and us lot arguing will wake her up. I'm not being funny, if she gets up, she will want to know everything and won't keep it quiet. You know her, she'd tell someone the ins and outs of a cat's arsehole.'

Lola stood her ground. 'I'm asking questions, Gina, that's all. Come on, what did you expect? That we would take this on the chin and not delve deeper? Of course we want to know what the hell has gone on and, yes, it could be you having me and Jess over. Has Taddy really had the gear nicked or have you fixed something to get out of paying us? Honest to god, Gi, you've changed. You're talking like you don't need Scott, like you don't need us. I'm just saying, it's a bit convenient the drugs have vanished.'

Gina moved so she could look Jess in the eyes. 'And do you think I'm part of this too?'

Jess looked down at her fingernails. 'Gina, we're not accusing you of anything, but you said yourself, we've all sleepwalked through too much. We didn't ask the fellas enough, so now I figure we're both entitled to know what has gone on. So wind your neck in and chill out. Tell us the facts, that's all we want. Let's go and see Bethany and listen for ourselves. If this was the other way around, you would be the same as us.'

'I can't even believe I am having this conversation with the both of you. Do you think I'm that low to have you over when you two have been by my side all along? For fuck's sake, now I've heard it all.' Gina started to march off.

Jess looked at Lola and sighed. 'Why didn't you wait until we had heard the story first? Bleeding hell, Gina is on one now and how awkward is it going to be when we go in the house and speak to Bethany?'

Lola was still furious. 'Gina promised me money and I want what's mine. Mike has been given the run around by Scott for years, and I'm damned if I'm letting a Gilbert walk all over me too. Now let's go and hear Beth's version.'

Jess walked in first. She popped her head inside the living room and clocked Gina stood at the front window. 'Where's Bethany?'

Gina kept her eyes on the window. 'She's on her way. Any minute now she will be here, sit down.' Lola followed Jess inside the room. This was nothing like Gina's old house, this was a home crying out for a makeover. It looked tired and dated – like something from the eighties. There was lots of brass everywhere, an old-fashioned navy floral sofa with protectors on the arms, a chunky fake-stone fireplace around a gas fire that looked lethal. China figurines were lined up over the mantel and Lola stared at them. Fragile little things.

Bethany rushed into the front room and closed the door behind her. 'I've just come from Taddy. You should see the state of his face, Mam, they've messed him up good and proper. He said there were loads of them, tooled up, shooter, knives, machetes. He got one of them pretty good, but the others jumped on him and made sure there was nothing he could do. He ran after them, told them he would find out who they were and that there would be a price on all of their heads.'

Jess and Lola could see that this was kosher, no lies, no bullshit. Bethany was shaking like a leaf, traumatised. She was a good actress, sure, but not this good. She was a frightened girl pleading with her mam.

'I think we should leave this world alone. Imagine anybody finding out we were behind it all. We could be killed, shot, anything could happen. This is my dad's world not ours. It's too big for us.'

Gina shook her head and paced the floor. 'Be quiet and let me bleeding think. Beth, you're spooked, that's all. It's Clarkson's gear so every man and his wife will know about this soon. We will have to keep our ears to the ground and find out if his boys were the ones who took it back, or if not, who's got it now.'

'Mam, are you not listening to me? Taddy is one of the hardest lads I know. If they have taken him down, then what chance do we stand? We don't have back-up. I'm the Londoner who he thinks is the big man, are you forgetting this, Mam? You have the money what you took from my dad already so cut your losses and be happy with that. Cut four ways that's still enough to leave town.'

Gina was raging. 'I call the shots, so fucking stop panicking. You know how it all works, somebody will blurt it out soon and we'll be straight back on it. Taddy will want blood and he'll do all the donkey work for us.

We're at an advantage here because people think us women can't do shit, so they don't mind talking in front of us. In fact, they think it makes them all Billy Big-Bollocks. We just have to sit back and listen. Sure, we might need to apply a bit of gentle pressure but it's not like we're getting our hands dirty. Beth, when you have calmed down, get on the blower to Taddy for one last performance as the big man and tell him to fucking get his boys out hunting for the weed. Really put the pressure on him. Tell him you'll blow his fucking legs off, anything to put the shits up him.'

Bethany was about to say something, but the look on her mother's face told her she meant business. Bethany lowered her head and left the room. Gina sat down and punched her clenched fist into the cushion. 'We all need to calm the fuck down and get our heads back in the game. Do you not think Scott will be all over this? He'll know the suspects, and you can bet my life on it that he tells me. Yep, it's shitty news but, come on, girls, if we fall down, we get back up again. Jess, someone said that Clarkson is back on the block. Give him a ring, say you've been worried sick, tell him you miss him in the sack, anything to get back in his good books.'

Jess licked her top lip. 'I can do that, not a problem. The guy can't resist me when I turn on the charm.'

'Let's hope you're right, Jess. We need as much infor-mation as we can get.'

Lola stood up and walked towards the window. 'I'm going to ring a taxi. My mam said she would stay over but I don't like staying out too late.'

Gina watched Lola ringing her cab and she could still feel the tension in the air. She needed to fix this before she left. 'Lola, sorry for snapping before, but on my children's lives, may they drop down dead and never breathe again, this is nothing to do with me. You're right, you do have to ask questions, but you know me better than that and know my morals. I would never have any of you over, cross my heart and hope to die.'

Lola softened. 'Yeah, well, I might have overreacted. I'm sorry too, but Gi, I'm bleeding skint. Mike's got no money left and you know as well as me that I don't have any other income coming in. But you're right – we can do this. I'll give you a bell in the morning.'

Gina double-locked the doors as they left, then turned all the lights off after she looked around the living room. She closed her eyes and she could see herself as a kid running about this front room playing. The family had always been poor, and her father's drinking never made her life any easier. He had been pissed up all the time, slapping her mother about, shouting, screaming, having the house up in the early hours. Standing here now as a grown woman made her heart heavy. She'd thought it was normal when she was tiny, then her fault when she was a bit older, and then guilty she couldn't stop it when she hit her teens. Probably why she'd run off to Sonny and then Scott. She'd messed up big time with that. She should have settled for one of the other guys who were interested in her, one who would have given her a stable, safe life. She went quietly up the stairs to bed. As she walked along the landing, she could see her mother's bedroom light on, a soft yellow glow creeping from under the door. Mildred had never been the best of sleepers. She would have only an hour here and there, never a full night's sleep. She understood now – you never really switched off as a mother. She pushed the door open with a flat palm and popped her head inside.

Mildred was reading and looked up. 'Are you alright, love?'

Gina could have fallen to her knees and told her mother everything, but she held her emotions in, put that familiar smile on her face and pretended everything was going to be fine. She sat down on the edge of the bed and touched her mother's warm hand. It felt frail in hers – nearly transparent, thin skin. Her mother was old now and she knew it wouldn't be long that she would have her there with her. But despite all that she felt safe with her. That was something the men could learn – sometimes safety wasn't a weapon, it was a feeling. She'd not spent a lot of time with her mother over the last few years. She was regretting that now and she certainly wasn't going to dump her troubles on her.

'I'm good, Mam, just a bit tired. Never mind me, how's that pain been in your back, have you taken your painkillers?'

Her mum winced, her face creasing with every movement she made. 'The painkillers don't touch it anymore. It's pointless taking them now, pointless.'

'Mam, you need to go back to the doctors' and let them see if there is anything else for you to take. You can't be expected to have pain like this every bloody day.'

'They upped my morphine patches but all that's done is make me sleep more. That's not living, it's just existing. I can't win.'

Mildred held her daughter's hand to her warm cheek. 'I know you're sad that you have lost the house, but I'm glad you came back here with me for a bit. I've missed our chats, missed the grandchildren.'

'I know, Mam. I've been caught up in stuff recently after the trial. I've been that busy I've met myself on the way back.'

'How is Scott, how's he coping? It must be so hard for him being away from you all. The next time you see him, send him my love. You've got a good man there, always there to look after you.'

Gina squirmed. 'Mam, he left us vulnerable, left us homeless.'

'Come on, love, don't be giving him a hard time. You knew the business he was in. The time to get mad with him was when you first knew. This was always coming down the line. You've had your head in the sand if you pretend any different. Anyway, that man would move mountains for you. He'll fix everything. You just watch.'

'I won't depend on Scott ever again. Look at my life, what have I achieved: nothing. I've been a housewife, never done anything for myself, always thinking about other people. What happened to my dreams, Mam? What happened to the person I said I wanted to be growing up?

And yes, I'd never admit it to anyone but you, but yes, you're right. It's as much my fault as his. Who did I think I was, living a charmed life? Just because I wasn't dealing the blows didn't mean I'm not guilty of enjoying the money Scott's work brought me.'

Mildred never said a word. She simply listened as her daughter poured her heart out.

'Age gives you wrinkles, Mam, but it's regrets that shrivel the soul. I should have gone to college and had a career. I wasn't thick, was I? I was bright enough. But I thought marriage was a shortcut – turns out it was a dead end.'

Mildred spoke with confidence. 'You're not wrong about your brains, darling. Me and your dad always said the world was your oyster and you could have done anything you wanted to in life. You had the looks, the confidence, but you chose Scott. I can still see your face now when he walked into your life. You had the biggest smile I've ever seen on your face, and you were smitten from the first second you saw him. Come on, don't you remember coming home to me and your dad telling us you had found the man of your dreams, your Prince Charming, your happy ever after? The day you two got married, your dad turned to me and had tears in his eyes and said, 'I'll never have to worry about her again. The man she's marrying will make sure she has everything she needs.' Mildred wiped the single tear that had fallen onto her cheek and raised a smile. 'Everybody goes through hard times, love, and we all question the choices we have made in life. We all make some daft decisions along the way. But life isn't always about right and wrong choices – it's about making the best of that path we've taken. Look at me and your dad, if I had a pound for every time I told him I was going to leave, I would be a rich woman. I know he was a drinker, but he did have a caring side., He just didn't show it much.'

Gina smiled and dropped her head onto her mother's lap. 'God, life is complicated, isn't it? He had the devil in him sometimes, but I miss my dad. He was so certain about things. Even if I hated what he said or did sometimes, I always knew where I stood.'

Mildred laughed out loud, 'That's one way of putting it! When he hadn't had a drink, he was sound, but you wouldn't wish him back after closing time.'

'And back then I hated him for the way he treated you. I'm just saying, despite all that, I miss him sometimes.' Gina lifted her head up as her mother started coughing. She opened the drawer at the side of the bed and pulled out the grey inhaler. 'Open your mouth, Mam. Come on, you need a few puffs on this and you'll be fine.'

Gina pulled her forwards and started patting her back. The coughing fit was over soon enough but she could see it had taken the wind out of her mother's sails. Soon she was drifting off to sleep. 'Mam, if you need anything, shout me. I'll leave the bedroom door open so I can hear you. And thank you, for the chat.'

But there was no reply from Mildred. She was fast asleep.

Gina snuggled into the duvet and looked out of her childhood bedroom window. The skyline was different but at least the sky was the same. She stared at it for a few minutes, then rolled onto her side. She had one last look at her mobile and quickly sent a message to her daughter.

Love you, be strong. It will all work out well and for the better.

She placed her phone on the bedside cabinet and started to drift off to sleep. A few precious hours of oblivion were what she needed. Tomorrow was do or die time.

Chapter Thirty

Jenkins tried opening his eyes as the morning light crept through the blinds. But they felt badly swollen and remained half closed.. Every time he tried to move his body, he screamed out in pain. Ryan was at his side and spoke in a quiet voice to him. 'Mate, I really do need to get you to the hossy. I've stopped the bleeding, but you can bet your life, if you don't get it looked at, you will get an infection and that will be the end of you. We'll give a false name, say you fell on an iron fence. Who's going to say anything different?'

Jenkins cringed in pain. 'Bro, what the fuck happened?'

'It was messed up, mate. That was Taddy who you were up against. He is one hard nutcase. Didn't you tell me you had beef with him a while back and twatted him when he was giving it the big-un with your sister?'

Jenkins closed his eyes and nodded. But even that movement sent waves of pain and nausea through him. 'You're right. I need to get sorted, bro, take me to the hossy.

Honest, I feel like I'm going to pass out.' Jenkins closed his eyes. His body was shaking slightly as if a cold wind had hit it.

Ryan panicked. 'Stay awake, Jenks. Mickey, get your arse in here and let's get him to the hossy. Honest, mate, if we don't get him there fast, I think he'll be brown bread. Hurry up, come and look at him and see for yourself. He's grey, and he's lost a lot of blood.'

Mickey came into the room and stared down at Jenkins, who looked the nearest thing to a corpse possible. 'Yep, come on, no messing.'

They struggled to lift Jenkins. Still injured themselves, the fight had gone out of them. Suddenly the three lads looked barely more than little kids again. Little kids who'd seen too much.

Gina parked up outside her old house. Sadness filled her body, heart heavy, eyes clouding over. She inhaled deeply. 'Come on, Gina girl, get what you need and go.' She was glad she'd been able to move things bit by bit – it was too much to face all at once, let alone find room for everything. Most of it was in a storage unit across town by now, but she still kept remembering cupboards she'd not cleared, or a bag left in the loft. If she left it much longer, she'd come back one day and the locks would be changed.

Gina looked about the front room, puzzled. Something wasn't right and she froze on the spot as she clocked a towel full of blood on the floor. Pretty fresh too, the deep red only turning brown at the edges. She listened carefully and looked around the front room for something she could use to protect herself if the intruder was still in the house. She walked slowly to the hallway and shouted up the stairs. 'Hello, is somebody there?' No reply. Slowly, she picked up an umbrella and gripped it tightly. 'Hello,' she said again. Still no reply. Gina checked every room, and nobody was there. Finally, she could breathe out. But somebody had definitely been at the house. The closer she looked, the more she could see blood stains splattered about. Her heart was in her mouth as the penny dropped. Her son still had a key to the house. Maybe he'd brought one of his friends here who was injured and cleaned him up. His dad was always telling him not to trust anyone, keep where he lived to a selected few. But he never listened, always thought he knew better. Gina went into the kitchen and opened the door that led to the garage. She flicked the light switch on. Her hands covered her mouth as she clocked the smashed-up motor. What the hell had gone on here? She stared at the car for a few seconds and with caution walked over to it. She saw large boxes on the back seats, more boxes behind the car, a strong smell of weed in the air. With haste she opened a box, her hands shaking. She saw the weed and froze on the spot. Her head spun as the pieces of the puzzle came together. What a mess.

But after the penny had dropped, another thought struck her. Yes, people had got hurt, and all because they were after the same grow, even though they were meant to be on the same side. Nevertheless, the weed was here, back in her hands. Like it was meant to be. She knew Jenks had been busy, and she knew he was impatient to make his mark, so she felt sure her son was the one who'd had Clarkson's grow, the one who'd had Taddy over. He wouldn't have risked everything if he was grafting for someone else. No, he wanted to be top dog. Like father like son, she thought. She felt the cold grip of guilt around her chest – if she'd involved Jenks, could they have avoided this? The blood spilt, Taddy's injuries? Maybe. But she also knew that he would never have taken orders from her. She'd have been back sitting at home waiting on a bloke to call the shots. Gina walked one way then the other, thinking. She had a decision to make.

Gina's car was soon loaded up. She was sweating buckets. Before she left, she covered her hand with a tea-towel and smashed the windows in the back patio doors, one two three bangs, glass spraying everywhere. She kept her head down and sprinted straight into the car. Somebody must have been looking down on her, because what were the chances of her getting all the weed back? But what would Jenkins say when he knew he'd lost his graft?

Gina made a call. 'Hiya, it's me. Panic over. I'll be dropping it off in about half an hour. Keep this between me and you, nobody else must know. I'll tell you everything when I get there.' The call ended and she carried on driving with the radio on low, always making sure nobody was following her.

Jenkins was seen straight away when he was rushed through A&E. He'd got even worse on the way to the hospital and, once the doctor had triaged him, they rushed him behind a curtain. Mickey and Ryan sat in the waiting area and looked at each other. 'Who's going to tell his mam? She needs to know, doesn't she? But, what the hell can we say happened? Gina will have us both sat there with her giving us the third degree. What if she gets straight on the phone to Scott?' They shuddered. They'd dealt with Gina in the past when Jenkins had been in trouble growing up, and she never ever went easy on her son's friends. She would never admit Jenkins was as bad as them, always protected him saying they had led him astray.

Mickey got the short straw now, and he stood up, still with one hand down the front of his trackies. 'Right, I'll go outside and give her a bell. Wish me luck.'

Ryan smirked. 'You'll need more than luck, bro. She is going to go mental.'

Mickey dashed outside, already dialling. The sooner he got this out of the way the better. And at least this way he could call her with uncertain news rather than bad. Gina's phone was ringing and ringing, no answer. He'd have to leave a message on her voicemail. He'd keep it short and to the point. 'Gina, Jenkins got attacked by a few lads last night. He's at North Manchester General Hospital. Me and Ryan brought him here first thing this morning. He's lost a lot of blood and the doctors are with him.' He ended the call and hoped for good news when he went back inside. He hated hospitals. He'd seen too many mates go in and not come out. Surely it wasn't Jenks's time. Not yet. Not now.

Chapter Thirty-One

Scott sat down in the hospital waiting room. They'd planned every detail for the last few days, looked at all the options. Scott coughed and the screw knew it was time to get this show rolling.

'I need a piss, boss,' said Scott.

Dave Planer stood up and sighed at the other officer. 'I'll take him. You have a read of the newspaper.' The other screw looked older, ready to retire from this job, turning up every day until his retirement came. 'Cheers, Dave. My feet have been playing up and the gout's so painful lately I can only just get my shoes on with it.'

Dave walked over to Scott. 'Come on, then, and you'd better be quick. I want a coffee and a read of the newspaper too. It's not just you lot who look forward to getting a break from the wing.' Dave unlocked the handcuffs from the metal chair and placed the cuff around his own wrist. They walked down the corridor and, once they were at the toilets, the plan kicked in. Dave opened the toilet door and let Scott go inside before he unclipped the handcuffs. The rest happened so fast. The screw was dragged inside and the door was slammed shut behind him.

Scott walked out of the toilet dressed in green scrubs, a face-mask pulled over most of his face. His pace was quick, and he knew he didn't have long before the screw was found in the toilets. Scott kept his head low and followed the signs for the exit. He was nearly free, he could practically taste the freedom, the double doors the only thing stopping him from being out in the fresh air. Once he was through them, Scott made a beeline out of the hospital grounds. He nipped up a side street, took a right, then a left and ran towards a black transit van that had the side door open. He flung himself into the back of it and lay on the floor trying to regain his breath. 'Fucking drive, Jim!' he roared.

Jim was a top driver, one of the best this side of Manchester. He was older now, but back in the day he'd been a boy-racer. He still loved speeding and putting the pedal to the floor. And he'd not lost his talent, weaving in and out of the traffic like it was a video game. He yelled over his shoulder. 'Can you hear the sirens, pal? Keep your head down and I'll have you there in no time.'

Scott was on an adrenaline high. 'Throw us a cig back in here, pal, and a lighter. My nerves are shattered. I'm not as fit as I was. I'm breathing through my arsehole, can you hear my chest rattling?'

Jim didn't look over his shoulder, he launched the fags into the back with a yellow clipper lighter. 'Yep, me too, mate. I need to pack the cigs in and get a vape or something. You should hear me coughing in the morning. I'm like a pensioner. The Mrs is always telling me to pack the fags in, but I can't bring myself to. I've smoked for too long now. You can't teach an old dog new tricks, can you?'

Scott lit his cigarette and sat with his knees held up to his chest. 'Fucking hell, is that the helicopter I can hear too?'

Jim dipped his head and looked up into the grey cloudy sky. 'Yep, the whirly bird is out. We need to get off the main road now and out of sight. The other car is waiting for us about two mile up this road. We'll ditch this fucker and torch it before we get off, though, sack my prints being all over it. That's the last thing I need, aiding and abetting a fucking convict to escape from the chokey. I'm on my last legs, the judge told me when I was up at court the last time, and if I get nicked again it will be a long stretch for me.'

Scott closed his eyes and held his head back against the cold metal. His heart was racing and he wasn't out of the woods yet. Jim kept his eyes on the road and shouted into the back of the van. 'So, did it all go like clockwork?'

Scott laughed out loud. 'Sweet as a nut. The greedy screw even took a beating; he said it needed to look real. I mean, he got a right few quid for it, so a busted nose, a black eye and a few bruises is still a bargain. I would get leathered every day if I was getting the kind of cash he got.'

Jim roared laughing. 'Everyone is as bent as fuck, aren't they?'

'Everyone's got their price, Jim, every one of us.'

Scott only really started to believe he'd got away with it when he walked into the house. A nice place it was, set up in the hills overlooking Manchester. Nobody would bother him here. The only living things he could see were a couple of sheep and a few dopey cows in the fields nearby. Scott stared out at the view as Jim come to join him. 'Please tell me you've got me some beer in. I've dreamed of this moment. A cold bottle of lager is just what the doctor ordered.'

Jim left the room and went into the kitchen, bottles clinking together as he walked back.

'There you go, lad, get that down your neck. I got us a few boxes to keep us going.' Jim sat down and guzzled a large mouthful of lager. 'So, you're definitely not telling the Mrs where you are yet?'

Scott shook his head. 'Nah, telling no one, pal. If she knows, she will be a liability, won't she? The police will be at her door soon enough and she'll be as shocked as everyone else when she knows I got on my toes. I'm not even going to ring her for now. I'm out here to sort my shit out, sort my kids and Gi out, and when I've done that, I can either do a bunk or, if I know my family are safe, I'll hand myself back in. It's not that I can't do my stretch – it's not like I'm afraid of anyone in the Ways – but it was messing with my head being in there and not knowing if everyone on the outside was safe. So, no, I'm not saying a word for now. Not til I've seen what's what.'

'She'll go ballistic, mate. Gina is a force not to be messed with and she'll go ape that you've not told her.'

'I have my reasons, Jim, trust me on this one.'

'It's not Gina who'll be out for your hide. Tommy will be fuming he's not been on this breakout. I've had text after text off him. He as good as said that Dave bloke was going to spring you both at once.'

'It is what it is. The screw told me straight he could only get me out. I had a hospital appointment. What was Tommy going to do – try and get sent down Manchester General with an ingrowing toenail? And then what? It would have been sus if two cons escaped via the hossy only weeks apart. I know he would try anything, though. He said he would tell the dibble he wanted to admit to some more crimes in the area. That's a better plan, get a few TICs.' Jim looked confused. '*Taken Into Consideration*. Time off your sentences if you admit to a few jobs. The police take you out and about and you have to point out what jobs you've done.'

Jim turned his nose up. 'That's almost like being a fucking grass. Wow, no way would I have that on my criminal record.'

'It's the way it works, Jim lad, and if he can get a trip out, then it's all gravy, isn't it? Otherwise, he'll be sweating his back out in that shithole for years. And Tommo's got enough sense to only fess up to some harmless old shit. It's not like he hasn't got enough minors to choose from.'

Jim swigged another mouthful of beer. 'So, boss. What's the plan?'

Scott smiled. He was loving being back in the game. 'I want the fucker's name who took my money and drugs from Tall Paul's. I want Paul put on a lie detector test too.

I trust nobody in this world, Jim, as you know. He's a decent guy and all that, but where money is concerned never say never. It's not how a man fights, Jim, it's what level of fight they have inside them. My old man taught me that, and,' he spoke through clenched teeth, 'I'll fight to the death for what is mine and what I love.'

'I think everyone knows that, Scott. Imagine everybody's faces when it's all over the news that you're back on the streets of Manchester. There will be some arses twitching, let me tell you. A few people will be sleeping with one eye open, for sure. Don't forget, although Clarkson has been quiet since we let him go, you know as well as me that he'll want revenge somewhere along the line.'

'So be it. If that what he wants, we'll have a straightener. The truth is, someone had me over and he's the fucking prime suspect. He'd do the same if he was in my shoes, he's a liar if he said he wouldn't.'

Jim nodded, stood up and looked out of the window, pulling the blind back slightly, hills in view. 'We should be sound here for a bit while we investigate. It's like a Yonner village, real carrot-crunchers. You know the sort, if it grows above the ground they make a soup out of it.'

Jim laughed at his own joke and Scott raised a smile. Jim was a good friend, and they went way back. Jim was loyal, a real old-time crim. He had morals and played by the rules in their world. Sure, he'd cut anyone who crossed him, but he'd never go off script, never showboat or drag women or little kids into his work. He also knew the city like the back of his hand – from every alley in the city centre, to all the towns and right out to these villages where no one would ever think to look for Scott.

'Order some scran, then. I've not had decent food for moons. Call every takeaway that'll deliver out here. I want a doner kebab with salad and hot sauce, some chips, and a garlic naan and, oh, tell them to throw a couple of onion bhajis in too. On my life, I've been dreaming of a feed like this. Eh, see if they do a spicy beef pizza as well. I've not eaten proper since before the trial. Stressed out of my head I've been.'

Jim got on the blower to order the feast. Scott Gilbert was a free man for now and sooner or later his enemies would be feeling his presence. But tonight, he could enjoy the fruits of freedom. He had one call to make first, though. He scrolled through his phone and found his son's number. He'd not spoken to him for a couple of days, he had too much of his own shit going on planning the escape. But, if he didn't check in with Jenks, he worried he'd go and try something daft. Scott rang the number and listened to it ring. There was no answer.

Once he'd spoken to him, he'd decide if he could let his boy know the score. His son was sound, but he loved to talk a good game. If he told Jenks even some of what was going down, it would be like telling half of Manchester, which wouldn't be a bad thing, but he wanted to pick his moment. Scott Gilbert was back on the streets of Manchester. He wasn't a man who'd hide for long. You live by the sword, you die by it had always been his motto. Now it was time to test it out.

Chapter Thirty-Two

Gina was lying on the bed in her childhood bedroom when she heard loud knocking at the front door, a gaggle voices shouting. She jumped up and went to the front window. The street was swarming with dibble. As she turned to run down the stairs, she heard more banging, voices getting louder. For crying out loud, they were taking the front door down. Gina stood frozen at the top of the stairs.

Her mother shouted from her bedroom. 'Gi, what's all that noise, is something wrong?'

Gina popped her head inside. 'Everything is fine, Mam, you stay there.' She raced down the stairs and met the officers head on. They pushed past her, nearly sending her west, and ran up the stairs. 'Can somebody tell me what's going on or what? This is my mother's house. You have no right coming here taking her bleeding door off its hinges.'

A female officer came and guided her into the front room. 'Sit down and let the officers do their job.'

She sat there in shock until three more officers came in. It was obvious they hadn't found what they came for.

Gina was losing her patience. 'Is somebody going to tell me what the hell is going on?'

The policewoman got the go-ahead from her colleague and took a deep breath. 'When was the last time you saw your husband, Scott Gilbert?'

'Last week. Is that a bleeding crime now too? You can see right down to the minute when I signed in and when I signed out. And that visitor centre is crawling with CCTV so you don't have to ask if I can prove that.'

'Scott Gilbert has absconded. Are you telling me you didn't know anything about this?'

Gina let out a sarcastic laugh, thought they were making it up. 'What, like he's just slipped through his window bars and you think he's here at my mam's with me? Are you sure you've got the right name? My husband is Scott Gilbert and he's banged up in Strangeways.'

The officer started to fill Gina in on the details and by the end of the conversation the colour had drained from her face. 'Hold on, let me get my head around this. You're saying my husband has done a bunk?'

'Correct, although we're hot on his trail. If you know anything regarding his whereabouts, then you need to let us know, because harbouring a criminal is a criminal offence and carries a large jail sentence.'

At least Gina didn't have to fake her surprise. 'Like I said, I know nothing, this is all news to me. How on earth did he vanish into thin air in the middle of a hospital?'

'He attacked one of the guards. So, when we catch up with him, and catch him we will,' the officer added, 'he'll be looking at adding another ABH charge to his rap sheet along with everything else.'

Gina's rage at being the last to know powered her on. 'He's never mentioned a word to me about any of this, but why does that not surprise me? The man is a down-and-out liar. Full of shit.'

The officers looked at each other, not knowing if she was covering up for her man.

'Look, I'm living at my mam's now and all I want is a quiet life. I've lost my house and my self-respect because of Scott, and now he's gone and done something like this to add to my stress. On my life, nothing surprises me with him. Wanker. As if getting on his toes is going to solve anything.'

The policeman at her side was on his radio now and walked out of the room. She could hear him in the hallway telling the caller they'd found nothing.

'So, what now? Do I have to put up with you lot at my mam's door every two minutes? Because, like I said, I know nothing. Do you think if I knew he was planning something like this I would still be here? Come on, think about it. I would be straight on a plane away from here. I would be long gone – certainly not at my mam's house.'

The policewoman rolled her eyes. She was used to people telling tall tales. This woman could be putting on a big show to protect her husband. She'd seen it many times before, the lengths people would go to protect their loved ones. 'It means we will be watching your every move-ment, Gina. Sooner or later, Scott will be in touch with you. He'll want to see you and the kids and, when he raises his head, we will be here to arrest him.'

Gina sneered, 'So now you've seen he's not here, you can piss off, can't you? How embarrassing is this for my mam having you lot kicking her door in. I hope you're going to pay for that door. Like I said, she's a pensioner.'

'We'll send somebody around to sort the door out, but I'll tell you something for nothing, we'll be back. Scott Gilbert is your husband and where you are, nine times out of ten, we'll find what we are looking for.'

Gina had heard enough. She made her way to the living room door and stood waiting for them to leave. 'Bye, then. Come on, no need for you lot to be here anymore. Piss off. You've done your job, so do one.'

The policewoman stood up, flipped her black notebook shut and headed for the way out. She stopped and handed Gina some paperwork. 'If your husband does get in touch, there is a number here to contact us. Maybe you really didn't know anything about this, but do yourself a favour and give us a call the moment you hear from him. Like I said, it's a serious charge if you're harbouring a dangerous criminal.'

Gina had heard enough. Her head was spinning and she was feeling sick in the pit of her stomach. She flung the paperwork on the side and watched as the officers left.

Beth came rushing in through the front door only moments later. 'Mam, what is it? Is it dad, has he been hurt again? Or Nana. Please tell me she's alright. Has she died, Mam, tell me what has happened?'

Gina watched the officers go down the garden path and gestured at the broken front door. 'Cheeky bastards, the bleeding lot of them. Look at the state of Nana's door. Your nana's fine, apart from the shame of this. And your dad, well it sounds like he's more than fine, too.'

She kicked some debris from the door to the side and stormed back into the living room. Bethany was right behind her. 'So, are you going to tell me what on earth is going on?'

Gina sat down and spoke in a low voice. 'Your dad has escaped from prison. They thought he was here.'

Bethany covered her mouth. 'No way, what the hell, Mam?'

'Exactly what I thought. How can he do this to us? Never a word of warning, never a thought about how this would affect us. It's always the same, all about him and his great big fucking ego.'

Bethany sat next to her mother. 'Bloody hell, just when I thought it couldn't get any worse. This family does my head in.'

Gina closed her eyes. 'Ring Jenkins and tell him what's happened. He'll be over the moon. You know what he's like: "my father, my pissing hero". In fact, maybe your dad is with him, or has at least told him, since it seems he doesn't trust the little women at home with his business.'

Bethany pulled her phone out and noticed a few missed calls, two from Taddy and one from a number she didn't recognise. She hit Jenks's number and it rang and rang. 'He never answers his phone. Imagine if I really needed him. Bobbins he is at picking up.'

Bethany rang the other number that had called her and waited apprehensively for the call to be answered. 'Hi, who's that?' she asked. 'Oh, hiya Mickey, I'm glad you phoned. I've been trying to get hold of our kid.' A look of concern washed over her as she listened to Mickey's words. 'What, when? Where is he now?'

Gina turned and looked up at Bethany. She could see she was tearing up. 'Beth, what's up?'

The mobile phone dropped from Beth's hand. Her voice was shaky. 'Jenkins is in hospital, Mam. He got stabbed up last night when they were walking home from the Cobra. Mickey said he's not good and to get up to North Manchester General Hospital as soon as possible.'

Gina sprang to her feet. 'Where's my car keys, Beth? Look for my bleeding keys. My boy, not my boy. I can't take much more of this. I'll be six foot under if anything else happens to this family.'

Bethany rushed around the living room and found the car keys. 'Here they are. Come on, let's get up there.'

Gina grabbed her leather coat from the chair and rushed upstairs to speak to her mother before dashing back out and through the remains of the front door. The neighbours were out in full force, whispering and point-ing at the wreckage the police had left, as she climbed into her car where Beth already sat waiting. Yes, she'd be the topic of all the gossip today, like she always had been when she was living here before. She turned the engine on and, as she checked her mirrors, she could see two police cars parked up. 'Like I need this lot following us all bleeding day,' she stressed. She rammed two fingers up at them and pulled out. She knew the police would be hot on her tail but as she headed for the hospital she didn't care if she broke the speed limit. Her foot was down and she was driving like a woman on a mission.

Gina and Bethany rushed in through the main entrance. Gina looked one way then the other. 'Excuse me,' she said as a doctor walked past her. 'My son Jenkins Gilbert is here, where would he be?'

The doctor was in a rush and in no mood to be of any help today. He looked tired, overworked, and ready for his bed. 'Go to that desk over there,' he said in a flat voice.

Gina couldn't keep still as she waited for the receptionist to finish speaking on the phone. The moment the call ended she made sure she had her full attention. 'My son is here, Jenkins Gilbert. I'm his mother and I want to see him as soon as possible.'

The nurse could see this woman was bubbling with rage and quickly started typing the name in the computer. She gave them a ward number and Gina and Beth were off again.

A nurse stopped her at the door to the ward. No sister wanted a hysterical relative tearing onto their territory and, after she'd got the details, she briefed Gina on what to expect. The doctors had stitched Jenkins's stomach up and the few other cuts on his arm. She told her to brace herself though, her son didn't look his best. But he was alive. That was the good news.

Gina gripped the door handle and pushed it open. This took her back to when she was younger and Scott had been attacked by a rival gang. She didn't recognise him: cuts, bruises, all over his body. Gina was at his bedside now and the nurse was still next to her. 'He may still be tired. The doctor gave him some strong painkillers and the drip in his arm is antibiotics for the infection.'

Gina's hand trembled as she reached over and stroked her son's warm forehead. She swept his thick dark hair back so she could see his full face. He was still her baby, still the person she would fight the world and his wife for. 'Jenks,' she whispered. His eyes flickered and slowly began to open. The bruises, deep purple, the swelling under his eyes, stopping him opening them fully. 'What happened, who did this to you? Give me names, son, tell me who it is, and I'll have someone around at their house before the day is out.'

His voice was weak, no strength to have a full conversation. 'Dunno. Walking home from the club, gang of them jumped on me, fucked me over.'

Gina sat down on the grey plastic chair next to the bed. 'Bastards, starting on someone who's got no beef with them. This world has changed. There are some sick twisted people out there.'

Bethany whispered something under her breath and Gina shot a look over at her. Gina knew Bethany wouldn't dare say anything, but her expression was enough to tell her mother not to get on her high horse now after her husband had probably done the same thing to innocent people. Bethany moved in closer and looked at her brother's injuries. She wasn't buying his story. If she knew Jenks, he would have been ballooning at some lads, mocking them, calling them names maybe. He was like that when he'd had a beer, a bully, thought he could fight the world. But now wasn't the time to dig deeper, so instead she blurted out all the tumultuous events of the last twenty-four hours. 'Dad's escaped from the nick. The dibble have just been to Nana's and kicked the door in, said he attacked a screw in the hossy.'

Jenkins tried to lever himself upright in the bed and his face creased in pain. 'When? Where is he?'

Gina knew she'd have to explain now and sighed. 'Your guess is as good as mine. I knew nothing about it.' She stopped as she spotted a police officer stood outside the room; his head had been pressed against the glass having a good butcher's inside. 'You need to rest now, let the antibiotics kick in. It makes me realise how lucky you are. It could have been a different story; you could have been dead, and what then?'

Bethany tried to lighten the mood to stop the misery of this situation seeping into her veins. 'Two more days and your sister hits the main stage with the leading role. Do you think they might have discharged you by then?'

Gina let out a sarcastic laugh. 'Will he bleeding hell. He will be in here for at least a week and I'll be telling these doctors to make sure he's fully recovered before they let him go anywhere. I've heard so many stories about this lot in here sending people home when they're not ready and they last a few days at home and drop down dead. It's all about needing the beds, you know. The NHS is on its arse. They should sort it out, before we have no NHS left and everything has to go private.'

Bethany folded her arms tightly. It was all about Golden Balls again, sonny boy. But Bethany knew Jenks would go ape if he knew what his mother and sister had been up to. Jenkins looked up at his mother and gripped her hand. 'I need my dad, Mam. If you speak to him, please tell him to get in touch with me.' He looked desperate.

'You need to get some rest, son. I'll settle now that I've seen you. On the way up here, everything was running through my mind. I thought you were on your last legs. I mean, if you were gone,' she choked up and her bottom lip trembled. 'I would never be the same, my life would be over.'

Bethany agreed. 'She would, you know. Look at Sadie Manion. They all say the same about her. She's a different woman since she lost her son. Nuts she is, couple of butties short of a picnic.'

Gina stood up and leaned over to kiss her son. 'You get some rest and I'll be back up later on. Bleeding hell, Jenkins, try to keep out of trouble in here, will you? I take my eyes off the ball for a few seconds and this family goes to pot. Never again, trust me. I'll never let any of you out of my sight again.' Her words were from the heart and at that moment she revealed what her weakness was. Her children.

Jenks watched his mother and sister leave. He hadn't told her he'd noticed the copper outside his room too – and he knew they weren't there to protect him. Still, at least Tate couldn't get to him in here. There was no way he could tell his mother about the world he'd been living in recently, the people who he'd rubbed shoulders with. But, hey, he could fix all that now he'd got the weed to sell. So what, he got a beating, it was a right of passage. What doesn't kill you makes you stronger, he thought, as he slipped back into the fuzzy embrace of the morphine.

Chapter Thirty-Three

Jenkins looked around the dark ward room, a gentle yellow light creeping under the door from the corridor outside. Even at night there was always a few lights on, endless bleeps and alarms. But he felt clearer-headed than he had done since he got here. He struggled to lift his arm up to look at his injuries. Bleeding hell, his mother was right, he could have been killed. But he survived, didn't he? He'd completed the job.

The door handle moved slightly, and he kept his eyes fixed on it as it slowly opened. This was no nurse. A silhouette of a man, dressed in black, his face covered. Jenkins swallowed – this was either his saviour or his nemesis. 'Dad, is that you?'

The figure moved closer to the bed and still he couldn't see who it was. The man sat down next to the bed and dropped his head low. Jenkins rolled on his side to get a better look. 'Dad, if that's you, stop fucking about. You need to get out of here, the police will be all over here. They will have coppers everywhere looking for you.'

The man lifted his head and Jenkins could see his eyes, his mouth covered by a black scarf. Jenkins screwed his eyes up to get a better look. Big brown eyes stared back at him, colder and darker than his father's.

'Yo, bro, told you man waits for nobody.' The man stood up, reached inside his coat and pulled out a handgun, with the distinctive long muzzle of a silencer added. He pressed the metal hard into Jenkins chest and his eyes were wide open as he dragged a pillow to put over it too. 'Told you, bro, told you time and time again. Nobody fucks with me and gets away with it.'

Tate pulled the trigger and Jenkins body shook as it absorbed the impact, thudding back into the hospital bed then falling still. Tate stared down.

'Job done,' he whispered.

Chapter Thirty-Four

Gina dropped Bethany off at her friend Hayley's. She was practising her script tonight, making sure she was ready for her first night. As the car pulled up outside Hayley's, Bethany turned to her mother. 'I should be back in an hour or so. I just need to make sure I'm on the ball with this script. I have so many people coming to see me and I don't want to mess up. Taddy and a few of his boys wanted to come but I told him the tickets had sold out. I'd go to pot if he was there watching me. He said he's going to come anyway, but I think he was joking. I didn't have him down as the theatre type. Do you think my dad might show?'

Gina chuckled. 'Don't be bleeding daft, Beth. Your father has every copper and crim in town after him. A night at the theatre isn't high on his agenda right now. Right, I'm off to see the girls. Stay safe.'

Jess and Lola sat waiting for Gina in the pub, huddled in the corner, whispering. Gina walked in and spotted them straight away. She walked to the bar and spoke to the barmaid. 'A gin and tonic, please, with ice.' Her phone started ringing in her handbag, but she couldn't face talking to anyone apart from her mates. Whoever it was could wait. She needed some time to think, to relax. Today had been a stressful day. Her boy was lying in hospital and her husband had escaped from prison. Yes, she definitely needed to chill out.

'Move over, then,' Gina said as she joined her friends at the table.

Jess reached over and took a large mouthful of her drink as Gina sat down. 'You look done in, Gi. Is everything alright?'

'How long have you got? Just when I think it couldn't get any worse, something bloody else happens.'

'What's up?'

She faced Jess and sighed. 'Don't tell me you've not heard Scott has escaped; it's been all over the bloody news. And our Jenkins got stabbed up last night on his way home from the Cobra club. I've just been to see him. The doctors said he should recover but still, it put the fear of God in me.'

Lola moved in closer and rested her elbows on the table as Jess said, 'I've had loads of missed calls from Tommy today. I bet he was going to tell me about Scott. But I can't be arsed with him anymore. All he does is throw insults at me and tells me how much of a slag I am. I'm going to block his number at this rate. Anyway, girls, enough about that prick of mine. Carl Clarkson is plotting something. I was with him last night and he was acting all shady when anyone rang, going into the other room so he could speak to them. I'm not one hundred percent sure but I think he was talking to Zac Manion's mob.'

Lola chirped in. 'I've heard from Mike that Zac is trying to make a comeback at his new jail, apparently doing everything he can to get Scott shipped out to the jail where he is. The guy's still in a bad way and he's throwing money around like nobody's business with a price on Scott's head.'

Gina sighed. 'And how does Mike know all this? Has he told Tommy? I thought you said Mike's mental health was bad and he wasn't even speaking to Tommy and Scott anymore.'

'I did. They had beef, didn't they, but come on, everyone in the jail is talking about it. Mike is on a downer every bleeding day and there is nothing I can do to help him.'

'Sad to hear that, Lola. Prison messes with a man's head and, although a lot of inmates say they can do time on their heads, they are lying. I've seen it so many times before with Scott's mates when they've been released after a long stretch. They're like zombies. I hope Mike gets sorted out, though. It might just be a passing phase. Scott never understood mental health and you can bet your life he's told him to man up and stop being a fucking idiot. He has no patience with any of us who suffer with our mental health, says we are weak.'

Lola shook her head, clearly worried her man would never be the same again. 'Do we have news on any money yet, Gina? I'm on my last legs and need something fast. The bills are piling up and the pot is completely empty.'

Gina picked her glass up and looked away as she sipped at her drink. 'Afraid not, girls. Taddy has not heard a peep about who did him over. It's all quiet on the western front and nobody is talking. It doesn't sound like it was Clarkson who took it back, from what Jess says, so I think we'll never get to the bottom of it.'

Jess jumped in. 'For fuck's sake, Gi. So, what now? Don't say that's it for us. I have plans, a new life and all that. We can do another job. Clarkson will have something else we can take. We've proved we can do it. I'll make sure I find out some details and we can set it all up again. We've done it before, and we can do it again.'

Gina shook her head. 'No, that's me done. I had a shot at it and messed it up. I've got Scott's money from Paul's house and the money from the cocaine I sold. I'll give you both something from that to keep you going. Who did I think I was, trying to be some kind of gangland big shot? From now on, I'm keeping out of it, getting my kids sorted and out of this world.'

Jess snapped. 'No, Gina, we're all in this together. We quit when we all have what we need. It's fucking selfish of you to even say you're pulling out of this. We all helped you get Scott's money and, now you're sorted, you think you can bail on us. Out of fucking order.'

'Exactly what I was going to say,' piped in Lola.

Gina practically had steam coming out of ears, her fist wrapped in her other hand. 'Listen, I've said I will give you both some money for helping me, but my hands are tied after that. It's dangerous out there. We nearly had it all, but we lost it. Taddy is a mess from getting done over. That could have been us, we could have been shot, sliced up. Is that what you want? Because I'll tell you now, I don't.'

Jess wasn't quitting. 'We know. We all knew what this world was about when we decided to join it. If my memory serves me right, we were the ones who said no, and you were the one telling us we could do it.'

'I did, and I thought we could. We had a few good runs, but our luck has run out. I can't put us all through it again. I was an idiot thinking we could do what the men do. We're not made like them. I'm always going to have an Achilles heel, caring too much about my family.'

Jess stood up. 'If that's how you feel, then fine. We'll do it, Lola. Like I said, Clarkson will have a few targets for us, and we've done it once, we can do it again. We don't need you, Gina.'

'Jess, take your head out of your arse and think about this properly. You have no man-power, nobody backing you now Taddy's been hammered.'

'We had no back-up when we worked with you, Gina, not at Tall Paul's, so why do we need manpower now? All we need is the information and Jess will get that. The rest of it is easy. We can pay Taddy to back us once he's healed up, and his boys will do the donkey work again.'

Gina was backed into a corner, and she knew it. 'Let me think about this, girls. I can't think straight knowing Scott is on the run and that he might be watching my every move. He will be in touch sooner or later, so just hold fire until I know where he is lurking.'

'And, then you're back in?' Jess asked with excitement.

Gina closed her eyes and blew out a laboured breath. She looked at them both and nodded slowly. 'Yes, I'm in. But just one last job. One last hit and I'm out, so make sure it's a big one, Jess. I'm not getting involved for peanuts.'

'I'm all over it. I'm with Carl tomorrow for the full day so be ready to get your arses into gear when I find out what's next. Gi, get your Beth to put Taddy on alert too. Make sure we can contact him at the drop of a hat. This job needs no fuck-ups this time. I want this more than ever and I know Lola does too. We just need you in, too, Gina. I mean fully in, not half-hearted.'

Gina's mobile phone was ringing again. 'All day that's been ringing, an unknown number. I want a bit of peace. They can piss off, whoever they are. My phone's not getting answered tonight. Anyone who really wants me WhatsApps. I need a bit of headspace. It's our Beth's show soon, girls. I've got us front row tickets so put it in your diaries for Friday night at eight. It's all she's gone on about for these last few months. She better be good after all this, let me tell you.'

Jess smiled. 'She's going to be amazing. Honest, that girl always surprises me. With all she's had on her head and she's still learning her lines. I would have folded.'

'She's got star qualities, Gina. You should praise her a bit more. You can see her trying to please you and you don't seem to give her your time.' Lola was clearly feeling dangerously honest.

Gina was straight back at her. 'If you've got a problem with me, come out and say it. Don't beat around the bush.

Say what you have to. Don't start chatting shit about my parenting and my kids, because, if you want to bring this to the table fully, I'll hold nothing back.'

Lola was bright red. 'I speak the truth and you know it. Jenkins is in the world with his dad and has been from as long as I can remember, so don't be that thick to pretend otherwise and think that we don't know. And don't even get me started on Bethany. You think she's sweet and innocent, but she's been sleeping with half the bloody estate since she was fourteen years old. People talk, Gina, so wake up and smell the coffee. You're just the same as me and Jess, no fucking different. You can take the girl out of Harpurhey but you can't take Harpurhey out of the girl. Fact.'

Gina looked ready to punch Lola's lights out. Jess bolted up from her seat and stood between them, aware eyes were on them all from every side of the pub. 'Girls, wow, calm down, will you. Everyone's bloody looking at us. Lola, keep your mouth shut, and Gina, sit back down and stop making a show out of us all.' She pulled Gina back to her seat and snarled over at Lola. 'Button it, the pair of you. Tensions are high, I get that, but slagging each other off and getting personal is out of bloody order. How is this helping anything?'

Lola folded her arms. Gina was fuming and keeping quiet was a task. She opened her handbag and searched for her cigarettes. 'I'm going outside for a cig. I'll be back in a minute and, if Lola knows what's good for her, she'll keep her mouth shut because, trust me, Jess, I'm ready to scratch her bleeding eyes out. How dare she call out my kids.'

Jess let Gina past her. 'Yeah, go and have a fag and calm down.'

Lola knew the moment Gina was gone Jess was going to go in on her. But why should they all pussyfoot around Gina? She was the same as them, no different.

Jess watched Gina go out the door and she turned quickly to face Lola. 'Are you right in the bleeding head, woman? If I hadn't been here, you would have been on the floor now with a chalk mark drawn around you. And chatting shit about her kids, saying Bethany is a slag, what on earth is that about? If she is or she isn't, it's none of your bleeding business. Have some respect, Lola. Gina's having it hard, and you've just gone to town on her.'

'It's what she needed to hear. Mrs Fucking Prim and Proper needs to know a few home truths. She thinks she can say what she wants to us and we are supposed to sit there and take it. Not a chance, sick of listening to her bullshit. She knows something about that weed and I'm not having it that it got taken like that. I have a gut feeling, Jess, and I'm never usually wrong. If we do this last job, I work for you, not her. I don't trust her. Shady she is, out for herself, not a team player.'

'Calm down. We need to stick together for one last job. After that you won't have to speak to her again. So, listen to me and do yourself a favour: keep that big mouth shut.'

'I will, but tell her the same. I'm not scared of her, Jess.'

'I know that, but for now keep it zipped.' Jess slid her index finger across her mouth. 'Zipped, do you hear me?'

Lola was calming down now and nodded. Jess watched the door with eager eyes, waiting for Gina to return. She was taking ages. Jess went outside and scanned the area. There she was, in the far corner of the car park with her mobile phone held to her ear. Jess walked towards her. Gina was walking around in a circle and her voice was raised. 'I'll meet you wherever you want, Scott. But the police are all over me. I don't care how much you want to see me, you should have thought about this before you went on the run. Did you not think about running this past me at any point?' She paused, then her face changed as she continued, 'You don't run anything past me anymore, do you? Shady you are, secrets, lies. What happened to us being a team?'

Gina turned and clocked Jess. 'I'm going, Scott. You do you and I'll do me and the kids. Our Jenkins is lay in hospital and he's my main concern at the moment, not you.'

The call ended and Gina stood looking up at the night sky. Jess was by her side. 'Was that Scott? What's he saying?'

'The usual crock of shit, all about him again. He wants to meet, but he can piss off if he thinks I'm getting caught harbouring a fugitive or whatever they call it. I'm done jumping through hoops for him. This is my time.'

Jess moved in closer to Gina. 'This has to go down properly, Gi. If Clarkson knows I'm the mole, my life won't be worth living. I've got Tommy on my back too, and it's only a matter of time before that idiot sends some heavies through my front door. You know more than me what he's capable of when his cage is rattled. The guy is a maniac.'

Gina let out a laboured breath. 'This job will go down, I'll make sure of it. After speaking to that dickhead just now, I've realised that the sooner I'm gone from around here the better. I want peace, a normal life and I don't see Scott in it anymore.'

Before Jess could reply, a black car came speeding towards them. Gina dragged Jess by the arm and both of them dived into the bushes.

'Fucking hell, they only just missed us. It was a woman driving,' Jess stammered as she dusted herself down.

Gina's mobile phone started ringing again and she was ready to give Scott a piece of her mind. 'Will you fuck off mithering me...'

Gina went white and her legs buckled as she listened to the caller. Her mobile fell to the floor, and she collapsed to the ground. Jess was by her side in seconds, holding her. 'Gi, what's wrong? Don't let any man get to you like this. Ignore the prick, that's what I do with Tommy. Or is it some prick after Scott?'

Gina looked up into the night sky and howled out like an injured animal. 'No,' she screamed. 'Not my boy, not my boy.'

Gina was taken home and the police were there waiting for her. From the moment she set foot inside the house, they were firing questions at her. 'Did Jenkins have any trouble with anyone? Who did he chill with? Did he owe any money? Did he have any addictions?' Gina tried to answer until it got too much. She covered her ears with her hands and screamed, 'Find out who has done this to Jenkins. Find out who it was.'

Bethany sat on the sofa next to Gina as if she was in a trance, not taking it in. Both women too trapped in their own pain to help each other.

Chapter Thirty-Five

Scott had been ringing Gina's phone constantly and up to now she'd refused to talk to him. Their son was dead and today was his funeral. Gina was so thin, grey skin, cheeks sunken. She'd barely eaten a thing since receiving the news of her son's murder. The police were doing their best to catch the person who had done it but so far all they had was CCTV footage of a man running down the hospital corridor, his identity hidden beneath the same hats and scarves every dealer wore on every street corner.

'Mam, what are we going to do without him?' Bethany had been aged by the news and the days since. Hollows under her eyes, a permanent frown.

Gina was staring into space, twisting her gold wedding band around her finger. Jess came into the room. 'The funeral cars are here, Gina. It's hammered with people outside, a good turnout for him.'

Bethany wobbled as she stood and had to be held up by Lola. Jess went to help her, but she refused. 'I'll stand on my own,' she hissed.

All of Harpurhey seemed to be outside the house today. Jenkins's friends, neighbours, family friends were all here to show respect and to send Jenkins on his last journey. Gina kept a stiff upper lip as she walked slowly down the front path. She stopped and looked at the hearse with the light oak coffin inside it. There were so many flowers: son, brother, friend, all names made up with red and white flowers. Jenkins was a proud Manchester United fan and she could see a United shirt draped over his coffin.

Mickey walked over to Gina. He was a mess, eyes red raw. 'Mrs Gilbert, I'm so sorry. Jenkins was one of my best friends, top lad he was. He will be missed forever. I'm gutted, we all are.'

Gina stared right through him. 'If you're his friend, find out who did this to him. That's all I ask, find out who took his life.'

'I will, Gina, trust me, I won't rest until I do.'

Bethany guided Gina to the car and helped her get inside. But where was her dad? Surely, he couldn't stay away and miss his own son's funeral. Where was his heart?

The police had had the same idea and were at the church and at the graveside when Jenkins was finally laid to rest. They stood back from the mourners, but everyone knew they were there. Half the congregation looked scared to death they would get nicked themselves. Like Gina, everyone else thought Scott would be there no matter what, that he would show even if it meant being rearrested and taken down. This was his son, his blood, his boy. What kind of man was Scott Gilbert to put his liberty before his love for his own son? So, it was Gina who stepped forwards alone at the graveside and held a single red rose tightly in her hand as she watched the casket get lowered into the cold earth. This was the last goodbye.

'Son,' she whispered under her breath. Then the emotion overtook her. 'I can't do this; I can't do this.' She looked at the people stood around. 'Someone knows who did this. This is my son I'm burying. Tell me a name, tell me anything so I can avenge my son's death. I will give you everything I have, everything I own. Somebody, just bring him to me.' Jess and Lola stepped to Gina's side and held her up. The three women huddled together and cried. Gina Gilbert was a broken woman. Bethany joined them and together they walked away from the graveside.

It was past midnight in Moston Cemetery. Scott Gilbert was on his knees at his son's grave, crying his eyes out. His hands gripped large handful of the thick brown earth. He looked up into the night sky as tears rolled down his cheeks. 'You could have had anything from me, anything, but not my family. As long as I have a breath left in my body, I won't rest until I find the bastard who took my boy from me.' Scott roared like a caged lion.

Jimmy was at his side and slowly lifted him to his feet. 'Scott, it's not safe to stay here any longer. Come on, I need to get you away before the police are on your back.'

Jimmy choked back tears as he listened to Scott crying. He'd never seen any emotion from this guy in all the time he'd known him. Finally, Scott walked back to the car. 'Get me a bottle of whisky, the biggest bottle they have.'

Chapter Thirty-Six

E verything had been on hold in Gina's life for the last few weeks. She wasn't taking any phone calls from Scott. Although her husband had spoken with Bethany, Gina still refused to speak to him. Grief had taken over every inch of her body and either Jess or Lola were with her around the clock for support. Gina was smoking non-stop and it was rare that she ate anything. Bethany's show had been postponed and everybody who knew the family was giving them time to grieve. But that left a void. Nothing seemed to be able to fill it. Even the police weren't round as often, giving up hope that they'd find Scott through his wife.

Jess moved in closer to Gina and Lola was all eyes. They both wanted this conversation to happen but didn't know when the time was right. Jess coughed to clear her throat. Gina was talking a bit more today and it seemed right to see what the future held. 'Gina, I can only imagine what you are going through but you need to start looking after yourself. You're worrying us. You won't speak to Scott, you're not eating and all you've been doing is staring into space every day. I'm your friend and I need to help you through this. You're stronger than you think, and God knows everyone is out there trying to find out who ended Jenkins's life. You need to find your inner strength and carry on, for us, for Bethany, for your mam.'

Gina nodded. 'I have no fight left in me. I'm drained. I just want each day to stop. I want this nightmare over.'

'And it will be, Gina. But I have to say this, nothing will bring Jenkins back. You know that, in your heart, but it's like you're still waiting for him to walk through the door. I know you can't let him go, no mother could, but you have got to keep going.'

Gina growled, 'He's my bleeding son, not a fucking family pet that's died. Nobody can tell me how long I should sit here crying. My heart is broken into a million pieces and I'm not going to pretend it's not.'

Jess was right back at her. 'You are not weak, Gina Gilbert. Get up them stairs and get a bath, get dressed and sort yourself out. You're a fighter. This is what you would be saying to any of us, isn't that right, Lola?'

Lola nodded. She knew Jess needed some back-up.

Gina swallowed hard as big bulky tears rolled down her cheek. 'I do want to fight the world, finish what we started, but where do I find the strength when I feel my heart has been ripped out?'

Jess moved in closer and cradled her friend in her arms. 'You find your strength in us, love. We carry on with the plan and we take it all. We take the money and we use it for us, not against us. Your Jenkins loved you, Gina, and, if he knew you had given up just when we were about to make it big, he would be the first one on your case.' Jess knew this was what Gina needed to hear. 'Clarkson has got something big going down and I know every last detail. We can do this, Gi. This is the job that will set us up for life. And not just life here – but wherever we want. Because, for the record, Carl is searching high and low for Scott. He's not forgotten what happened at his gaff and he wants his blood. If the dibble don't find him first, Carl definitely will.'

Gina nodded. The lioness in her was waking. She looked at the girls. 'OK. We'll do it. For us. For Jenkins. For every woman who's ever been told she's not strong enough.'

Chapter Thirty-Seven

B ethany had butterflies. Tonight was her time to shine on the stage. At one point, she'd been sure she wouldn't be able to do the rescheduled shows, but Gina gave her the pep talk of her life and told her acting was her superpower – her ticket to be someone else, anyone she wanted to be. Her mother's words were exactly what she needed to help calm her nerves before the big show. 'I'm doing this for our Jenkins, Mam,' she sobbed, but then she dried her eyes. It was true, being someone else for a little while, away from all the pain of her own life was exactly what she needed.

Gina looked at the clock on the wall. It was still early. She had time for a really important visit before heading to the theatre. If it went smoothly, she might even have time to spare for a drink before she went into the theatre. She wondered if Scott would show tonight – a drink might steady her in case he did. She gripped her car keys and hooked her black bag over her shoulder. She shouted up the stairs before she left. 'Mam, I'll see you later. Beverley will be in soon, so you won't be on your own.' Gina could just about hear her mother's voice replying. 'See you later,' Gina shouted back up the stairs, and she was gone.

---

15 Burnside Road, New Moston. Gina had memorised the address that first day she'd read it in the evidence papers. Now she was finally ready to knock on the door of the house facing her. She lit a cigarette and opened the car window to let the smoke out. In the last few weeks, she'd often park up at this house and sit looking over at it, this place her husband had so often visited but never told her about. It was now or never. Gina got out and flicked her fag. Her shoulders were pulled back, and she looked one way then the other as she crossed the road. She walked down the path and looked around the front garden. It was clean and tidy – nothing like the stash houses or grow houses she knew Scott ran and that made up most of the other addresses in the evidence pack. She knocked several times and stood back from the door.

A young woman opened it, wrapped in a towel. 'Bloody hell, I was just getting some clothes on. If it's about donating money, the answer is no. I give money all the time to cancer research and I can't afford to start subscribing to something else.'

Gina coughed slightly and her eyes opened wide. 'I'm not here for money, I'm here for the truth. I'm Gina Gilbert, Scott's wife. And you are?'

The woman went white and tried to close the door quickly, but Gina's foot rammed inside the door stopping her from closing it. 'I don't know anyone called Scott. Let me go back inside, please. I'll ring the police if you don't leave me alone, honest I'll have you arrested.'

Gina didn't give the woman chance to say any more. She pushed her way into the house and pinned the smaller woman up against the wall by the scruff of her neck. 'Get your arse in there and you better start talking, bitch, because my husband has been here a hell of a lot, and I want to know the reason why.' She dragged the woman into the living room and flung her onto the sofa.

'You've got the wrong woman. I don't know anyone called Scott.'

Gina had heard enough. She wasn't listening to more bullshit. She took her coat off and tied her hair back. 'We can do this the easy way or the hard way, love, but let me tell you something for nothing: I'll slice that cocky face up if you carry on lying to me.'

Gina pulled out a small kitchen knife and held it over the woman. 'Park your arse there and take a few minutes. I'll tell you what I know, shall I, before you start trying to lie to me?'

Gina knew every detail she was going to tell this woman: dates, times, the full monty. There were only one or two missing pieces. 'So, let's start with your name, shall we? Or shall I just call you the slut?'

'I'm not a slut. My name is Carol, and it wasn't me who started this, it was your husband. I told him I didn't mess with married men, but he told me you were going through a divorce. My friend was seeing his mate Jimmy and at first Scott used to come and have a few drinks with us all. I never made any moves towards him, it was all him. He told me he could look after me, make sure I had decent holidays every year, have nice clothes.'

Gina had to take a few moments to regain her composure. She sucked in a large mouthful of air before she spoke next. 'How long, how fucking long has this been going on?'

Carol sat chewing on her fingernails, trying to straighten her clothing, tears flooding her eyes. 'A while,' she snivelled.

Gina's voice got louder. 'A while? Are we talking months, weeks, years, how long?'

Carol cringed as Gina's drilling tones met her ears. 'Years, it's been six years. I met him when I was eighteen. But, like I said, it was him who come on to me. I told him time and time again to leave me alone, but then —' She froze and stopped talking, eyes looking one way then the other. Gina sat on the edge of her seat ready to pounce if she didn't carry on. Carol played with her fingers and dropped the bombshell. 'Then, I got pregnant.'

Gina was sweating now, her mouth moving, no words coming out.

'Maisy is three now and Scott comes to see her whenever he can. He told me, if I ever told anyone about this, he would deal with me. He'd take Maisy and make sure I never saw her again. I'm scared of him. He rules my life even when he's not here.'

Gina looked like a puppet with her strings cut. She'd come to destroy this woman, the home-wrecker she'd been sure had caused all the rot between her and Scott. But now she was here, the truth looked very different. This girl was Jenkins's age – and Scott had got her pregnant. Gina was disgusted. It wasn't even Scott's lies that were stinging her the most right now – it was how easily she'd believed them, and how fiercely she'd defended him.

'So, you believed he was going through a divorce? Come on, love, we've all heard that one before. Why wasn't he in your bed every night, if he loved you? We are saying he loved you, aren't we?'

Carol sat back in her seat and lowered her head. 'He said he loved me at first, when he was drunk, but he never said it when he was sober. To tell you the truth, I was just happy to be getting looked after. I left home when I was sixteen and I was working at the club trying to make ends meet. Everyone knew who Scott was and, at first, I was infatuated by him, by how he could change my life, but after time had passed, I realised he was lying to me. I told him I was going to come and see you and tell you all about us, but ...' She lifted up her white bath towel. 'This is the scar he left on me; told me it would be my face if I ever rocked his boat again.' A livid X of red scar tissue cut across her midriff.

Gina was done in, her heart not able to take any more. The last shred of comfort she'd relied on – that Scott might be violent, but he'd never hurt anyone who didn't deserve it – was smashed to pieces, like her heart. 'So, since he's been in jail, has he been in contact with you?'

'Yes, I take Maisy to see him once a month. If it was up to me, I wouldn't go near that place or him. I mean I was relieved when I heard he got a ten-stretch. But he told me he's got eyes on me. If I miss one Maisy visit, she'll be taken. But since he escaped, I've not seen him. Just a few texts and calls. He likes to know where I am even if I don't know where he is.'

Gina felt a physical pain in her chest. She could have dealt with another woman, a fling, a quick shag, but a six-year affair and a child, no, not even Gina could get her head around this. She said softly, 'I pity the poor kid, like I do you. I wouldn't touch the man with a barge-pole now. You'll probably talk to him before I do. Tell him we'll see who has the last laugh, that's all.'

Carol looked relieved that Gina wasn't going for her throat. 'I'm not saying anything to him, he's a nutter. Gina, I'm so sorry. I was a young fool back then and now I'm older I realise exactly what I've done. I'm not proud of the way that I've acted.'

'Not your fault, love. It's Scott who's the twisted one. Don't you worry your sweet little head about me. Women like me fall down but get back up again stronger than ever. I'm going now. Good luck, you're going to need it.' She scribbled her phone number on a piece of paper from her bag. 'There. I can't give you cash at the moment, but I can give you contacts. Consider that your insurance if he ever tries any shit like that scar again.' Gina gripped her black jacket and rushed out of the front door like she had a fire under her. She jumped into her car and started the engine. Her fist smashed against the steering wheel. 'Bastard, low-life woman-beating bastard,' she shouted out. 'Watch this space, Scott, you just watch.'

Chapter Thirty-Eight

B ethany was on the stage and Gina sat watching, completely enthralled. She was good, her girl, amazing, in fact. Playing Ronnie Kray had taken Bethany out of her comfort zone, and yet she was spot on – her slim frame in a dark suit, hair slicked back, and the voice made her utterly convincing. More than that, there was genuine menace – in her words, in her body language, in the aura she gave off. This was a girl who knew how to play a bad guy down to her very bones. The audience sat quietly, and you could have heard a pin drop as the Kray brothers acted out a brutal scene. Gina, Jess and Lola were as appalled as they were hooked – was this what their men were like when they were attacking somebody?

At the end of the row, Taddy sat on the edge of his seat as he watched Bethany beat the living daylights out of a man. It was all acting, but it looked so real. Taddy froze as Bethany spoke again. It hit home and he bolted up from his seat and quietly left the auditorium, looking haunted.

And right at the back was Scott Gilbert hidden away in the shadows, enjoying the cover given when the house lights came down. Everyone was rapt, looking ahead at the stage rather than at the guy in black anyone might have mistaken for an usher. His plan was to watch the first half of the show then get on his toes in the interval before anyone clocked him. Jimmy had told him he was mental for going and that he was a sitting duck if the dibble were there tonight. But the temptation was more than seeing Beth in the spotlight. He could see his wife at the front. He hated that he wasn't sat next to her, hated that she refused to talk to him. This might be his chance to tell her how much he loved her. Tell her how much his heart was broken, how much he loved and missed his son. But the dibble would likely still be watching her, waiting in the darkness to spring on him if he went near his wife or his daughter. No, this was enough for now. Family had to come second while he rebuilt things. His empire was back on track and already he was calling the shots back in his area, even hidden away up in the hills.

Gina stared at the stage, in a world of her own. Jess whispered into her ear and made sure nobody else could hear: 'After the show we will go to the pick-up point and make sure this shit goes down properly. Taddy and his boys will be there and this time he's more than ready. He got a few shooters and he said he's willing to use them if it comes on top. I was there when Bethany spoke to him and it's game on. No mistakes. Taddy's only interested in the cash, nothing more, nothing less.'

Gina was aware they should be quiet and nodded at Jess. 'We can speak in the interval. This job has to be perfect because I'm taking me and Bethany as far from Manchester as I possibly can. A new start, a place where we can just be us, nothing to prove, no police knocking on our door all the time. Bethany has talent and she'll waste it if she stays here.' Gina sat back in her seat as the actors came to the edge of the stage, voices raised and Bethany in full view. She felt a wave of warm emotion filter through her body: this was her baby on the stage, her daughter. Maybe she had neglected her over the last few months, not been there when she should have been. Grief had isolated her, she'd wanted time on her own. The more she thought about it the more she should have been supporting Bethany. The scene finished and the curtain came down for the interval.

Gina listened to all the great reviews the show was getting from audience members as they left their seats. The three women walked to the door and the bright lights hit them as they approached the bar. It seemed everyone in the building wanted to speak to Gina, congratulating her on Bethany's performance. 'Can you get the drinks in, Lola? I'll be there in a minute. I'm going to nip to the loo.' She needed some peace to get her head together. Head low, no eye contact with anyone else, she headed straight for the toilets. At last, she was inside a cubicle. She pulled her mobile from her handbag and smiled when she read a message:

Not long now.

Gina finished and opened the cubicle door, only to come face-to-face with the last person she wanted to see. 'Can you move out of my way, please?' she hissed.

Sadie Manion smirked, the pungent smell of alcohol surrounding her. 'Look what the cat's dragged in,' she stuttered.

'Move out of my way, woman. Go and sober up, for fuck's sake.' Gina pushed past her.

'You're no different than me, woman. A husband that rules you, no life, expected to sit at home all day waiting for them. Go on, tell me I'm wrong. And I bet he's got women all over the place, just like my Zac has. I've seen it, Gina, seen where this life is going for you. You're more like me than you think. I lost my son too. Broke me in two it did.'

Gina turned around from the sink. 'I'm nothing like you, love. You wait and see.'

Sadie stood with her back to the wall and closed her eyes. 'I've already seen the future, seen your girl playing with my son's head. Remember, I've got the gift. Do you expect me to sit back and watch it all? No, I'm going to enjoy what'll happen next.'

'Piss off, Sadie. I don't even know why you're here tonight. Go home and sober up, you lush.'

Sadie cackled. 'I'm a lush, yes, I drink to forget, to blank out the things that have hurt me. Like I said, I see it all, so be careful, love, very careful indeed.'

Gina was spooked, didn't want to hear anymore. She'd heard the rumours that Sadie could predict the future, but she'd assumed it was a load of bullshit, like everything else that family said. She shot a look at Sadie one last time and spoke to her through clenched teeth. 'Sort your fucking head out, woman. I'll be fine, we all will. You worry about your own lot and what they're doing.' Gina rushed out from the toilets and looked back over her shoulder to make sure the crazy woman wasn't following her. She needed to be on the ball tonight with her head clear.

Jess held a drink out to Gina. 'Bleeding hell, hurry up. They've already announced the show will be starting again in five minutes.'

Gina necked the drink in one and passed the glass back to Jess. 'Come on then, the sooner this show is over the faster we can finish what we started. And I'm not messing. You might as well know, I'm carrying tonight. I've got a gun for back-up.'

Jess's eyes widened. She'd not signed up for anyone getting killed, and where the hell had Gina got a gun from?

It had been one of the last things to come out of the old house when she emptied it. She'd gone to get a few things from the garage and she found an old towel with something wrapped inside it. It was a gun; she wasn't sure whose, but one thing was for sure: she was taking it with her. It was her protection now, and she'd got used to the weight of it reassuring her.

'Gina, we are paying Taddy and his boys to do all the dirty work. We don't want blood on our hands. I'm having nothing to do with anyone getting shot.'

The last call to be back in their seats silenced them. As they were walking back into the theatre, Gina felt a shiver and she turned around. She was sure she'd just seen her husband rushing past. She looked again and studied the area, but nothing. Her heart was pounding inside her chest as she sat down, her stomach turning like a washing machine on a full spin cycle. She was terrified she was losing her mind – it was all getting too much – but there was no turning back this time: she was all in.

Chapter Thirty-Nine

The sky was pitch black and only a few stars were out. The rain was coming down in sheets and seeing more than a metre ahead was nigh on impossible. The three women sat in the car in the side street watching every movement they could. The wealth and the glamour of Manchester city centre were side by side with the worst parts. Only metres away from party-goers and late-night shoppers, you could find the other side of the city. Pick-pockets, drug deals and brasses selling their bodies. Cars crept past the working girls, the men inside looking at them, deciding which one would be their guilty pleasure tonight.

Lola was intrigued more than surprised. 'Look at her over there. She looks like she's ready for the knacker's yard – but a lot of the johns must like the older women. Half of these should be claiming their pension!' Then she grimaced as she saw a much younger girl. 'But that one – I bet she's only just turned sixteen, if that. The poor thing is all skin and bones. It breaks my heart how girls like her end up on the streets. Where the hell is her family, somebody who cares about her?'

Gina watched the young girl walk over to a nearby car. 'Never mind the girl, that dirty bastard pulling over is probably someone's husband. I bet his wife think he's working or having a few pints with the lads down the boozer. Dirty twat he is. I hope the police come and arrest him and tell his Mrs.'

Jess was slumped down in her seat, eyes on the ball, not taking any chances that she'd miss Clarkson and his boys dropping off the swag.

Lola stopped looking at the young girl. Her heart was low. She was sick to death of being on her own, skint, merely existing. 'Gina, I know we've not been seeing eye to eye lately, but I've always looked up to you. You seem to have it all held together no matter what happens. How do you do it?'

'I don't, Lola. I just put a smile on my face and pretend everything is rosy in the garden when in fact the foundations I built it all on, my marriage, has been one big lie.'

Jess turned to face Gina now. This was not what she was expecting to hear. 'Give over. Scott idolises you. Ask any of the lads. He worships the ground you walk on. Times have been hard for you lately. I mean losing Jenkins and Scott not being with you must hurt you more than anything, but he'd not do you dirty.'

Gina cringed as she spoke the words out loud, her eyes flooding with tears. 'That's what he wants everyone to think. But in fact Scott is a lying cheating bastard.'

Jess reached over to grab her hand to comfort her, but she snatched it away. 'I'm fine, Jess. I need to get this off my chest so you both know Scott is not all he makes out to be to everyone. My husband has been having an affair for over six years. He has a three-year-old kid too.'

Even Lola was trying to comfort Gina now. 'Fuck off, Gi, it's all bullshit. Someone is making stuff up to try and hurt you. How many times have you said to me to ignore the rumours when I've been upset about the stuff I've heard about Mike?'

'I found an address in Scott's depositions that kept appearing and for weeks I was scratching my head thinking why Scott would be calling there all the time. I hoped it might be another stash house. Every night it played on my mind, and something didn't sit right with me. For months I've been going to the address and sitting outside trying to work out what the connection was. Once I worked out it was another woman, I was ready to go in steaming—'

Lola was fuming. She hated any man who cheated on their partner. 'We'll go there. I'll scratch her eyes out. Honest, you take me and Jess there and I'll make sure that woman never sleeps with another married man in her life.'

Jess nodded. 'Fucking dead right, Gi. I'll boot her right in her fanny.'

Gina lifted her head, knowing her friends had her back. 'No need. I went to see her myself and, yes, I went in hard but, when I saw her, heard about the kiddie, it changed everything. She didn't lie. She confessed everything to me, told me Scott had threatened her not to tell anyone about the kid, said he would end her, take her daughter. Carol she's called. Eighteen years old when she first met him, and he's been shoving his dick in her ever since. I must have been blind. Why the hell didn't I see it, see the signs, know something was going on?'

Lola chirped in again. 'Because they are snidey bastards, Gina. They all have each other's alibis. They can barely get through a sentence without lying through their front teeth.'

'Apparently, Jimmy was screwing one of them too. I've been debating going around to his Mrs's house and filling her in. Why should she not know what they've been up? That fucking Jimmy has been in my house and sat with me, and he knew all along about Scott and his fucking affair. He's a two-faced prick and somehow, some way I will make sure he doesn't get off with this, either. His wife will know, trust me.'

Jess turned back to look through the windscreen, her eyes wide open. 'Clarkson's just pulled up. Quick, keep your eyes on him. Where the fuck are Taddy and his boys? He knows he needs to grip him before he goes inside that house. He's got fucking minutes, where the hell is he?'

Gina reached inside her jacket pocket and pulled out the gun. 'If he doesn't get here soon, I'm running over there myself and taking the fucker down. I don't care anymore. It's do or die time. Girls, get them ballies on and cover your faces. If Taddy isn't here quick, then the plan is this: Jess, you drive over to the car and T-bone it, and I'll fucking shove the gun in his face. Hopefully I won't have to use it. We only want them bags he's carrying.'

Lola's hand squeezed the back of the seat, her knuckles turning white. 'Look, here's the boys, two black cars.'

The three women sat watching now as Taddy and his boys stormed in and attacked Clarkson and his boys. There was no messing about, machetes swinging in the air, every window on the car smashed with hammers. It all happened so quickly. Taddy gripped the bags, still booting Clarkson when he was down.

'Fucking make sure you don't lose them, Gina. Put your foot down and get on that road there. Ring Bethany, Lo, and tell her to get on the blower to Taddy, tell him she's coming to pick up the man's share.'

Lola was shaking from head to toe as she gripped her mobile phone. 'Beth, it's gone down. Ring Taddy and meet him, take the money and fuck off out of there as soon as.'

The call ended and now Gina was on the main road with Taddy in full view. Jess punched her clenched fist into the air and started to celebrate. 'Get in there, you beauty. Girl power! I knew we could pull this off. Get me on that plane as soon as possible. The moment I've got my cut, I'm gone.'

Lola chuckled. 'Me too. I'm booking a few weeks in the sun with the kids. Hopefully I might meet a new guy who wants to give me a better life.'

Gina didn't speak, eyes fixed on the road, head still in the game.

Taddy sat counting the money out when Bethany entered the house. She walked straight into the front room and clocked the piles of cash stacked high on the table. Taddy nodded at his mate. 'Give me a few minutes, eh?'

The man walked out of the living room and shut the door behind him.

'Bleeding hell, Tad, this was a big job, wasn't it? Plenty here for everyone.'

Taddy flicked a bundle of cash near his face. 'Yeah, there sure is. Why don't you tell your man to come and meet me so we can celebrate properly together.'

Bethany gulped, thinking on her feet. 'You know he won't. The deal is he gives you the jobs and you split the money. You agreed to this at the start. He still spends most of his time in London where his proper patch is. These jobs are just his expansion plan.'

Taddy stared at Bethany. 'Crafty little bitch, aren't you? I never thought in a million years it was you, but I went to your show tonight and I knew I'd heard that voice somewhere before.'

Bethany went white, sat down, playing with her fingers. 'I don't know what you mean. Split the money and stop wasting time.'

'Nah, don't you tell me what I should or shouldn't do. You're the fucking big-man Londoner, aren't you?'

Bethany let out a nervous laugh, making no eye contact with him. 'Taddy, what the hell are you going on about? Your head has gone west if you think I'm the bloody brains behind this. This isn't a woman's world.'

'You're an actress. That's what you are. And you fuck-ing played me. I know I'm right, so, unless you start talking, you won't be getting a carrot. Honest, you can go from here with nothing, or you can spill, your choice.'

Bethany was on the spot. Her phone was vibrating in her pocket, and she knew her mother would be waiting on her. She inhaled deeply and stood tall, her voice louder than it was before. 'Listen, Taddy, don't mess me about. It's like this: hand the money over, otherwise I'll make a call to the man and then you'll see what he's about. But, before you make a choice, be mindful that you will never get work from this guy again. You've seen the jobs he's put you on to and each one of them has been big money. So, if you want to go down that road, just say the word. I'll bell him and tell him the score.' Bethany's heart was in her mouth, poker-faced, watching Taddy.

'Sit back down, Bethany. No rush is there?'

'No, you can piss off now, Taddy. If I don't call it in soon, there'll be trouble. Why on earth would you even say something like that? If I wanted some grafters to hit somebody, I could go to anyone – Jenks, family, the firm. Think about it. But I came to you as I thought we were friends. Thought we might have something else.'

Taddy started to share the money out into different piles, but Bethany was sweating. The sooner this was over the better. Her phone vibrated again. Taddy shot a look over at her. She said, 'That will be him. Told you he doesn't fuck about. Honest, if I don't have the money soon, he will have a crew around here in seconds. Your choice.'

Taddy counted out the last pile of money. 'Fucking having it your way, then. That's your lot. I'll shove it in the bags, and you can get gone. Tell the man I'm ready when he is for the next job.'

Bethany couldn't wait to get out of this gaff. She watched the cash being loaded into the sports bag and quickly picked it up to leave. Taddy stood up and walked closer to her. 'Any chance of a kiss, then?'

Bethany dropped the bag to the floor and used one hand to hold his face and kiss him. She'd been acting all night – this was the finale. Their lips parted and she smiled at Taddy. 'I'll be in touch.' She was free.

Bethany struggled carrying the bags and each step felt like an age. Her mother had parked about four streets away and every step she took she was in pain. Her phone started ringing again. She dropped a bag on the floor and rummaged in her pocket to get the phone out. Her eyes focused on the screen and her trembling finger went to press the green button to answer the call.

She fell to the ground when a wooden bat smashed over her head. Her eyes barely open, voices above her, her body flung one way then the other. She could only see the shadows of two people stood over her. Her head was dragged up from the floor and she could feel the breath of her attacker in her face. A woman's voice: 'Did you think we didn't know what you were up to, eh? Two can play at that game, Bethany. Look who's laughing now.'

The woman let out a menacing laugh. Reece Manion stood over Bethany and spat in her face. 'Once a Gilbert, always a Gilbert.'

Sadie dragged the bags towards her feet. 'Come on, son, leave her to rot.'

Reece bent down and looked deep into Bethany's eyes before he planted his warm wet lips onto hers. 'Could have been good, me and you. Shame, eh?'

Sadie pulled at her son's arm. 'Come on, like I said, leave the poisonous bitch. Grip the bags.'

The Manions had a car waiting and jumped straight into it. As Reece looked back through his rear-view mirror he could see three people stood over Bethany. She wouldn't die, but she would know never to think she could have the Manions over again. Game, set and match.

Chapter Forty

Gina stood outside the hospital and sobbed her heart out. She couldn't lose another child, no way, it would end her. She walked to a nearby bench and sat down holding her head in her hands. The doctors had been to see Bethany and, after a brain scan, they were happy there was no permanent damage. Bethany was lucky though; it only took one blow to end someone sometimes. Gina hadn't been able to rest until all the tests were done. It was half-four in the morning and there were only a few people about on the street. A fox ran across the road beside her as a voice from behind made her jump.

'It's me, Gina, don't turn around, just stay there. Jimmy told me what's happened, and I can't believe it. Our baby in hospital, what the fuck is going on? My boy has gone, not my girl too.'

Gina kept her eyes focused in front of her. 'Fuck off, Scott. I don't want you near me. Not now, not ever.' She got her phone out of her bag, typing out a message.

'What the fuck are you going on about, Gina? I'm your husband. I did what I did for us. We're back on the up.'

There was no way she was sitting down for this. No, she wanted to see his face when she told him what she knew. She turned slowly. She could see him now, unshaven, long hair, a mess. 'I've been to see Carol. She told me all about Maisy, about your seedy fucking secret. Six years it's been going on, fucking six years you've been lying to me.'

Scott swallowed hard, tried to grip her to pull her into the shadows, but she wriggled free.

'Take your fucking hands from me. You will never touch me again in your life. I'm going, Scott, leaving Manchester and never coming back. You can rot in jail for all I care, because you won't stay on the outside for long. Oh, and, for the record, it was me who took your money from Paul's, me who took your drugs. So I'll be fine for money. Don't worry about me, you won't need to support me any longer. Concentrate on your new fucking family.'

Scott lunged for her, but she swerved. 'Fuck off and leave me alone before I ring the police and tell them where you are.'

Scott roared into her face, and he was about to skull-drag her to the floor when a group of men jumped on him, grunting, booting, kicking him.

'Get him in the back of the van,' Carl Clarkson growled. Scott was dragged to the white transit van a few paces from where she sat. She could hear his screams and watched the van drive away with her husband in the back of it. Clarkson walked over to her side and passed her a large brown envelope.

'Cheers for that, darling. All the money is in there. I'm glad you've seen him for the prick that he is. He sent people through my door, Gina, hurt my boy. Nobody gets away with that. Don't worry, he will live, like we agreed, but he will never ever cross me again, mark my words. Might even leave him outside the cop shop when we're done.'

Gina lifted her eyes to Carl and smiled. 'You can't trust anybody these days, can you?'

Chapter Forty-One

Gina went to see Bethany every day for the following weeks. She was on the mend and the doctors said she would be out any day. She sat looking at her daughter, reached over and held her hand tightly. 'Nana will give you an envelope when you get home with enough money in to make sure you don't need anything. I'm leaving Manchester and starting over again. When I've got settled, I'll send for you. You know I need to go now. You don't expect me to be even near your dad after finding out about his affair, do you?'

Bethany clung tightly to her mother's hand. 'Mam, I just want you to be happy. I'll stay with Nana for now. After the show, there are so many opportunities coming my way and some of them are here in Manchester. You might even see me on *Corrie* next. I love you, Mam, always will. That means I want what's best for you, and I know Harpurhey and you are done.'

Gina started blubbering, couldn't get her words out. 'I have to go, love. I'll be in touch as soon as I find my feet. I'm only ever a phone call away, remember that.'

Bethany smiled at Gina. 'Go and be happy. It's your time now.'

Gina picked her handbag up and kissed her daughter on the forehead. If she didn't leave now, she would never get the courage. One last look, and she was gone.

———

Gina jumped into the white car that had just pulled up outside the hospital. Sonny Lawson reached over and patted her leg. Gina smiled at him as he pulled off from the side street. What was that saying – the best mirror is an old friend? It was true. Gina could see her younger self reflected in his eyes. The self from the days before she was a Gilbert.

———

Gina had everything she needed packed. All that was left now was to say goodbye to her mother. She took a few deep breaths before she went into her mother's bedroom and slowly edged inside. Mildred was reading and half asleep as Gina sat on the edge of the bed. 'Mam, I'm leaving now. There are two envelopes here, one for Bethany and one for you. You and Beth will be golden, I know. But I need a new start.'

Mildred dragged her daughter to her, stroked the top of her head and kissed it. 'You've been a good wife and mother, Gina, but this is your chance. Go and be the person you should have been all those years ago. I'll miss you every day, but I know you will be happy and that's enough for me.'

Gina felt like a little girl again in her mother's arms. She stood up from the bed and dried her eyes. 'I love you, Mam. Don't forget, ring me if you need me. I might never set foot in this place again, but Beth can always bring you to me.' She hurried downstairs and shut the front door on her memories of that place.

As she walked down the path, a car pulled up honking its horn. Jess and Lola hadn't asked about the money since Beth had been done over. They'd all agreed that the Manions would get what was coming to them in time. Jess said she'd set Clarkson on them, and Lola was sure Mike could get a name from the inside to put a hit out.

Before she left the garden, Gina walked over to a potted rose bush plant that sat next to a hole neatly dug for it. She'd bought it for her mam and Beth to remember Jenks by. Before she put the plant in, she put a carefully wrapped package in the soil. The pistol was better there than in her new life. 'One day I might need you again,' she whispered. 'But I hope not.' She put the rose in on top, stamped the earth down around it and walked away to Sonny's waiting car.

It was time to go. 'Stop off at Tavistock Square before we hit the motorway, Sonny. I need to see someone before I go.'

Sonny followed instructions and turned the radio down slightly. 'Have you got everything else you need, Gina? Said all your goodbyes and that?'

'Yes, it's broke my heart, but sometimes you just have to do what is right for you, isn't it? I'll keep in touch with Bethany and my mam but, as for that prick Scott, I wouldn't piss on him if he was on fire. Hopefully he's back in custody now and back behind his door.'

Sonny carried on driving. 'I always told you he never deserved you, didn't I?'

'You sure did, Sonny. I should have listened, but hey, sometimes you've got to make your own mistakes.'

Sonny waited on the edge of the square while Gina dashed across, looking one way then the other. A man came towards her, head down, smoking a cigarette. Gina stood tall and spoke with confidence. 'Alright, Jimmy, a few minutes late but better than never. Did you get the money from Sadie Manion, or what?'

Jimmy passed over a bag and spoke through clenched teeth. 'Yes, I did. Slapped her up too, just like you asked. Slapped them all up. So, that's us sorted now, isn't it, never to be spoken about again?'

Gina took the bag from Jimmy and looked inside it. The money was all there. 'Yep, a small price to pay for my silence, isn't it? Might I suggest you keep your snake in its cage the next time a young bit of arse comes your way? You could have lost it all, Jim, lost your wife and your family. All for a quick shag. I mean, look what's happened to me and Scott.'

'I know, Gina, fuck knows what would have happened if my wife had found out. I'm grateful for your silence and, like I said, this stays between me and you, nobody else.'

'Fine by me, Jimmy. No one buys my soul, but this will buy my silence, trust me on that.' If there was one thing she had a black belt in, it was keeping secrets. She turned on her heel.

Gina threw the money on the back seat of the car and clipped her seat belt in. 'That's me done. See you, Scott, see you, Manchester.'

Sonny gunned the car and the city blurred past them. Soon he took the turning for the airport.

As he pulled into the drop-off zone, he leaned across. 'I wish you'd let me come with you, Gi.' He squeezed her hand.

'Not this time, Sonny,' Gina said as she pulled her hand away. 'I've never been by myself. Daughter, wife, mother. Don't get me wrong, I've loved playing all of them. I mean, maybe Beth isn't the only actor in the family. But I've never just been me. Maybe that's why I let Scott fool me for so long. I'll call you when I'm sorted.'

Gina climbed out, grabbed her case from the boot, and as she felt the airport doors slide open, she smiled. She was alone. And stronger than ever.

ACKNOWLEDGEMENTS

To Gen and all the team at HarperNorth and HarperCollins - thank you for all your hard work and backing.

Thank you too to all my readers and followers for your continuous support and reading my books.

Harper North

Book Credits

We would like to thank the following staff and contributors for their involvement in making this book a reality:

Sarah Allen-Sutter
Fionnuala Barrett
Peter Borcsok
Laura Braggs
Sarah Burke
Alan Cracknell
Jonathan de Peyer
Anna Derkacz
Tom Dunstan
Kate Elton
Sarah Emsley
Simon Gerratt
Lydia Grainge
Monica Green
Natassa Hadjinicolaou
Emma Hatlen
CJ Harter

Megan Jones
Jean-Marie Kelly
Taslima Khatun
Holly Kyte
Rachel McCarron
Alice Murphy-Pyle
Adam Murray
Genevieve Pegg
Amanda Percival
Florence Shepherd
Colleen Simpson
Eleanor Slater
Hilary Stein
Emma Sullivan
Katrina Troy
Daisy Watt
Sarah Whittaker
Ben Wright

For more unmissable reads,
sign up to the HarperNorth newsletter at
www.harpernorth.co.uk

or find us on Twitter at
@HarperNorthUK

Harper
North